# Making the 'Invisible' Visible?

# New Trends in Translation Studies

## Volume 39

PETER LANG
Oxford - Berlin - Bruxelles - Chennai - Lausanne - New York

# Making the 'Invisible' Visible?

## Reviewing Translated Works

Martyn Gray

PETER LANG
Oxford - Berlin - Bruxelles - Chennai - Lausanne - New York

Bibliographic information published by the Deutsche Nationalbibliothek.
The German National Library lists this publication in the German National Bibliography; detailed bibliographic data is available on the Internet at http://dnb.d-nb.de.

A catalogue record for this book is available from the British Library.

Library of Congress Cataloging-in-Publication Data

Names: Gray, Martyn, 1992- author.
Title: Making the 'invisible' visible? : reviewing translated works / Martyn Gray.
Description: Oxford ; New York : Peter Lang Publishing, 2024. | Series: New trends in translation studies, 1664-249X ; volume no 39 | Includes bibliographical references and index.
Identifiers: LCCN 2024007428 (print) | LCCN 2024007429 (ebook) | ISBN 9781803740300 (paperback) | ISBN 9781803740317 (ebook) | ISBN 9781803740324 (epub)
Subjects: LCSH: Translating and interpreting--Evaluation.
Classification: LCC P306.2 .G73 2024 (print) | LCC P306.2 (ebook) | DDC 418/.02--dc23/eng/20240508
LC record available at https://lccn.loc.gov/2024007428
LC ebook record available at https://lccn.loc.gov/2024007429

Cover design by Peter Lang Group AG

ISSN 1664-249X
ISBN 978-1-80374-030-0 (print)
ISBN 978-1-80374-031-7 (ePDF)
ISBN 978-1-80374-032-4 (ePub)
DOI 10.3726/b21881


Published by Peter Lang Ltd, Oxford, United Kingdom
info@peterlang.com – www.peterlang.com



This publication has been peer reviewed.

A translated text, whether prose or poetry, fiction or nonfiction, is judged acceptable by most publishers, reviewers and readers when it reads fluently, when the absence of any linguistic or stylistic peculiarities makes it seem transparent, giving the appearance that it reflects the foreign writer's personality or intention or the essential meaning of the foreign text – the appearance, in other words, that the translation is not in fact a translation, but the 'original'.

– Lawrence Venuti, *The Translator's Invisibility: A History of Translation* (1995: 1)

# Contents

# Figures and tables

## Figures



## Tables

# Acknowledgements

The foundations for this book were established during my period of PhD study between 2015 and 2021. First and foremost, therefore, I would like to express my sincere gratitude to my two main supervisors during that period, Dr Kathryn Batchelor and Dr Alex Mével, for their continuous support and enthusiasm throughout the research and writing process, as well as Dr Yvonne Lee who kindly stepped in as a supervisor once Kathryn had left for pastures new. I really could not have wished for a better supervision team – The 'Dream Team'.

A special mention for Alex: you have become not only a much-valued colleague but also an excellent friend. You know how much I appreciate all your support, both personal and professional.

I would also like to thank my colleagues in the Department of Modern Languages and Cultures at the University of Nottingham for being generous with their time and providing feedback on my ideas for this book. There are too many of you to name, but I appreciate your valuable input into my professional life daily.

A massive thank you to my family, too, and particularly my Mum and Grandad who have supported me the whole way through my academic career and beyond. You both know how much your support is appreciated.

Last, but certainly not least, thank you to Rachel for believing in me, for encouraging me and for making me want to be the best person that I can possibly be.

# Introduction

In his 1995 seminal work, *The Translator's Invisibility*, Lawrence Venuti introduces the notion of invisibility, a term that he uses to describe the translator's situation and activity in contemporary British and American cultures. The renowned translation scholar believes that the work of British and American translators is concealed not only by the way in which the translators themselves seek to use the target language to naturalise the cultural elements and linguistic features of the source text for their target audience but also by how translations are read and evaluated by publishers, reviewers and general readers. Venuti (1995: 1) asserts that a translated text is judged acceptable 'when it reads fluently, when the absence of any linguistic or stylistic peculiarities makes it seem transparent, giving the appearance that it reflects the foreign writer's personality or intention or the essential meaning of the foreign text', or, more precisely, when it does not read like a translation at all. Venuti (ibid.: 1) finds this status quo troubling, as the illusion of transparency 'conceals the numerous conditions under which the translation is made, starting with the translator's crucial intervention', and leads to what he terms a weird self-annihilation for translators. In other words, translators undertake translation in such a way that reinforces its marginal status in Anglo-American cultures and maintains its second-order status, simply being considered a copy of the all-important original text.

Venuti provides several distinct examples of ways in which translation and translators are marginalised. First of all, he discusses copyright law and contractual arrangements. On the one hand, British and American copyright laws allow the translator's name to appear in the copyright of the work and thus openly acknowledge that the translator 'uses another language for the foreign text and therefore can be understood as creating an original work' (ibid.: 8). Yet, on the other hand, Venuti (ibid.: 8) also demonstrates how translation is defined in British and American law as 'an "adaptation" or "derivative work" based on an "original work of authorship", whose copyright [...] is vested in the "author"', ultimately meaning that the translator is subordinated to the author of the original text. Copyright law, then, essentially does not allow the author of the original work and the translator of the translated work to have an equal status, furthering the notion that translation is somehow second-rate. The way in which translation contracts have often been formulated is inherently tied to these copyright laws. Venuti (ibid.: 9) shows how translators are frequently required to assign the copyright to the original author, meaning that translators are often paid a 'flat fee per thousand words of the translating language, regardless of the potential income from the sale of books and subsidiary rights'. The scholar provides the startling example of American translator Paul Blackburn, who, in 1965, produced an English translation that filled 277 pages as a printed book and received a total of $1,200 for his services. The original author, Julio Cortázar, on the other hand, received a $2,000 advance against royalties, amounting to 7.5% of the list price for the first 5,000 copies. Once more, then, the work of the translator has frequently been underestimated and undervalued in contracts. Venuti does acknowledge that translators have, over the past twenty years or so, received an improvement in their financial terms, often receiving an advance against royalties. And yet this improvement has been small and still does not allow for the work of the translator to be recognised in the same way as – or even close to – the (financial) recognition an author of an original work could expect.

Another significant way in which translators and translations are marginalised in Britain and America, according to Venuti (ibid.: 11), is through book production. He demonstrates how, despite a huge increase in the overall number of books published in the two countries, the 'number of translations has remained between 2 and 4 per cent of total annual output': in 2001, for example, 190,001 books were published by British companies, yet only 1,668 were translations (or 1.4%); American publishers, in a similar vein, published 195,000 books in 2004, and only 4,040 of these were translations (or 2.07%). This is particularly startling when compared to the figures that Venuti provides for Britain's western European neighbours, such as France and Germany. Venuti (ibid.: 11) claims that the translation rate in France 'has varied between 8 and 12 per cent of the total', backed up by the fact that 9.9% of the 29,068 books brought out by French publishers in 1985 were translations. The translation rate has been almost as high in Germany, too: in 2004, Venuti finds that German publishers brought out 61,015 books and 8,716 of these were translations (or 7.3%). Venuti believes that such publishing statistics and patterns themselves 'point to a trade imbalance with serious cultural ramifications' (ibid.: 11), with British and American publishers making huge profits from translations out of English and successfully encouraging the promotion of their own cultural values in a foreign context, whilst making their English-speaking readership 'accustomed to fluent translations that invisibly inscribe foreign texts with British and American values and provide readers with the narcissistic experience of recognising their own culture in a cultural other' (ibid.: 12).

Venuti's figures are very convincing and depict an alarming situation for translated works in the Anglo-American world. However, the use of percentage rates to compare publishing practices in different countries could be misleading, as pointed out by Anthony Pym, who questions whether such figures really reveal much. Pym (1996) asks us to consider the years which are central to Venuti's period of analysis (1960–1986) and shows how the *Index Translatonium* lists more than 2.5 times as many translations in Britain and the United States (1,640,930) than in France (624,830). He claims, then, that 'risking a fair extrapolation, there were far more translations into English than into French' (ibid.: 167). However, the extrapolation that Pym risks does not allow us to make a certain conclusion about the number of translations to which English-speaking readers had access compared to their French-speaking counterparts. Furthermore, the *Index Translatonium* is not the most reliable of sources, depending completely on libraries and other institutions providing them with bibliographical data. Venuti's data, then, may well hold up to scrutiny after all. If we look at more recent figures relating to publishing practices, a picture similar to the one painted by Venuti does indeed emerge.

Comprehensive publishing figures, particularly for translated works, are difficult to find in the United Kingdom. Given that the 'generally accepted and often-cited translation rate [in the United Kingdom] is approximately three per cent' (Donahaye 2012: 4), it seems acceptable to extrapolate this percentage to the 188,000 books which were actually published in 2018 (WIPO 2020). This gives rise to an approximate 5,640 translated books published in the United Kingdom in the year 2018. The publishing figures for France and Germany are, on the other hand, much more comprehensive, up-to-date and accessible, which is perhaps rather revealing in itself. For the year 2018, 12,591 of the 82,313 books released by French publishers were translations, or 15.3% (Observatoire de l'économie du livre 2020). Similarly, German publishers released 71,548 titles in the year 2018, of which 9,803 were translations, or 13.7% (Börsenverein des Deutschen Buchhandels 2020). These statistics reveal a significant difference not only in the translation percentage rates but also in the actual number of translated books published in the United Kingdom in the year 2018. These figures thus provide greater weight to Venuti's argument than his original statistics.

## The role of reviewers

Yet, according to Venuti (1995), the most significant manner in which the invisibility of the translator becomes most apparent is how translations are reviewed. In *The Translator's Invisibility*, Venuti examines a sample of translated literature from a range of British and American periodicals, both literary and mass-audience, across a sixty-year period (1946–2005). He chooses examples with various kinds of narratives and from different genres, ranging from novels and short stories to philosophy and politics. Many of these translations were commercial successes in English; some were initially successful, but then became marginalised; yet others came to market with very little notice. Venuti discovers that reviewers very rarely address the translation in any meaningful way, but if they do, their comments usually 'focus on its style, neglecting such other possible questions as its accuracy, its intended audience, its economic value in the current book market, its relation to literary trends in English, its place in the translator's career' (Venuti 1995: 2). Ultimately, the reviewers in question 'have grown amazingly consistent in praising fluency while damning deviations from it, even when the most diverse range of foreign texts is considered' (ibid.: 2). This assertion overlaps significantly with the findings of previous scholars, such as Christ (1984) and Maier (1990). Christ (1984: 8) describes how translations tended to be reviewed in the 1980s in his contribution to *PEN American Center Newsletter*: many newspapers 'do not even list the translators in headnotes to reviews [and] reviewers often fail to mention that a book is a translation while quoting from the text as though it were written in English'. Maier (1990: 19), in a similar vein, discovered that North American reviewers of a translation in the late 1980s 'focus almost exclusively on [its] potential role in English, comparing it to "similar" works in North American literature and evaluating the ease with which it can be read'. This certainly adds weight to Venuti's argument that the work of the translator is very frequently concealed.

Venuti supports his central argument with a selection of excerpts from the reviews under investigation. The reviews commend translations which are elegant, flowing and fluid. West refers to Rabassa's translation as 'a triumph of fluent, gravid momentum, all stylishness and commonsensical virtuosity' (*Book World* 1970, in Venuti 1995: 3). The *Times Literary Supplement* assesses a translation to be 'pleasantly fluent', so much so that 'two chapters of it have already appeared in Playboy magazine' (*Times Literary Supplement* 1969, in Venuti 1995: 3). On the other hand, those translations which are wooden, unidiomatic or clumsy are overwhelmingly castigated by reviewers. Anthony Burgess (*New York Times Book Review* 1990, in Venuti 1995: 3), for example, appears to criticise Helen Lane's translation of the title of the book, as it is 'faithful to Mario Vargas Llosa's – "Elogio de la Madrasta" – but not quite idiomatic'. Balderston (*New York Times Book Review* 1992, in Venuti 1995: 3), on the other hand, assesses a translation to be 'wooden', 'careless' or 'inaccurate', claiming that it shows 'all the signs of hurried work and inadequate revision'. Translations, therefore, do seem to have been judged acceptable when they read fluently and idiomatically.

However, Venuti does not elaborate upon whether the authors of these reviews provide any justification or examples from the translated text to support their comments and indeed implies in his broader argument that they do not. Yet, in at least one case, namely that of the 1990 *New York Times Book Review*, the extract is taken out of its context. The reviewer,

Burgess (1990: online), expands on his comment, providing a justification which is difficult to criticise:

> Helen Lane's translation of the title of this book is faithful to Mario Vargas Llosa's – 'Elogio de la Madrasta' – but not quite idiomatic. Since it reproduces the title of an essay written for a school assignment by a villainous young character, Alfonsito, something like 'I adore my stepmother' might be better than 'In Praise of the Stepmother'. The definite article sits awkwardly, turning the lovely stepmother, Lucrecia, into a kind of monument (like those statues in Italian stonemasons' yards that represent 'The Poet'), when she is all too warmly carnal.

Burgess' criticism of the title of the translation is not simply due to the lack of fluency and idiomaticity here; rather, it is more about how impersonal the title appears to the English reader and the fact that it does not appropriately reflect the close relationship between the narrator and his stepmother. Moreover, Burgess (ibid.) goes on to defend the translator later in the piece, explaining that it is the differences between the two languages and cultures which are to blame for general elements of loss in Lane's translation of Vargas Llosa's novel:

> I'm not greatly impressed. The erotic tradition doesn't belong to English literature, except briefly in the 18th century with 'Fanny Hill'. That book, stupidly banned, had a clean Augustan quality – exact, classical, humorous. Perhaps the English language, with its tendency to laugh at itself, is not suited to the expression of serious lust. Ms. Lane has done as well as she can – I have read her and the original in tandem – but what is passionate in Spanish is comic in English. And, of course, other people's copulation, not being our own, is always vaguely distasteful. Whereof one cannot speak one must be silent.

Furthermore, Venuti's investigation does not give us concrete insights into reviewing practices due to its brevity in combination with its diachronicity: any conclusions drawn from a study which examines reviews of fourteen translated books over a sixty-year period – indeed, it appears that Venuti only examines one review for each of the books – can only be described as tentative. Whether he is simply using these select reviews as illustration or whether his corpus is this small is admittedly difficult to ascertain, since the focus on *The Translator's Invisibility* is not on reviews of translated literature. In other words, his work is not conceived as an in-depth study of the kind of language reviewers use to discuss translations. But questions around the methodology, such as how those fourteen books and the reviews from different periodicals were chosen, do remain unanswered. Nonetheless, regardless of such potential criticisms of Venuti's brief survey, it is undeniable that it gave the issue of reviewing practices, and more broadly the translator's invisibility, much more prominence in the field of translation studies.

Venuti (1998: 16) also openly accepts that the picture is not entirely black and white and refers to the reviews of his translations of Tarchetti's tales *Un osso di morto*, in which he closely adheres to the Italian sentence construction and retains the archaising language, and *Fosca*, in which he makes the 'strain of archaism more extensive and denser, still comprehensible to a wide spectrum of contemporary American readers, yet undoubtedly enhancing the strangeness of the translation'. For the former, Venuti (ibid.: 16) finds that a substantial number of reviews made clear that 'the archaism called attention to the translation as a translation without unpleasurably disrupting the reading experience'. Indeed, the *Village Voice* praised the 'atmospheric wording of the translation' (Shulman 1992, in Venuti 1998: 15) and the *New Yorker* (1992, in Venuti 1998: 15) admired the fact that the 'translation distils a gothic style never heard before, a mixture of Northern shadows and Southern shimmer'. However, the latter translation found more favour with elite readers and was often heavily criticised by mainstream reviewers. *Kirkus Reviews* (1994, in Venuti 1998: 18) judged the translation to be 'sometimes stiff, with an occasional jarring phrase', whereas the non-fiction writer Barbara Harrison (1994, in Venuti 1998: 19), in a review for the *New York Times*, was much more scathing, stating:

> I am obliged to wonder if some of the problems presented by *Passion* have to do with the determination of the translator, Lawrence Venuti, to use contemporary clichés, and his failure to use 20th-century colloquialisms convincingly. Surely 19th-century Italian romantics didn't have 'siblings' (detestable word), and they didn't get into anything resembling a 'funk'; nor was a woman of lyrical violence capable of saying, on the eve of her rapture, 'Time flies when you're having fun.'

It is indeed intriguing to observe the extent to which reviewers do seem to interact with Venuti's translations given his assertions about the lack of engagement with translation by reviewers; however, it is also worth noting that any reviews of Venuti's work are likely to be polarising such is his stature and prominence in the field of translation studies. Whatever we may think about the validity of the conclusions of Venuti's innovative investigation into reviews of translated works in *The Translator's Invisibility*, it is clear to see that reviewing practices are a crucial, if not the most important, indicator of how translation and translators are perceived at any given point in time. Venuti's survey of reviews gave rise to a plethora of studies of reviewing practices in the late 1990s and early 2000s, mainly, but not exclusively, in the Anglo-American context. It also provides the inspiration for the present book which will undertake a cross-cultural and cross-platform comparison of how translations are reviewed in the United Kingdom, France and Germany.

## Aims and structure of the book

The purpose of the book is thus to provide the most comprehensive study of how translated works are reviewed to date, building upon Venuti's brief survey and subsequent investigations into reviewing practices. The book has three main aims. Firstly, it assesses whether the United Kingdom has seen an evolution in reviewing practices since *The Translator's Invisibility* was first published in 1995, that is to say, whether reviewers continue, as Venuti asserts, to contribute to the invisible status of translators. However, the book also aims to provide a cross-cultural comparison of reviewing practices in the United Kingdom, France and Germany. The discoveries that will be brought to light in this regard should allow us to go some way to determining whether Venuti was justified in focussing on the Anglo-American world in *The Translator's Invisibility* or whether the notion of invisibility may now be more productively used to describe the situation and status of translators and translation in other Western European countries as well. The third aim of the book is to offer a cross-platform insight into reviewing practices, examining how translations are reviewed depending on the popularity or specialisation of the platform on which the review is published. The study therefore incorporates reviews collected from three types of platform for each of the countries: popular corpora open for comments from the public; mainstream newspapers and/or cultural supplements; and specialised literary magazines. Although different platforms have 'particular restrictions, characteristics and intended readership' and thus 'the content or the methodology of the review is likely to be different' (Johnson 2005: 13), previous studies of reviewing translated works have tended to focus exclusively on broadsheets, despite the fact that they only form a small part of the network of reviewing, particularly in the twenty-first century. The book therefore engages with reviewing practices in three different countries and across three categories of platform in a number of significant ways.

Chapter 1, *What purpose(s) does a review serve?*, contextualises the book, firstly by defining what a general book review (in other words, not of a translated work) is intended to be and secondly by examining the current expectations of reviews of translated works. This chapter incorporates the thoughts of editors for various publications (e.g. the Books Editor for *The Guardian*, Claire Armitstead, and writer for German publication *Literaturkritik*, Ruprecht Frieling), authors/poets, academics and celebrated translators (including Daniel Hahn and Tess Lewis). Some attempt to be prescriptive and outline what a review should or should not include, but in the main this chapter demonstrates that there is little consensus on the purpose of a book review and certainly an extremely limited framework upon which reviewers can actually base their reviews. Whilst Chapter 1 examines what various individuals believe a review of a translated work *should* be, the second chapter is much more focussed on what reviews have tended to look like since the publication of Venuti's seminal work.

Chapter 2, *Building on The Translator's Invisibility*, therefore elaborates upon Venuti's discussion of how translations are reviewed and provides a comprehensive overview of the studies which have been published in this field since *The Translator's Invisibility*. Most of these studies focus on British reviews, but this chapter also examines the key studies which have shone a light on French and German reviewing practices. This chapter demonstrates that the findings of such studies support Venuti's previous assertions that reviewers play a significant role in maintaining fluency as the main criterion by which translations are assessed. However, the chapter also points out the limitations of these studies, such as their restrictive focus on broadsheets and their overwhelming focus on the UK context, and outlines the need for the current book. The final part of Chapter 2 discusses how the reviews in the corpus have been collected and how the reviews are analysed in the subsequent chapters, building upon models which have been used by other scholars. In other words, Chapter 2 sets out the theoretical framework for the remainder of the book.

Chapters 3, 4 and 5, entitled *Reviewing in the United Kingdom*, *Reviewing in France* and *Reviewing in Germany*, respectively, analyse the corpus of reviews which have been collected from each of the countries. A total of 881 reviews were collected from a variety of British platforms for this purpose: amazon.co.uk (popular platform); *Times Literary Supplement* and *The Guardian* (mainstream broadsheet supplements); and *London Review of Books* (specialised literary magazine). Another 1,058 reviews were collected from French platforms: amazon.fr (popular platform); *Le Monde* and *Le Figaro* (mainstream broadsheet supplements); and *Actualitté* (specialised literary magazine). A further 1898 reviews were collected from German platforms: amazon.de (popular platform); *Süddeutsche Zeitung* and *Der Spiegel* (mainstream broadsheet supplements); and *Literaturkritik* (specialised literary magazine). Each of the three chapters follows a similar structure, picking apart the reviews in a number of significant ways and providing different insights into how translations are reviewed and how visible translators can be considered to be. These chapters are particularly important, as they demonstrate that the situation has changed rather radically since the publication of *The Translator's Invisibility* for the first time in 1995.

Chapter 6, entitled *Reviewing the (in)visible: An entirely Anglo-American phenomenon encouraged by mainstream media?*, examines to what extent the invisibility of the translator is an entirely Anglo-American phenomenon, as Venuti seemed to assert back in 1995, or whether the notion can actually now be applied more productively to describe the translator's situation in France and Germany. It also analyses whether there are significant cross-platform differences in the promotion of the visibility of the translator between the popular platform, mainstream media and specialised literary magazines. Chapters 3, 4 and 5 provide in-depth insight into the situation in each of the three countries and across each of the platforms; Chapter 6 draws out the similarities and differences between the findings of those chapters. The discoveries of this chapter are somewhat surprising, showing that British reviewers are much more likely than their French and German counterparts to engage with translation at various levels. The chapter also explores the potential reasons behind the apparent increase in visibility for translation in British reviews. These include a much greater presence for translation associations and organisations; the importance of prominent book fairs for the promotion of translation; and the development of an entire range of courses, degrees and conferences in the field. The chapter also considers why French and German reviewers seem more loath to engage with translation in their reviews.

The book concludes by reflecting on the main discoveries, outlining to what extent translation and translators are visible in the three countries, thus focussing on one aspect of what Venuti defines as the translator's situation. However, the conclusion also disentangles the notion of invisibility, building upon the discoveries of the book and aiming at a redefinition of the very concept. It then demonstrates precisely what the book has contributed to our understanding of visibility in translation studies, but also identifies the many other aspects of the notion which require future research. The final aim of the conclusion is to discuss the moral and ethical ramifications of the invisibility of the translator.

CHAPTER 1

# What purpose(s) does a review serve?

This chapter defines what a review is written for and attempts to understand how and why reviews are written in the way that they are. It also examines whether reviewers are provided with any frameworks or guidance on how their reviews are to be written. It presents the assertions of people with a wide variety of different skills, backgrounds and knowledge bases – from journalists and editors, through academics and scholars, to poets and translators – in order to showcase the extent to which views on this topic diverge: there are those who believe that a book review should educate and inform the general public, whilst others assert that a book review is there to persuade the reader whether to buy the book or not. It therefore becomes clear that a review may be written differently depending on the ultimate purpose that the individual reviewer had in mind. Moreover, we quickly discover that, whilst many attempts to be prescriptive and define what a review should do, more writers and critics do precisely the opposite by outlining what a review should *not* be attempting to achieve. The chapter continues by discussing what people think we should expect reviewers of translated literature to write about in their reviews. It focusses particularly on what kind of engagement with the translation a general reader might expect to see in such a review: should this be a passing mention of the translator's name or a more comprehensive insight into the work that the translator has completed to bring the text to a readership in an entirely different language? We will discover that, if it is the latter and the reviewer does engage with the translator's work, there is once more a diverse range of views on what that engagement should look like and how the work of the translator ought to be presented to the reader of the review. The final section of the chapter examines what kind of reviewers are considered to be capable of reviewing a translation; in other words, what linguistic and cultural skills are expected of them in order to be able to write a proficient review.

## The purpose of book reviews

In response to the title of this chapter, there appears to be no general consensus on what book reviews are actually for; a book review is ultimately 'many things to many people. It is a judgement, a recommendation, a criticism, a job, an ego booster, interpretation, retelling part of the story, and others', ultimately meaning that 'when you ask what a review is, and what purpose it serves, you ask a simple question with a complex answer' (Calvani and Emmons 2008: 7). It is therefore to be expected that there are many varying opinions on what a book review should do and how it can achieve this. Reviewing, then, can become a rather opaque affair, due to the number of uncertainties that reviewers must face in the course of their work. Indeed, in her book *Inside the Critics' Circle: Book Reviewing in Uncertain Times*, Chong (2020) outlines three types of uncertainties that reviewers encounter when completing their work: *epistemological* uncertainty, whereby the 'procedures for assessing quality are not well defined' and therefore the 'aesthetic quality [of a work] is difficult to ascertain in a determinate way [since] such judgements often remain open ended and vulnerable to contestation' (ibid.: 8); *social* uncertainty, which refers to not only 'how individuals imagine others will react to their evaluations, but also what future consequences such reactions may have for the evaluators themselves' (ibid.: 9); and finally *institutional* uncertainty, which focusses on the 'more or less formalized and explicit consensus about the routines, norms, organizational forms, and meanings that anchor and give coherence to reviewing as an activity' (ibid.: 11). In other words, reviewing never takes place in isolation of other reviews, yet there is an 'absence of clear and unequivocal criteria of judgement' (Janssen 1997: 295) for reviewers to follow. Some would argue that it is precisely the lack of criteria of judgement which gives book reviewing its ultimate purpose, namely to be a creative art. Gibson (2014: online), for example, claims that

> there should be no hard and fast rules concerning book reviewing. That's because reviewing constitutes a worthy genre in its own right, one that should not be limited by guidelines or mandates. Criticism is a very important art. It is also a mark of our democracy. It should therefore enjoy the same freedom as other aesthetic forms such as poems, novels, plays, essays and so forth.

Whether we believe that reviewing should be subjected to the imposition of guidelines or theoretical frameworks or not, it is not surprising that most views on book reviews seem to be related to what a book review should not do, rather than what it should do. The most widespread view is that book reviews are not primarily intended to sell books. Indeed, the Associate Editor for Culture of *The Guardian*, Claire Armitstead, outlined her opinion in an interview with renowned translator, Daniel Hahn, that what 'book reviews are not for is selling books. This is where publishers come in, expecting us to be a sort of extension of the market. We're not. We're there for our readers' (Sedgman 2013). This notion is reiterated further by poet and essayist Elisa Gabbert (2018: online), who believes that whether a book review is positive or negative in nature, the review is not there to convince its readers to buy (or not buy) the book:

> The point of a piece of negative criticism should *not* be to make sure that people don't buy or read the book in question. Further the point of positive criticism is not to make sure that people do buy and read the book. [...] Good criticism is worth reading even if you've already read the book or never plan to. So what is criticism for, if not to tell you what to read? A piece of criticism should illustrate an engaged and considered approach to a book and, by extension, other books like it; it should demonstrate what good reading and good thinking about reading look like.

Both Armitstead and Gabbert argue therefore that it is the informative and educational aspects of book reviews which are more important than the persuasive element. This notion is supported by Dale (2014), who believes that the focus of a book review should rather be on enriching the lives of its readers. He asserts that it is 'about bringing ideas and information and entertainment and education to a wider public' and claims that book reviews, particularly those in newspapers, should 'serve as a barometer of a city's intellectual life' (ibid.: online). This idea of intellectuality is furthered by Janssen (1997: 275) who believes that book reviews can actually inform readers 'to a great extent which texts in a given period are held to be legitimate forms of literary fiction, [and] what ranks they are supposed to occupy within the hierarchy of literary works'. She also asserts that they may guide readers who read for more than mere entertainment to discover contemporary literature which is considered to be 'legitimate' or elite in some regard.

However, there are others who believe that, if reviewers were really to consider what their readers want from a book review, then they would conclude that it is to receive a recommendation as to whether they should read a book or not. Award-winning writer, Anna Holmes, fits into this category since she believes that 'most readers of general-interest book reviews in general-interest publications look to them to provide entertainingly but clearly stated answers to fairly simple questions: (1) is a book good? (2) is a book good or interesting enough to justify buying it?' (Holmes and Parker 2015: online). Frieling (2015), a writer for *Literaturkritik* in Germany, takes a similar view, asserting that the evaluative and subjective judgement of the reviewer is not something which should be undervalued, nor which should be kept from the reader. He claims that 'the opinion of the reviewer counts: a reviewer does not have to be the author's friend, nor the author's executioner or teacher. But, out of respect for the public, the reviewer does have a duty to not mince his/her words' (ibid.: online, my translation). Depending, then, on the perspective of the individual book reviewer and what their main aims are, this could, much like Calvani and Emmons suggest, lead to entirely different reviewers with very different purposes being written about the same book. No matter what is the purpose of the review, however, there seems to be a general consensus that a review 'should identify the central idea of the book, giving the reader some indication of the author's style, approach or premises, and then offer an overall evaluation' (Holmes and Parker 2015).

Nonetheless, offering an overall evaluation of the work does not mean simply providing a brief blanket judgement. Reviewers come in for huge criticism for passing judgement on the work using only one or two adjectives, not backed up with any analysis or examples. Yet books are frequently judged with what Boyd (2014: online) refers to as a 'perfunctory assessment' and what translator Esther Allen (in Wright 2016: 82) identifies as a 'single adverb approach'. Whilst, according to Brown (2014: online), it is important to include an opinion in a review along with some kind of description and the 'ultimate point of a book review is to make a recommendation', 'throwing around adjectives like "terrific" or "disappointing" doesn't really tell the reader anything about the book'. The evaluative aspect should rather, as argued by Holmes and Parker (2015: online), take the form of a 'considered, but not ponderous critique'.

However, Holmes and Parker (ibid.) also raise the question of how it is possible for reviewers to fit everything that they want to say into a single book review. Even if we take the following very brief checklist of what a reviewer should include in a so-called 'good' book review produced by novelist and reviewer John Updike (1975: 223), it is difficult to see how a reviewer can be expected to fit it all into the limited amount of space that they are granted:

1. Try to outline what the author wished to do, and do not blame them for not achieving what they did not attempt.
2. Give them enough direct quotation – at least one extended passage – of the book's prose so the reader can form their own impression, can get their own taste.
3. Confirm your description of the book with quotations from the book, if only phrase-long, rather than proceeding with fuzzy precis.
4. Go easy on plot summary, and do not give away the ending.
5. If the book is judged deficient, cite a successful example along the same lines, from the author's oeuvre or elsewhere. Try to understand the failure. Sure it's theirs and not yours?

Indeed, a lack of space is becoming more and more commonplace, particularly in mainstream broadsheets and supplements. Calvani and Emmons (2008: 18) find that some publications want very short reviews due to space constraints, so 'the review must be concise – less than 200 words. These review publishers like to see a brief two-or-so lines about what the plot is, comments on the writing, a brief opinion of the author and an opening with a definite hook.' Indeed, many broadsheets have now 'cut back on review sections and others have replaced it with the sort of feature articles or profile pieces which puff up celebrity at the expense of critical discernment', demonstrating the apparent 'dwindling status and prestige of the role of the critic' (McDonald 2022: online). The brevity therefore required of most mainstream publications means that a reviewer 'rarely has enough space to develop an idea or back up opinions with substantial argumentation. As a result, reviews are commonly shallow, full of unformed or ill-formulated thoughts [and] crude opinions' (Wasserman 2007: online). It may be down to the lack of space, therefore, that reviewers often resort to the much-criticised 'single adverb approach' to provide their overall evaluation of a work.

The dwindling amount of space assigned to book reviews is not just an Anglo-American phenomenon, either. Book reviews in Germany, for example, are also being afforded ever less space. As literary critic Weidermann (2013: online, my translation) asserts, the room given to book reviews in newspapers in particular 'is decreasing. The attention that book reviews receive is decreasing. Their value and the value of literature in general is dwindling. Book reviewers are quickly becoming a thing of the past.' Weidermann (ibid.) is also hugely critical of German newspapers for no longer producing neutral reviews independent of publishers, but rather only publishing those reviews which 'frequently enough come directly from the advertising or publishing industries and therefore do not really cost the publication anything. No negative criticism on the one hand; no money needs to be spent on the other.' This approach in Germany is rather problematic since the purpose of the book review is ultimately defined by an interested party who only has one ambition in mind: to sell the book. The situation is equally similar in France where the space 'assigned to the genre in the press has shrunk' and various critics and writers have been left 'sick to the stomach by the very little space given to literature in favour of cronies and other coteries' (François 2012: online, my translation). Flamand (ibid.), the Manager of the Book section of popular internet company Amazon, believes that this is partially down to the rise of the amateur online critic: '[N]owadays, book purchasers fall back on the opinions of web users, just like when they are choosing a restaurant or a holiday.'

Yet it would be difficult to claim that this issue with lack of space accorded to book reviews is simply down to the evolution of web users into online, amateur critics; indeed, as far back as 1946, George Orwell published his essay *Confessions of a Book Reviewer*, in which he developed the notion that the 'great majority of reviews give an inadequate or misleading account of the book that is dealt with' (Orwell 1946: 144), overwhelmingly because the reviewer does not have anywhere near enough space to provide a comprehensive account. Orwell (ibid.) believed that it is far better for publications to utilise the space available to publish longer reviews of fewer books, rather than to attempt to cover many books in a smaller number of words:

> The best practice, it has always seemed to me, would be simply to ignore the great majority of books and to give very long reviews – 1,000 words is a bare minimum – to the few that seem to matter. Short notes of a line or two on forthcoming books can be useful, but the usual middle-length review of about 600 words is bound to be worthless even if the reviewer genuinely wants to write it.

In addition to the lack of space available to reviewers, some writers and scholars have suggested that the alleged inadequacy of book reviews may also be down to who the reviewers are themselves. They may not be regular book columnists or reviewers and are often paid a poor wage to write about books that they may well not be interested in. Dale (2014: online) claims that book reviewing is 'not a financially rewarding occupation', which leads to the profession falling 'to the second-rate, the hack who skims the text and summarises the blurb and whose real motive for reviewing the novel in the first place is to see their name in the book pages'. In other words, there could well be another, rather more covert, purpose to a book review: to promote the image of the reviewers themselves. Sarah Fay (2012a), the editorial associate at *Paris Review*, goes further than Dale in her criticism of the people who review books and is extremely sceptical of the rise of the online critic. She believes that

> too few newspapers and magazines employ regular book columnists and reviewers. This is done in the spirit of egalitarianism, but in the digital age, where anonymous,

> poorly written 'customer reviews' sway readers, we need to establish relationships with our literary critics. We need to trust them as 'experts' hired and trained by publications that employ them or self-educated and trained as book bloggers. (ibid.: online)

Nonetheless, even if newspapers and magazines do employ regular reviewers, it may be the wrong people that they are employing. There is currently a 'tendency to ask novelists to review novels', which on the surface appears to make sense: after all, novelists 'understand the form, having practised it themselves and are, therefore, qualified to evaluate their fellows' (McDonald 2022: online). However, as McDonald (ibid.) asserts, there is a clear dividing line between the 'creative' and the 'critical' and 'one does not guarantee the other.' Not only are novelists happy to have extra income and keen to write reviews when 'the gig might increase their visibility', but they are also less likely than other reviewers to 'give a bad review to someone that might be reviewing their novel the following week' (ibid.). This view is supported by Calvani and Emmons (2008: 5–6) who claim that

> a reviewer does not just write a review and that is the end of it. Each review a reviewer writes has an impact on the reviewer's reputation as well as the author's. Too much praise for any book and the reader may be suspicious that the reviewer is either a friend of the author or afraid to write even a little critically of an author's work. Too much negativity in a review has the same effect. It either causes one to suspect the reviewer of playing God to build up his own ego or having an ax to grind.

In these instances, then, we might consider that one of the purposes of the book review is self-promotion – getting their name out there – and concurrently self-preservation – writing a positive book review to ensure that they do not receive a negative review themselves.

Readers of reviews may actually be well-served by the rise of the online critic. As we have seen previously, Fay problematises this development, since readers are being swayed by 'anonymous' and 'poorly written' reviews, and yet such reviewers may be less likely to produce a partial review than their professional counterparts. Furthermore, whilst all reviewers are to some extent inherently interested in reviewing books, it is the amateur reviewers who are doing this mainly for free in their own time and therefore the book which they are reviewing is likely to be one that they have read out of their own interest; this is not always the case for professional reviewers. Indeed, Orwell (1946: 144) raised this point in his essay in which he admits that 'books on specialised subjects ought to be dealt with by experts', but also claims that 'a good deal of reviewing, especially of novels, might well be done by amateurs'. To support his claim, Orwell (ibid.) states that 'nearly every book is capable of arousing passionate feeling, if it is only a passionate dislike, in some or other reader, whose ideas about it would surely be worth more than those of a bored professional'.

## Reviewing translated works

Bearing in mind what has been outlined in the chapter so far, what, then, can we expect from reviewers who are reviewing translated literature – that they read the source text and the target text? Is this a realistic expectation? What do scholars and translators believe that reviewers of translated literature should be doing? As discussed in the Introduction to the book, Venuti's (1995) investigation into how translated literature is reviewed turned the topic into a contentious issue, particularly amongst translators who have differing views on to what extent a reviewer should (or indeed should not) engage with the work of a translator. This is evidenced none more so than by the intriguing Words Without Borders (the self-proclaimed 'Home for International Literature') series, *On Reviewing Translations*, in which various translators had their say on what a review of translated literature should aim to achieve.

Two of the columnists for the Words Without Borders series assert their belief that it is not always necessary for book reviews to engage with or even to acknowledge the translation or translator in any regard. González (in Parr 2011: online) claims that the reason why translations are rarely reviewed is because of the 'irrational belief that the reviewer should assess the quality of the translation', but actually questions to what extent this is relevant to the reader. The esteemed author and book critic suggests that it should be down to the translator's notes, foreword or other introductory remarks, in other words the peritexts of a work, to 'provide for all readers some level of orientation' (ibid.) with regard to the translation, rather than reviews. The notion that the translation does not need to be commented upon is supported by renowned translator Daniel Hahn (2011: online) who draws upon his own practice to justify his approach: '[A]s it happens, I don't often mention the translator of a book I'm reviewing. I don't feel any obligation to do so. In a five-hundred-word review there will be any number of things I'm not going to write about.' However, Hahn (ibid.) also expands upon this initial remark to assert that this is only acceptable if the reviewer does not engage with the work of the translator at all and focusses primarily on features which would have been present in the original text:

> What makes me crazy is when the reviewer praises something *that I did* and gives the impression that I'm not there. By all means, compliment the author on the tightness of the plotting, on the deftness of the characterisation and ignore me – they're supported by my work, of course, but marginally. But a reviewer who thinks he can praise the rhythm, the texture, the beauty of the prose, the warmth and wit of the voice, without acknowledging who's responsible, that's a reviewer who simply has no understanding of what translation is.

Hahn's assertion is supported by Schimmang (1996), who states that there is no need to engage with the work of the translator if, and only if, the primary focus is on the author of the original book. He claims that 'the German reviewer of foreign-language literature is nonetheless encouraged to focus his/her main attention of the work of the author, not on the work of the translator' (ibid.: 26, my translation).

However, there are also scholars and translators who take the opposing view and believe that reviewers should dedicate part of their review of translated works to discussing the quality of the translation and the work of the translator. Klein (2014: online), writer and Chinese–English translator, puts this is no uncertain terms in his Words Without Borders article entitled *Name the Translator*:

> I would find it unconscionable not to discuss the translation and the specific performance of the translator. Can you evaluate an actor even when you haven't read the script she's acting from? Can you evaluate an artist even when you haven't seen the model he's painting, or a musician when you haven't read the score? Can you evaluate a dance you didn't choreograph? Then you can discuss a translation of a book of fiction or poetry for how it contributes to the overall effect of the work under review.

This view is echoed by Sirviö (2006: 4, my translation) who claims that those reviews which do not engage with the quality of the translation or which, worse, do not even acknowledge the fact of translation, simply entertain 'the simplistic opinion of some people that a translation is just a direct transfer from one language to another, a transfer in which, contrary to the reality, the personal choices of a translator do not have any impact'. Ultimately, there is a lack of consensus amongst scholars and practitioners about the importance of a comment upon the actual translation in a review of translated literature.

However, there is clear agreement as to how the reviewer should comment upon the quality of the translation if indeed they choose to do so in the first place. Schulte (2022) discovers that there is a status quo in how translations tend to be reviewed following a browse through various American and British publications. He asserts that if a translation is reviewed in the first place, then the 'repetition of the same clichés applied to the characterization and the evaluation of translated works is predictable: "beautifully translated", "a fine job", "this apparently ungraceful translation", "the translation holds up well", "sensitive and truly faithful in spirit"' (ibid.: online). Whilst French and German to English translator Lewis (2011: online) readily acknowledges the 'satisfaction even a single adjective – supple, fluid, accomplished – can bring', happy to 'take the reviewer's judgement on face value, without expecting any examples or justifications', she provides an example in her article of where such a brief blanket judgement does not do justice to the translation. A generally positive review of her own translation of *Splithead* by Julya Rabinowich called the text 'clunky in places'. Whilst she accepts that the reading experience will indeed by clunky for English readers, she also feels that the reviewer rather lost the point of her translation style, explaining that

> this is a novel about the dislocation a young girl experiences when she was suddenly uprooted from her native Russia at the age of seven and transplanted to Vienna without any warning or preparation from her parents. The clunkiness is intentional and had to be recreated in the English language version. (ibid.)

This so-called single adverb/adjective approach, which has also been employed by reviewers of books which have not been translated and subsequently hugely criticised, is frequently used for reviewing translated literature. At the end of her article for the Words Without Borders series, Lewis (ibid.) adds that 'if you're going to pass judgement on a translation, whether in one word or several paragraphs, whether laudatory or condemning, whether you know the original language, you should provide evidence to support that judgement'. This point is put across in even stronger terms by Esposito (2011: online):

> Please, do not disrespect the hard work of the translator you have just read with one of those pat-on-the-head adjectives: 'so-and-so's lucid, sparkling, fresh, estimable, crisp, fine, readable translation …'. If you're going to talk about the translation, tell us something by which we can know you have actually appreciated the work involved and thought about the fact that this book was originally written in a completely different language.

Nonetheless, this kind of evaluative approach is often still used by reviewers of translated literature. The reasons behind this remain unclear, but it could well be down to the lack of space available to the reviewers. Klein (2014: online), however, does not accept this excuse for using the single adverb approach, asking why 'is talking about translation a "distraction"? Why do we trust translators so little that their work always has to be "judged" as if it were a foreign language exam? In short, none of these defences is defensible.' It has also been argued that this approach is so prevalent because the reviewers feel unable to assess the translation in any greater depth, since they do not know the language of the original text.

Other scholars and renowned translators have attempted to take a more structured and prescriptive stance in response to this allegedly poor standard of reviews of translated works by providing guidelines for what such reviewers should write about. Schulte (2000) believes that the ideal critic would first situate the author and work within its literary tradition before moving on to engage with the translation in a more comprehensive manner. He acknowledges that the 'delicate threads of what is foreign in a work can never be fully transplanted' in the translation process, but suggests that the critic examines the translation in such a way that they 'delineate the contours of that foreignness which would take the reader deeper into an understanding of a foreign culture and how the language of that culture creates its own, specific perspective of interpreting the world' (ibid.: 2). Susan Bernofsky, Jonathan Cohen and Edith Grossman, all three acclaimed translators, submitted a joint essay to the Words Without Borders series, *On Reviewing Translations*, with six points that they believe every review of a translated work should attempt to include, building on and going beyond what Schulte (ibid.) suggested. The six points are as follows:

- Always include the translator's name in your initial mention of the book and in any bibliographic sidebar.
- If the translation stands out because of its elegance, panache or daring word choices, by all means say so. If it drags and stumbles, this too is worthy of note, particularly if your conclusions are backed up by examples.
- If the translator has included a note describing his or her approach to the translation, it is useful to summarise the principles mentioned in the statement and to indicate whether the translator's aims have been achieved.
- When previous translations of a work exist, compare parallel passages so you can indicate the contributions made by the new one.
- If the work of the original author is celebrated for particular literary qualities, it is valuable for the reader to know whether they appear in the translation.
- Most interesting of all for you to consider is this: does the translated work contribute to the literary life of the English language, to our speech, art and sensibility? (Bernofsky et al. 2011)

From the point of view of translation studies, it appears extremely difficult to argue with this comprehensive checklist; however, with a limited amount of space available to reviewers and the reviewers themselves perhaps not in a position to read the original text, such extensive engagement with the translation is highly unlikely in the 'real' world. This view is echoed by Flad (1996: 46, my translation), German editor and publisher, who believes that, whilst the name of the translator absolutely must be included in the bibliographic information and there should be a reference in the text that the book under review is a translation, 'a detailed review of the translation itself will only be of interest to specialists and consequently should only be published in specialist magazines; such a review is not necessary for every book'. However, point four introduced by Bernofsky et al. (2011) – that the reviewer should compare parallel passages if previous translations of the same work exist – may be the most relevant. Indeed, one review editor, during a panel with the editor of the *On Reviewing Translations* series (Varno 2011: online), claims that there are essentially two kinds of reviews of translated works: 'one for the books that are appearing in the language for the first time', whereby the focus will be firmly on the author, the content, the plot, and 'another for books that have been translated before', where clear comparisons can be made between the new and existing translations.

At the same panel of book review editors, one editor said that he 'expects an overall level of expertise from his reviewers on both the writer and the language', whilst another claimed that 'a reviewer does not need to be a specialist in the language the book was written in' (ibid.); in fact, she encouraged people to cover works from languages outside of their knowledge to follow their interest in contemporary literature. These two opposing views encapsulate the important debate which exists in this field regarding who the actual reviewers are and whether they should be able to speak the language of the original text; the key question is whether the reviewers are actually in a position to assess the text if they do not speak that language. Reviewers of translated literature are much the same as reviewers of works not in translation; in other words, they are often not regular, professional columnists, but rather 'almost always complete beginners in the field of translation studies' (Sirviö 2006: 10, my translation). Often, the reviewers will be 'reading a work in translation by an author they've never read before, from a language they don't know first-hand' and then only have 'three sentences (if that many) to comment specifically on the subject of the translation' (Blitzer 2011: online).

However, this is a contentious issue amongst editors. Racz (2022: online), editor of the journal *Translation Review*, outlines that some reviewers are unable to read the source language, even in leading media publications, but insists that reviewers for *Translation Review* must be 'translation "professionals" – academics and/or practitioners – most holding a Ph.D. in translation studies or, more frequently, a related field of expertise'. Schell (2014: online), contributing editor of the site *Reading in Translation*, believes that reviewers 'must have knowledge of the original language and culture of the work in order to be able to really evaluate the translation'; however, she openly admits that reviewers are 'often ill-equipped to evaluate the aspect of the translation', seemingly reviewing the translation as if it were originally written in English, since they do not know the language of the original text. If they do attempt to evaluate the translation, Schell (ibid.) claims, then they do so with the single adverb or adjective approach. Calvani and Emmons (2008: 27) suggest that if 'you're not fluent in the language in which the original text was written, you may review the book just as if you were reviewing any other book. However, you should state in your review that you're only evaluating the story and *not* the translation.' Lorraine Adams (2011: online), novelist and acclaimed journalist, believes that reviewers who do not speak the original language must be 'humble'; in other words, they should always take into consideration 'their narrow set of references and permit wide latitude to the translator in terms of the book's style, phrasing and dialogue, and, to the author, in terms of his or her structure, ideas, insights and characterisations'. However, this approach does not relieve them of their duty to provide judgement; otherwise, the review would be what she terms 'worthless'. Prize-winning translator, Susan Bernofsky, is firmly of the belief that reviewers do not have to know the language of the original to review the translation. In an interview with Randol (2013: online), she claims that

> in some cases, you might be able to pick apart which is the author and which is the translator. If the book is composed of excruciatingly long sentences that seem strange in English, you can assume it was the author's style in the original, so you should feel free to have opinion on whether the translator has successfully communicated the long sentences. [...] If it is plot boredom, it's the writer. If the book is poorly written on the sentence level, chances are it's the translator. Usually things that are poorly written don't get translated that much. There are exceptions, but we tend to pick from books that were well written in the original. If the writing is poor, chances are you can blame it on the translator.

In these instances, however, reviewers can never be entirely sure of what they are asserting. Despite this, it does seem to have become a widely accepted notion that if the writing of a translation is poor, it is probably down to the translator. This is precisely the kind of quick judgement that Venuti (1995) outlines as being problematic and damning for translators.

Many scholars and translators believe that it is the monolingualism of reviewers which is at the root of the alleged poor quality of reviews of translated literature, but others have tried to find further reasons to explain it. Schell (2014: online) provides two reasons to explain why translation is very rarely engaged with in reviews: firstly, even if the reviewers are not monolingual and can speak the language of the original, it would 'take extra time and research that most reviewers do not have' to read both the original text and the translated text and to compare the two; and secondly, there simply 'isn't enough room to adequately discuss both the original work itself and the translation' due to the strict word limits imposed upon the reviewers. Indeed, space is always an issue even when only examining a book written in the original language. Mela (in Sirviö 2006: 76, my translation), much like Schell, also believes that it may be down to economic reasons linked to 'the time that the work takes and the payment the reviewer receives for it'. Maier (ibid.), on the other hand, agrees with Venuti (1995) that translation is simply viewed as a second-rate activity and claims that, whilst translation remains undervalued in the Western world, the quality of reviews of translated works will not improve: '[A]fter all, it is the lack of status accorded to translation in the Western world which ultimately determines the quality of reviews of translated works.'

## Conclusions

Throughout this chapter, it has become clear that reviewing is a contentious issue. Reviewers face a great deal of uncertainty when reviewing works, whether it be epistemological, social or institutional, as there are no set guidelines or a framework within which reviewing takes place. It is not surprising, therefore, that there is no one set answer to the question posed as the title of this chapter: *What purpose(s) does a review serve?* We have seen that, often, people outline what a review should not do, rather than what it should do. For those who attempt to define what a review should do, there is a broad division between two camps: those who believe that a review should inform and educate and those who believe that a review is for providing a recommendation as to whether to read the book. Depending on the ultimate purpose of the review, it may therefore be written in very different ways. But what has become clear throughout is that book reviews, regardless of their purpose, are being allocated less and less space by publications which, in turn, has led to the rise of online reviewers, further problematising the notion of the purpose of a book review. Ultimately, reviewers are never operating in isolation of their context; a review can be vastly different depending on what the reviewer is trying to achieve and for whom they are writing. The uncertainties and issues that reviewers of works in the original language face become even more complex when reviewing translated works, as there is the added complexity of the transfer from one language to another. The general consensus is that it is fine to not comment upon or assess the translation in any way as long as the reviewer is not engaging with the translation at all. However, if the reviewer does engage with the work of the translator, this has frequently taken the form of a single adverb/adjective which tells us very little about what the translator has done; this approach is therefore highly criticised by scholars and translators alike. The question of who reviews also becomes more important, and we have seen various views on whether reviewers need to be able to speak the languages of both source text and target text to assess the quality of the work. Again, though, a lack of space and time very frequently mean that reviewers simply cannot do this. Overall, this chapter has outlined how various groups of people discuss reviewing translations in rather abstract terms; Chapter 2 now examines the actual practice of reviewers of translated works over the past thirty years or so.

CHAPTER 2

# Building on *The Translator's Invisibility*

The impact of Venuti's (1995) brief investigation into practices of reviewing translated works should not be understated. Although the validity of any conclusions based around the apparent small number of reviews over a prolonged period has been questioned earlier in the book, it is undeniable that his investigation gave rise to a good number of studies in the field, particularly in the late 1990s and early 2000s. The first aim of this second chapter is therefore to provide a comprehensive overview of the studies which have been published in this field since the release of *The Translator's Invisibility*. However, as pointed out by Schulte (2004: 1), there still exists 'no comprehensive anthology of reviews of translations', despite the fact that this could be the 'starting point for the development of strategies to review translations'. Schulte (ibid.) also asserts that we need 'a study of the reviews that are published in international newspapers and journals in foreign countries', since most existing studies in this field focus on the British context, neglecting to critically analyse how translations are reviewed abroad. The second aim of this chapter is to outline the need for the current book and to discuss the framework behind the study, examining how the corpus of reviews has been compiled and how the reviews are analysed in the subsequent chapters, and building upon models which have been used by other scholars. The study not only examines reviewing practices in the United Kingdom, France and Germany but also attempts to determine the similarities and differences between how translated literature is reviewed depending on the platform on which the reviews are published. Even though previous studies of reviewing practices have been no longer than article-length, the findings of each of them have been indispensable in determining to what extent Venuti's (1995) conclusions can be seen to be valid. All of the studies have taken slightly different angles in their analysis, but as Fawcett (2000: 295) outlines, they can broadly be broken down into two main branches: (a) those which research 'how a particular author has been received in translation in the British press, which is the most usual aim of review studies'; and (b) those which look at 'how translation is perceived as a general phenomenon […] and how this perception differs from the views of both theorists and practitioners'. There are also studies which combine the two: Johnson (2005: 129), for example, 'examine[s] claims that reviews of translated literature are characterised by certain tendencies' by looking at a selection of reviews of Pablo Neruda's *Canto general*.

## Subsequent studies of reviewing translated works

Three years after the publication of the first edition of *The Translator's Invisibility*, Munday (1998) released a study of the reviews of translations of works written by the prominent Columbian novelist Gabriel García Márquez, whom Munday refers to as a 'notable exception', given the amount of his works which are translated and published for the English-speaking world. The paper examines 'reviews of his work in *The Times Literary Supplement* and […] look[s] more deeply at a range of reviews of two of his recent translated works, *Strange Pilgrims* (1993) and *Of Love and Other Demons* (1995)' (ibid.: 137–38) to explore the critical reception that García Márquez has received. Munday (ibid.: 139) discovers that reviews in the United States are particularly 'adulatory' in tone towards the works, with Paul Gray in *Time* outlining that *Strange Pilgrims* reveals 'the enchanting density of García Márquez at his best', and John Bayley, in *The New York Book of Reviews*, considering 'most of the stories to be undoubted masterpieces'. However, despite the praise towards García Márquez, the integral work of the translator in bringing these texts to an English-speaking audience is frequently overlooked and not discussed by many reviewers. Munday (ibid.: 139–40) discovers that *Time*, *Booklist* and *Atlantic Monthly* 'do not even mention that the book is a translation', whilst *Library Journal* 'does at least give a credit to Edith Grossman' and *New York Review of Books* gives Grossman 'a passing accolade'. Most problematically from the point of view of the visibility of the translator, in this latter review, Munday (ibid.: 140) finds that the reviewer refers to a 'characteristic Márquez sentence', despite the fact that there are various translation shifts in the sentence, such as dividing the original sentence due to its complexity in Spanish. In other words, the 'translated text has passed for the original; in fact, for the reviewer, the style of the translation is the style of Márquez'. This is remarkably consistent with what Venuti found in *The Translator's Invisibility*. It is a similar story in the UK, where 'the paucity of references continues: of seven reviews which were studied, only three (*The Sunday Times*, *Independent* and *TLS*) mention the translator in the credits' (ibid.: 142). Similarly to the American reviews, many reviewers make reference to the style of the work, but only two reviewers actually reflect on the role of the translator: Kemp, in *Sunday Times*, 'lauds the "polished lucidity" of García Márquez's prose', whilst Winder, in *The Independent*, 'considers the content to be more important than the style "even in Edith Grossman's vibrant translation"' (ibid.: 142). Ultimately, Munday's (ibid.: 144) findings corroborate what Venuti discovered, as the reviews in question seem to give the illusion that the 'prose has not only been *translated* into English – in the eyes of many reviewers it *is* English'.

Two years later, Fawcett's (2000) paper on translation in the British broadsheets focussed on translation assessment and criticism. His body of reviews was collected over a seven-year period, 1992–1999, from British broadsheets, mainly *The Observer*. Whilst we may expect this to give rise to a large number of translation reviews, his study found that '11 translations of novels, short stories, poetry and biographies came up for review' (ibid.: 295); however, the study only includes reviews which wrote explicitly about translation or, in other words, excludes those reviews which treat the work as if it were originally written in English. Despite the small number of reviews, the study provides a crucial contribution to our understanding of the field as it reveals certain critical parameters or features by which translations tend to be assessed by reviewers. Firstly, the most common quality preferred in a translation by reviewers is 'transparency, the feeling that one is not reading a translation at all' (ibid.: 296). Fawcett (ibid.) provides an example from the review of Musil's *The Man Without Qualities*, in which reviewer Coe approves of the work, as 'Sophie Wilkins has translated the novel into good, idiomatic American English, making it far more accessible than in the earlier translation'. On the flipside, there is a clear dislike of source-language contamination in translation: Birnbaum criticises the translators for their work in translating *A Diary of Darkness*, because 'the English, too often retaining the constructions of the original, is laborious' (ibid.: 297), whilst Romney castigates Baignère's translation of the biography of Almodóvar for being 'cumbersome'. Fawcett (ibid.) also discovers that a sweeping judgement is generally 'supported by what, to an academic, is the flimsiest of proof (a few examples at most, and very often none at all)', meaning that a reader might believe a whole translation is poor, 'because the reviewer has noted a handful of clumsy phrasings (of a kind not after all uncommon in English original texts)'. In a similar vein, reviewers do not frequently make clear why they find some of the translated text poor, but also 'do not allow that absence of analysis to soften the severity of the judgement' (ibid.). Another important issue that Fawcett (ibid.: 298) identifies with the reviews in question is that 'we are not given the information we need to establish on what basis of authority the reviewer is making judgements'; in other words, we do not know whether the reviewer has read the source text or even if they speak the original language. Only Mars-Jones, in his review of Pamuk's *The New Life*, admits that he 'cannot read Turkish and so has to hedge his criticism of what he himself sees as faults of English with the admission that they may correspond to stylistic choices in the original' (ibid.). Fawcett (ibid.: 305) therefore concludes rather strongly that the reviews under study are 'an exercise in institutionalised irresponsibility', as they 'used a limited physical space to brand a translation and a translator as poor in relation to a criterion assumed to be universal and unassailable [transparency]'. This conclusion certainly backs up previous discoveries.

Johnson's (2005) paper is the most recent to be published in this field which focusses exclusively on the Anglo-American context. Its main purpose is to 'test and develop the claims made by analysts of translated literature reviews' by examining reviews of 'translations into English of *Canto general* by the Chilean poet Pablo Neruda published in the US and the UK during 1950–2004' (ibid.: 130). Much like previous scholars, Johnson discovers that the fact of translation tends not to be acknowledged; however, she does not take issue with this. Indeed, if a translation is not marketed as such, she claims, it 'might be a way to enter the target culture; a way for the readers to acquire a taste for foreign literature; and a way for the author to reach a wide audience' (ibid.: 139–40). Johnson (ibid.: 137) also asserts that the preference for 'a readable [or target-oriented] or an accurate [or source-oriented] translation depends on the reviewer', and that a monolingual reviewer 'may be more likely to prefer a readable translation since s/he does not have the capability to evaluate the accuracy of the translation'. The scholar does not believe that either approach is necessarily better than the other, but this builds upon the idea introduced by Fawcett (2000) that readers should know whether reviewers of translated literature are able to speak the language of the original text and therefore upon what basis the reviewer is making their judgements. Despite Johnson's (2005) positive tone towards the work of reviewers, her study does still show that translators ultimately continue to be invisible in reviews.

In the United Kingdom, Venuti's (1995) assertion that translations are judged as 'acceptable' by reviewers if they read fluently was supported by subsequent studies in the 2000s. But does this also apply to reviewing practices in France and Germany? Vanderschelden's (2000: 273) article on quality assessment and literary translation in France examines how translated works are reviewed exclusively in the French context, thus enabling us to make 'further comparisons [...] between the French, British and American contexts'. The body of reviews upon which she draws is collected from *Le Monde* and *Libération* over an eight-year period, 1991–99, which makes it the most comprehensive study of French reviewing practices of translated literature to date. However, at no point does the scholar actually provide the number of reviews yielded by this collection or indeed any indication as to what kind of reviews (e.g. fiction/non-fiction, prose/poetry/drama, etc.) were included in or excluded from her study. Her work suggests that the situation in France is similar to the picture that Venuti paints of the US and the UK, the 'reviews themselves tend[ing] to follow certain patterns which do not promote the visibility of translation' (ibid.: 282).

Whilst Vanderschelden (ibid.) found that the fact of translation is often mentioned in the title of a review, she also discovered that the 'status of the book as a translation is of secondary importance and, most of the time, not worth commenting upon in the body of the review'. Indeed, the overwhelming majority of reviews 'make a brief blanket judgement, often in the form of a single adjective such as "excellente" or "remarquable", or cite the translator briefly in parenthesis' (ibid.: 285). Vanderschelden (ibid.) argues that a single-word comment on a translation 'is of little value and has limited impact; if anything, it reinforces the general attitude of casualness towards the work of the translator'.

However, Vanderschelden (ibid.: 286) does not castigate reviewers as it is impossible to have a complete understanding of the circumstances under which they are working; indeed, she asserts that, in addition to the limited space available for reviews, reviewers 'may not know the source language and therefore may not feel competent to judge the translation; the editorial policy may encourage the invisibility of translation; or no adequate criteria for assessing translations may be available to the reviewer', reinforcing the points made by Fawcett (2000) and Johnson (2005) in the British context. In addition to this, Vanderschelden identifies that the style of the translation is invariably treated as the style of the original text. Whilst she does not heavily criticise reviewers who comment on the translation using a single word, Vanderschelden (ibid.: 284) is much more unforgiving when reviewers make no distinction between the styles of the source and target texts, ultimately treating 'the French translation of the book as the original'. She provides the example of a review by Albert Bensoussan, 'active defender of the status of translators and [...] a renowned literary translator' (ibid.: 285), and is shocked that his review treats the translation as the original Spanish novel. Indeed, the review contains the phrase 'finally, at the end of a trying narration, written with clinical precision, in the right tone and with impressive rigour, all of which make Muñoz Molina such an immense writer, we gain a message of hope' (ibid.: 285, my translation), without attributing any of these features to the work of the French translator, Philippe Bataillon. The picture painted here by Vanderschelden demonstrates clear similarities with studies of reviewing translated literature in the United Kingdom in the early 2000s, with translators continuing to be relatively invisible in the reviews included in her corpus.

Another paper which deepens our understanding of the reviewing situation in France is that of Bush (2004). He examines the reviews of translated literature in a handful of broadsheets and specialised publications in three diverse cultural contexts – the United Kingdom, France and Spain. Bush (ibid.: 30) analyses a two-month period and acknowledges that his study only provides a 'somewhat arbitrary, impressionistic state of play'. The majority of his paper focusses simply on the quantity of reviews of translated literature published in the different publications and what the subject of these reviews was; however, the fact that only thirty-one reviews of translations appeared in *Times Literary Supplement* and four reviews of translations appeared in *London Review of Books* provides us with interesting insights into the state of play of translated literature in the British market, especially when compared to the much greater figures for the French (and Spanish) equivalents in the study. In France, Bush (ibid.: 37) discovers that *Le Monde* published significantly greater numbers of translation reviews than its English counterpart in the study, *Times Literary Supplement*, with around 'eighty reviews of works of fiction, science, history and politics alongside a large number of reviews of books written in French'. It is predominantly the quantitative element upon which Bush (ibid.: 38) focusses again for the French context, but he does nevertheless attempt to provide a single qualitative comment about his collection of French reviews: 'Reviewers always include the name of the translator in the heading of the review and almost never comment on the quality of the translation.' This qualitative comment only provides a basic insight into French reviewing practices, but it does indeed seem to support the initial findings of Vanderschelden's (2000) study. Bush's conclusions for reviewing practices in each of the two countries are, however, extremely different. Although it would seem very hard to justify based on his limited corpus and restrictive methodology, Bush (ibid.: 44) comes to the strong conclusion that Anglo-American culture 'prefers bombs to words and holds most things foreign as objects of suspicion', whilst as far as France is concerned, he claims that 'the newspaper reader in Paris [...]

faces no shortage of books pages or reviews of literature in translation' compared to the British reader.

In contrast to Bush's mainly quantitative approach, Gray (2018: online) attempts to take a mixed quantitative-qualitative approach to examine British and French reviewing practices in the year 2015. He draws upon a corpus of reviews collected from two broadsheet supplements in each country: *Times Literary Supplement* and *The Guardian* in the United Kingdom and *Le Monde* and *Libération* in France. The British broadsheets published 299 reviews between them in 2015 (211 in *Times Literary Supplement* and 88 in *The Guardian*), whilst *Le Monde* and *Libération* managed 550 between them, 429 and 121, respectively. Compared to the United Kingdom, then, the 'number of reviews of translated works published in French broadsheets in 2015 remains considerably greater' (ibid.). The scholar also delves into the reviews to determine whether and in what kind of ways reviewers engage with the work of the translator. He discovers that all of the reviews in *Times Literary Supplement* acknowledge that they are writing about translation, whilst 86.4% of reviews in *The Guardian* do so. More than 95% of reviews in both *Le Monde* and *Libération* include an acknowledgement of the fact of translation. In this regard, there seems to have been significant progress in the intervening years since previous studies, particularly in the United Kingdom, where it seemingly became commonplace to acknowledge that the work is a translation. Gray also examines the frequency of comments made on the work of a translator and discovers that just 7.04% of reviews in *Le Monde* and 4.31% of reviews in *Libération* go beyond an acknowledgement of the fact of translation to comment upon the work of the translator. Both of the British broadsheets, on the other hand, 'go on to comment on the quality of the translation after they have acknowledged the fact of translation relatively frequently' (ibid.) – with 78.1% and 55.3% of reviews in *Times Literary Supplement* and *The Guardian* doing this. Nonetheless, Gray (ibid.) still discovers that the comments on translation are done with the much-criticised brief blanket judgement approach, 'usually in the form of a single adjective, such as "fluent" or "accurate"'. He ultimately concludes that 'reviewing practices in the United Kingdom have improved to at least some extent over the past two decades in that translators and their work have become more "visible" in the British and French broadsheets in the present day' (ibid.).

Despite the fact that it was a German translation scholar, Reiss (1971), who produced one of the fundamental works for the development of assessing and reviewing translated works in the form of *The Potentials and Limitations of Translation Criticism: Categories and Criteria for Translation Quality Assessment*, there is only one key study of German-speaking reviewing practices, conducted by Lanschützer in 2010. Lanschützer (2010) begins her paper with some statistics about German publishing practices. For example, she discovers that 'in 2008, translations accounted for "only" 7.2% of all of the first editions published in Germany; however, a breakdown by genre shows that in 2008 at least 22% of all fiction publications were translations – and this looks set to increase in future' (ibid.: 159, my translation). Nonetheless, she also finds that translators are ultimately undervalued – or, even worse, ignored – by the general public. Lanschützer therefore conducts her study to delve deeper into reviewing practices in the German-speaking world and to discover the reasons behind the alleged invisibility of translators. One of her aims is to determine whether reviewers 'make readers aware of the fact that a work came from a different language, a foreign culture' (ibid.: 159–60, my translation). To investigate this question, the author collected the reviews published in *Die Presse* (Austria) and *Neue Zürcher Zeitung* (Switzerland) during the months April–June 2009 and those published in *Die Zeit* (Germany) in the months May–June 2009. The scholar discovers that twenty-six of the sixty-nine of the books reviewed in *Die Presse* (37.7%), twenty-four of the sixty-one books reviewed in *Neue Zürcher Zeitung* (39.3%) and thirty-two of the eighty-nine books reviewed in *Die Zeit* (36.5%) were translations. All three of the newspapers engage with the translation in some regard in all but one of their reviews.

However, when the author examines the type of engagement with translation, she discovers that the majority of the reviews in all three newspapers fit into her categories 2–4, which are defined as follows: category 2 is for a review in which 'the name(s) of the translator(s) are mentioned in the bibliographical information'; category 3 is for a review which 'acknowledges that a translation is being reviewed by including casual comments such as "now appearing in German", but without making the translator(s) explicitly visible'; whilst category 4 is for instances in which 'the translation is judged using a blanket comment (such as the two "prime examples", *congenial* and *clumsy*)' (ibid.: 160–61, my translation). These three categories are referred to as 'not overly satisfactory' by the author. None of the reviews in *Die Presse* and just four reviews in *Neue Zürcher Zeitung* (16.7%) are assigned to the so-called 'ideal category' six in which 'space is given to the translation – there is a comparison between the original and the translation or between two different translations' (ibid.: 161, my translation). Lanschützer (ibid.) also outlines that twenty of the eighty-nine reviews in *Die Zeit* (22.9%) are classified into either category 5 or 6, with category 5 being defined as 'the reviewers engage briefly with the translation beyond an initial blanket comment'.[1]

Another crucial point which Lanschützer makes in her study is that fluency is much revered by reviewers in Germany and that a translation which reads as though it was originally written in German is a positive outcome. This is demonstrated by the following extract from a review which she provides: 'Peter Knecht's translation reads once more as if the author wrote the German text himself' (ibid.: 166, my translation). She claims that the only criterion for the reviewer Harpprecht was that the translation reads fluently, thus promoting the invisibility of the translator. The author ultimately concludes that standard 'empty phrases' are used to assess the performance of translators and that the ultimate goal for translators, from the point of view of reviewers, is to produce a translation which reads as fluently as possible and which brings the author towards the reader by guaranteeing easy readability. Lanschützer (ibid.: 173, my translation) also suggests that translations are 'generally criticised or praised without any apparent objective assessment criteria' and makes a key distinction between how a translation may be criticised or praised, namely that 'criticism is made mainly at the lexical level, for example the title of the translation, whilst praise is in many cases based on stereotypical cliches'.

1 Incidentally, Lanschützer's category 1 is defined as 'no mention of the translator(s)'.

## Reviewing translated works as a 'normative behaviour'?

Translators and their work have therefore been relatively invisible in reviews of translated works across the three countries in the twenty years or so since the publication of Venuti's *The Translator's Invisibility*. For this reason, I would like to suggest that reviewing practices of translated works in the United Kingdom, France and Germany have become a 'normative behaviour', as introduced by Toury (1995). In 'The nature and role of norms in literary translation', Toury (1995/2012: 169) makes a clear distinction between 'rules', which are considered to be 'relatively absolute', 'idiosyncrasies', which lie at the opposite end of the scale, purely based upon the individual and his or her preferences, and in between the two, what he refers to as 'norms', which 'form a graded continuum along the scale: some are stronger, and hence more rule-like, others are weaker, and hence almost idiosyncratic'. Assuming that the conclusions of the studies discussed above are valid and reliable, then fluency and transparency have become the two main tenets by which translations are reviewed and evaluated; they have, indeed, become the 'norms' for reviewers of translated works, perhaps even verging on becoming a 'rule', where any deviation away from the two aforementioned criteria are seemingly highly chastised by reviewers. To refer back to Fawcett (2000: 305), the vast majority of reviewers seem more than willing to brand a translation as 'poor in relation to a criterion assumed to be universal and unassailable [transparency]'. Toury (1995/2012: 170) also asserts that, once norms have become accepted with a community, they will 'serve as criteria according to which actual instances of behaviour are *evaluated*'.

In this case, the community is the reviewers of translated literature, and the results of the above studies do indeed show that the suggested norms of fluency and transparency have become the main criteria against which translations are evaluated, making the reviewing process itself a normative behaviour. This, in essence, is reminiscent of what Chong (2020) calls the 'social' and 'institutional' uncertainties surrounding reviewing, where, in case of uncertainty, reviewers will tend to adapt their reviews to what is expected. This phenomenon can clearly be linked to what Janssen (1997: 277) describes as a process of 'orchestration', whereby 'critics and other connoisseurs little by little attune their judgements to each other, without making explicit references to each other's work and without there being a single conductor who might be responsible for the harmony'. Whilst she introduced this notion to apply to book reviewers in general, it seems to be the case here that we can use it productively to describe the process that seems to occur when translated works are reviewed. Janssen (ibid.) asserts that 'the larger number of critics who agree on the nature and value of a work, the more critics are inclined to comply with assessment' and this certainly seems to be the case with translation reviews. In other words, there is a clear knock-on effect, with the larger the number of reviewers who agree that fluency and transparency are the notions by which translations should be reviewed, then the more and more reviewers who will also evaluate translations in an analogous manner.

Nonetheless, Toury (1995/2012) also claims that 'non-normative behaviour' is always a possibility. In terms of the current discussion, such non-normative behaviour would be defined as reviewers evaluating a translation by other criteria beyond fluency and transparency. However, Toury (ibid.: 176) asserts that 'non-normative behaviour tends to be the exception in actual practice' and this has been evidenced by the fact that a very small number of reviewers have gone against the accepted behaviour of reviewing translations in terms of fluency and transparency to focus on other important aspects of the translation. Yet Toury (ibid.) also acknowledges that 'deviant instances of behaviour may be found to have effected *changes* in the very system'. In other words, non-normative behaviour can lead to a gradual change in what is accepted as a 'norm' in the first instance. If, then, reviewers were to change their practices of evaluating translations, this may lead to a change in the criteria by which translations are generally evaluated. Nonetheless, a large number of reviewers would have to take this approach before the process of 'orchestration' begins to take hold. Determining whether such a change has happened in the field of reviewing translated works over the past ten years or so is therefore one of the key aims of this book.

However, it is also important to point out that, whilst these previous studies have made valuable contributions to the field, introducing different angles as to how one may examine reviews of translated works, they also have a few shared issues. The scope of the studies examined above is often relatively small. To be more precise, they focus on translations of one author or only deal with a relatively small number of reviews. Much like the criticisms of Venuti's (1995) brief study, this makes it difficult to provide any definitive conclusions on how translation is actually perceived by reviewers. Another issue with previous studies is their restrictive focus: with the exception of a brief mention of how specialised publications such as *Lire* and *Le Magazine Littéraire* review translations in the Vanderschelden (2000) paper discussing French reviews, the studies have all focussed on broadsheets. This has provided us with an in-depth knowledge of how translated works are reviewed by this kind of press. However, broadsheets only form a small part of the network of reviewing and there has been a neglect in this field of other such media as specialised literary publications.

## The current study

The study therefore incorporates what has been lacking from such studies so far, not only attempting a cross-cultural comparison, examining the criteria by which translations are assessed in the United Kingdom, France and Germany in 2022, but also assessing how translations are reviewed depending on the popularity and specialisation of the platform on which the review is published. Although each platform has 'particular restrictions, characteristics and intended readership' and thus 'the content or the methodology of the review is likely to be different' (Johnson 2005: 130), previous studies of reviewing translated works tend to focus exclusively on broadsheets. The corpus of reviews for this book includes reviews from broadsheets, but will also examine reviews from specialised publications and a popular platform open to amateur, general public reviewers. The addition of a popular platform is in fitting with the current digital age, given that consumers increasingly rely on user ratings to inform their purchase decisions, with 70% of respondents indicating trust in them (Nielsen 2012: online). Furthermore, according to a Pew Research study published in 2012, more than 50% of people 'obtain news and information – including book reviews – on digital platforms' (Fay 2012b: online).

Yet not everyone is in favour of reviewing being undertaken by amateurs. Schickel (in Wasserman 2007: online), critic for *Time* magazine, asserts his belief that reviewing is not a 'democratic' activity, not an activity to be undertaken by amateur reviewers. He claims that it should be

> an elite enterprise, ideally undertaken by individuals who bring something to the party beyond their hasty instinctive opinions of a book. It is work that requires discipline, taste, historical and theoretical knowledge and a fairly deep sense of the author's entire body of work.

And Schickel is not the only writer to take this view. Austrian writer and translator, Federmair (2016), stopped writing reviews of literature, because he believes that the whole practice is being problematised by the rise of the online critic. In his article *Warum ich keine Literaturkritik mehr schreibe* [Why I do not write any more literary reviews], he claims that reviewing should be left to 'experts', those who 'in some manner have developed the required skills and are capable of presenting and justifying their judgements' (ibid.: online, my translation). Nonetheless, no matter what we think about the validity of amateur reviews online, it is undeniable that more and more potential customers are getting their information from reviews posted on popular platforms and it is therefore important to include a popular platform in the study to cover the vast majority of the reviewing network.

The reviews for the study have been collected from the following platforms. The British platforms are: amazon.co.uk (the popular platform); *The Times Literary Supplement* and *The Guardian* (mainstream broadsheet supplements); and *London Review of Books* (specialised literary magazine). The French platforms are: amazon.fr (the popular platform); *Le Monde* and *Le Figaro* (mainstream broadsheet supplements); and *Le Magazine Littéraire* (specialised literary magazine). And finally, the German platforms are: amazon.de (the popular platform); *Süddeutsche Zeitung* and *Der Spiegel* (mainstream broadsheet supplements); and *Literaturkritik* (specialised literary magazine). The reason for choosing Amazon as the popular platform across the three countries is that it is currently the biggest e-commerce platform featuring a comprehensive literature section – including a subsection for translated/foreign literature – and its net revenue and number of users are continuing to grow at a staggering rate (Forbes 2018: online). The broadsheets were selected mainly based on the previous studies discussed earlier in this chapter, with the exception of the German broadsheets. *Süddeutsche Zeitung* and *Der Spiegel*, however, rank amongst the top five German broadsheets in terms of average daily circulation, with the former having a circulation of 361,507 and the latter a circulation of 113,716 in 2018 (Informationsgemeinschaft zur Feststellung der Verbreitung von Werbeträgern 2018: online). They are thus broadly comparable to the British and French broadsheets included in the study. The specialised literary magazines included in the study were chosen according to three criteria: (1) frequency of publication; (2) number of subscribers; (3) ease with which reviews can be retrieved. With regard to all three of these criteria, the three specialised magazines included in the study are broadly comparable.

The corpus for this study includes all reviews of translated works published in the aforementioned broadsheets/cultural supplements and specialised literary magazines in the year 2022, no matter whether they write expressly about translation or not. The present study will analyse how frequently reviews actually acknowledge the fact of translation and it was thus important to collect all reviews of translated works. With regard to Amazon, however, it would have been beyond the scope of the corpus to analyse all reviews of translated works published in 2022 because of the extremely high numbers that this would have involved across all three countries. It was therefore decided to only collect Amazon reviews of translated works for which a review had already been published in the respective broadsheets. Overall, the number of British reviews included in the corpus is 881, broken down as follows: 573 from amazon.co.uk; 173 from the *Times Literary Supplement*; 102 from *The Guardian*; and 33 from *London Review of Books*. A total of 1058 reviews were collected from French platforms: 604 from amazon.fr; 138 from *Le Monde*; 172 from *Le Figaro*; and 144 from *Actualitté*. The German reviews collected for this study form the largest part of the corpus, with 1,898 reviews included: 1,469 from amazon.de; 233 from *Süddeutsche Zeitung*; 43 from *Der Spiegel*; and 153 from *Literaturkritik*.

## Framework for analysing reviews

The framework for analysing the corpus of reviews is largely based upon two already existing models, as introduced by Gullin (in Sirviö 2006) and Lanschützer (2010). In her model for analysing reviews of translated works, Gullin (in Sirviö 2006: 23–24, my translation) attempts to distinguish between the numerous ways in which reviewers of translated works can engage with the translator and his or her work and comprises seven different categories:

0. Translator not mentioned at all;
I. Translator only mentioned in the bibliographical details;
II. Comment on the style without mentioning that the work is a translation;
III. Comment in the text that the work is a translation;
IV. Brief comment on the translation, but not justified;
V. Brief, justified comment on the translation;
VI. Longer and more detailed evaluation of the translation which may lead to a general discussion about the work of translators.

Categories 0, I and III deal with the question of whether and where the translator is mentioned within the review. Categories IV and V are extremely similar to the notion of whether a judgement remains a 'brief blanket judgement' using the single adverb/adjective approach or whether reviewers go beyond this and actually provide some form of justification for their comment. Category VI attempts to pick out whether further analysis and engagement with the translation is present in the review, something which previous studies have tended to suggest is a rather rare occurrence. Category II is then for those reviews which do not mention the translation or the work of the translator, but still comment upon the style of the target text, something which is highly criticised by Vanderschelden (2000). The scholar provided the example of acclaimed translator, Albert Bensoussan, reviewing a translation and praising certain features of the text without actually mentioning the translator himself.

This attempt at categorisation is reminiscent of a slightly different model used by Lanschützer (2010). Her classification of reviews into various categories was mentioned earlier in the chapter, but it is worth outlining these once again, as, along with Gullin's (in Sirviö 2006) categories, they form the basis of the framework used to analyse the corpus of reviews for this study. Lanschützer (2010: 160–61, my translation) draws upon six categories to classify her reviews, as follows:

1. No mention of the translator(s);
2. The name(s) of the translator(s) are mentioned in the bibliographical information;
3. It is acknowledged that a translation is being reviewed by including casual comments such as 'now appearing in German' in the text, but the translator is not made explicitly visible;
4. The translation is judged using a blanket comment (such as the two 'prime examples', *congenial* and *clumsy*);
5. The reviewer engages briefly with the translation beyond an initial blanket comment;
6. Space is given to the translation and/or translators – there is a comparison between the original and the translation or between two different translations.

Categories 1 through 3 refer to the question of whether the work of the translator is acknowledged and thus generally correspond to Gullin's categories 0, I and III. Categories 4 and 5 are precisely the same as Gullin's IV and V, discussing whether a comment is made upon the translation and whether this comment is further justified with a short piece of analysis. Category 6 of Lanschützer's model is broadly comparable with category VI of Gullin's model, both including reviews which refer to the translation and the work of the translator in a more extensive manner. These two models were therefore instructive in formulating the categories into which the British, French and German reviews are allocated in the subsequent chapters of the book. These categories can be seen in Table 1 below.

Table 1: Categories for classification of reviews

| Category | Name/description |
|---|---|
| A | No reference to act of translation at all, and no comment on the style of the target text |
| B | No reference to act of translation at all, but comments made about the style of the target text |
| C1 | No mention of the translator's name, but act of translation acknowledged not within the main text |
| C2 | No mention of the translator's name, but act of translation acknowledged within the main text |
| D1 | Mention of the translator's name in the bibliographical information |
| D2 | Mention of the translator's name within the main text |
| E | Short unjustified comment on the translation[2] |
| F | Short justified comment on the translation |
| G | Extensive engagement with the translation[3] |

This selection of categories will allow us to gain important insights into how translations are reviewed across the three countries in a number of significant ways. Reviews which are assigned to categories A and B will be those which contribute to the complete invisibility of translation and the translator. They conceal the fact that the text has been translated, either by not commenting on the work of the translator and focussing on other aspects of the translated work in the review in the case of category A or, worse, by commenting on aspects of the work to which the translator has contributed and not mentioning the fact that the text has been translated in the case of category B. Categories C and D are for those reviews which promote what I term the 'superficial visibility' of translation and translators for the purposes of this project. I use this notion to refer to those reviews which mention translation in the briefest way possible, either through

2 'Short' in categories E and F means that fewer than three sentences of the review are dedicated to such a comment.

3 'Extensive' in category G means that more than three sentences of the review are dedicated to such engagement with translation.

mentioning the word translation or containing an implicit reference to the fact a text has been translated (such as 'now appearing in English') in the case of category C, or through mentioning the translator's name in category D. Categories C and D are broken down into two sub-categories for good reason: the location of the acknowledgement of the translation or the mention of the translator's name – either within or outside the main body of the text of the review – seems to be correlated to the amount of the review that the reviewer dedicates to the work of the translator.

Reviews which are allocated to categories E through G are seen to promote what I term the 'embedded visibility' of translation and translators; in other words, this is engagement with the work of the translator in the main body of the text, beyond a simple acknowledgement of the fact of translation. These three categories see a vast difference in the quantity and quality of engagement with the translation – from a brief unjustified comment on the translation in the case of category E to extensive engagement with the translated text and potentially its context in the case of category G – but all reviews assigned to these three categories attempt to draw attention to the work of the translator in some shape or form, even if only in the guise of a couple of adjectives. Such classification of reviews into the seven categories (or nine if we consider C2 and D2 to be separate categories) will therefore allow us to evaluate the extent to which translators remain invisible in the different publications and across the three different countries. The book draws upon this method of classification for the following three chapters: Chapter 3 will focus on the British context; Chapter 4 will focus on the French context; and Chapter 5 will focus on the German context. These three chapters provide crucial comparisons with previous studies and allow a glimpse into how translated works are reviewed from a cross-cultural and cross-platform point of view.

CHAPTER 3

# Reviewing in the United Kingdom

Based on the findings of previous studies, the invisibility of the translator was seemingly encouraged at various levels by reviewing norms and practices in the United Kingdom in the late 1990s and early 2000s. Indeed, much of what was discovered during that period chimed with what Venuti (1995) outlined in *The Translator's Invisibility*. Bush (2004) found that just thirty-one reviews of translations appeared in the *Times Literary Supplement* and four reviews in *London Review of Books* over a two-month period, relatively small figures compared to several French and Spanish equivalents. Fawcett (2000: 296) discovered that the quality most commonly preferred in a translation was 'transparency, the feeling that one is not reading a translation at all'. In addition to this, source language influence was widely condemned by reviewers. However, the 2010s saw some evolution in reviewing practices: Gray (2018) discovered a clear increase in the visibility of the translator compared to the 2000s, with the *Times Literary Supplement* and *The Guardian* almost always acknowledging that they are writing about a translated work, and many of their reviews commenting on the quality of the translation. It is in this context that the present chapter intervenes: it outlines how reviewers for amazon.co.uk, the *Times Literary Supplement*, *The Guardian* and *London Review of Books* engage with translation in the year 2022. For this purpose, a total of 881 reviews were collected, broken down as follows: 573 from amazon.co.uk; 173 from the *Times Literary Supplement*; 102 from *The Guardian*; and 33 from *London Review of Books*. As the chapter progresses, we will analyse each of these platforms in turn, determining the extent to which they promote the visibility of translation and/or the translator at various levels, drawing upon the categorisation methods outlined in the previous chapter.

## Amazon UK

Out of the 573 reviews collected from amazon.co.uk, 446 do not engage with translation at all and are therefore categorised into either category A or category B. The vast majority of these reviews fit into category A where there is no reference to the act of translation at all, and no comment is made on the style of the target text. A total of 382 reviews, or 66.7% of all amazon.co.uk reviews, are assigned to this category. This is not entirely surprising since, although Amazon reviewers do not have a limited number of characters in which to write their reviews, most of them will in reality have a limited amount of time. In addition to this, Amazon reviewers are more likely to focus on the plot of the work than the actual writing itself, as the following review (Amazon UK 1: online) of Hannah Bervoets' *We Had to Remove this Post* shows:

> *We Had to Remove This Post* is the story of a content moderator and how she came to leave her job, looking onto the dark realities of what lives under our social media. The novel opens with Kayleigh explaining to a lawyer that she'll recount what happened when she worked as a content moderator for a social media platform she cannot name, and that's what she does: explains why she needed money, how she trained and became a moderator, made new friends and a girlfriend there, and then how things started to go downhill, with her colleagues' newfound interests in conspiracy theories. The question is, did the content affect Kayleigh too?

Here, we see the reviewer outline the main purpose of the story, discuss how the novel opens and pick out the key highlights which occur throughout the work. This review, 111 words in length, is representative of the vast majority of Amazon reviews, usually between 100 and 200 words in length and focussing exclusively on the subject of the work. In addition to this, a small number of reviews focus on the recipient of the book – 'Son wanted it so not sure if its [sic] good' (Amazon UK 2: online) – or are written to provide feedback on delivery times, costs and the condition of the product – 'Arrived on time in good condition. Bought as a gift' (Amazon UK 3: online). We must remember that Amazon reviewers are generally not professionals, not paid or even rewarded to write reviews, with a few exceptions, and are not given any specific guidelines to follow in their reviews. Amazon does provide its own 'Customer Review Creation Guidelines', but these are not specific to book reviews and certainly not to reviews of translated works: 'include the "why", be specific, not too short, not too long [and] be sincere' (Amazon 2022: online). Indeed, Amazon encourages its reviewers to focus on their experience and service received as well as the product, which explains the presence of the various aspects outlined above in the reviews of translated works, rather than any mention of the actual translation itself.

Category B represents the second largest group of reviews on Amazon, with sixty-four reviews making no reference to the act of translation at all, yet still making comments about the style of the text; this equates to 11.2% of all Amazon reviews. This is the category which most scholars and translators find to be problematic: Hahn (2011: online), for instance, says that 'a reviewer who thinks he can praise the rhythm, the texture, the beauty of the prose [...] without acknowledging who's responsible, that's a reviewer who simply has no understanding of what translation is'. And yet many Amazon reviewers do choose to comment upon the writing or the prose as if the translator has had no input into the process. Forty-two of the sixty-four reviews assigned to this category are positive towards the writing or style of the text, such as in the following example taken from a review of *Tomb of Sand* by Geetanjali Shree, translated by Daisy Rockwell: 'The prose is simply breath-taking, with an almost poetic rhythm, but also witty and very funny and pointed in places' (Amazon UK 4: online). Translator Rockwell is not acknowledged anywhere in this review, and therefore the praise for the writing in the target language is assigned to the original author. There is a disconnect here between who actually did the writing in the target language and who receives the praise.

Yet it is more problematic in instances when the act of translation is not acknowledged, and the writing style is judged to be poor in some regard by the reviewer. The remaining twenty-two reviews in this category all criticise the author for their writing, even though the vast majority of works which are considered to be poorly written in the source language would be unlikely to get translated. For instance, one reviewer criticises Orhan Pamuk for the writing in *Nights of Plague*, translated by Ekin Oklap, as it 'seemed unnecessarily verbose, and rather than conjuring up a picture of the life and times of the characters, it made me long for the end of the sentence' (Amazon UK 5: online); another reviewer believes that 'it shows' that Werner Herzog is making his fictional debut, given that there is a 'puerile attempt to be poetic' in his prose work, *The Twilight World*, translated by Michael Hofmann (Amazon UK 6: online). A quick look at amazon.de demonstrates that German reviewers disagree with this conclusion: one reviewer thinks the book is 'well-written', whilst another believes that it is 'masterfully narrated'. The English Amazon reviewer could therefore be passing comment on the work of the translator rather than the original author, yet does not mention the translator at any point. In many cases, then, praise or criticism is being attributed to the wrong person.

A total of 64 of the 573 Amazon reviews promote what I have termed the superficial visibility of translation; these are reviews which are assigned to categories C1/C2 and D1/D2. Of these sixty-four, forty-eight reviews fit into the two categories C1 and C2 – three in the former, forty-five in the latter – where C1 is for reviews which do not mention the translator's name, but acknowledge that the work is a translation outside of the main body of text (in other words, in the title of a review on Amazon), and C2 is for reviews which do not mention the translator's name, but acknowledge that the work is a translation within the main body of the text. Twenty-eight of the forty-eight reviews in these two categories are neutral in tone towards the act of translation and simply acknowledge that this work is now available in English translation for the first time. Six of the reviews are overtly positive towards translation as an act, with reviewers expressing their gratefulness for giving them access to authors whom they would not have been able to read otherwise: one reviewer, for instance, claims that 'it's always a joyful experience to read authors in translation' (Amazon UK 7: online) when reviewing Tove Ditlevsen's *The Trouble of Happiness*, translated by Michael Goldman. However, in ten of the reviews classified into these two categories, there is the development of a notion that translation is or could be at fault for a reader disliking a book, or, rather, that translated works are considered to be uncomfortable or difficult to read. A reviewer of *Scattered All over the Earth* by Yoko Tawada, translated by Margaret Mitsutani, asserts that the writing style was 'not my cup off [sic] tea' and adds that 'this could be due to the translation' (Amazon UK 8: online), without explaining why or how they believe this might be the case. Another reviewer, this time of Paula Rodriguez's *Urgent Matters*, translated by Sarah Moses, says that reading the work was 'a bit out of my usual comfort zone' due to the genre and 'the fact that it was a translated book' (Amazon UK 9: online); this reviewer does, however, finally claim that they were glad that they decided to try it despite initial reservations. Nonetheless, the initial idea is still present that a translated work is something which takes extra effort, which requires a reader to go beyond their comfort zone.

The remaining four reviews assigned to categories C1/C2 see the reviewer outline their belief that the translation is not to blame for issues with reading experience; it is particularly noticeable that they feel the need to do so, attesting to the fact that many readers would automatically place the blame at translation's door. For instance, a reviewer of *Three Assassins* by Kotaro Isaka, translated by Sam Malissa, queries how the author is an award-winning Japanese writer and asks which language he is supposed to be an award winner in. The reviewer asserts that it is 'not English' and feels the need to add 'that is not blaming the translation' (Amazon UK 10: online). In addition, in a review of Kwon Yeo-sun's *Lemon*, translated by Janet Hong, the reviewer claims that they 'had to work incredibly hard to work out what has happening' in the book, outlines that the work is translated from the original Japanese, but also claims that the translation 'can't account for a lot of the confusion' (Amazon UK 11: online). What becomes clear from the reviews assigned to these categories is that translation has a negative reputation amongst many non-professional readers and reviewers. Category D1 – for reviews which mention the translator's name in the bibliographical information – is not relevant for Amazon, as reviewers do not provide separate bibliographical details, but 16, or 2.8%, of the reviews on this platform are assigned to category D2 where the translator's name is mentioned within the main text. All of the reviews which are assigned to this category are purely factual, with the sole intention of providing information about who is responsible for the act of translation. We never see any of the pre-conceptions present in some of the reviews assigned to categories C1/C2 in these reviews, or, in other words, individual translators are not targeted as being expected to produce a text which is confusing or might detract from the overall reading experience.

This means that the remaining sixty-three British Amazon reviews promote the embedded visibility of translation, reviews which engage with translation in some way beyond just a mention of the act of translation or the translator's name. Forty-three of these sixty-three reviews are assigned to category E, where a short, unjustified comment is made about the translation. The most frequently used words to make a passing comment upon a translation appear to be rather general in nature and it is difficult to know precisely what the reviewer means through their use of such words without any context. The words 'beautiful' and 'well' appear six times each to praise a translation, whilst the words 'excellent' and 'good' appear three times each. Yet an 'excellent' translation could, for instance, be a translation which reads well in the target language or, equally, it could be a translation which has managed to capture many of the aspects present in the source text. Only in two reviews do we see a clarification from the reviewers regarding what makes them come to such a conclusion: one reviewer of Mieko Kawakami's *Heaven*, translated by Sam Bett and David Boyd claims that the text is 'so well translated you'd think the author's native tongue was English' (Amazon UK 12: online), whilst a reviewer of Bitter Orange Tree by Jokha Alharthi, translated by Marilyn Booth, reserves praise for the translator for 'rendering the original Arabic so well into English' to such an extent that 'I never felt as though I were reading a translation' (Amazon UK 13: online). The word 'well' is being used in both cases in relation to how the target language work reads and with no consideration for the source text, but we cannot simply assume that this is the case for all of the reviews in which these more general words are used.

Other words which appear less frequently in the reviews to comment upon translation without further justification are as follows:

- Words which appear twice: fluent; lost; praise.
- Words which appear once: amazing; brilliant; captures (the tone); conveys (a sense of the otherness); exemplary; fantastic; fluid; great; not the greatest; outstanding; professional; seamless; skilful; smooth; strange; superb; wonderful.

Amazon reviewers only draw upon a couple of words which explicitly refer to how the work reads in the target language. These words are 'fluent', 'fluid' and 'seamless' and they only appear a total of four times in the 573 Amazon reviews collected. However, on the flipside, only two words are used which are explicit in referring to how the translated work has managed to reflect aspects of the source text: 'captures (the tone)' and 'conveys (a sense of the otherness)'. The remaining words in the list are more general in nature and very rarely negative towards the individual translation. In fact, only three words are used to criticise the translation without a provision of further justification in this whole body of reviews: 'lost', 'not the greatest' and 'strange'. 'Lost', for instance, is used in a review of Kwon Yeo-sun's *Lemon*, translated by Janet Hong; the reviewer claims that the novella is 'beautifully written', but adds a criticism that 'some things are definitely lost in translation' without any further comment (Amazon UK 14: online). But the majority of comments are overwhelmingly positive towards the individual translation. The fact that so many of the comments in reviews assigned to category E are positive also demonstrates that reviewers feel less need to justify a comment when they are praising the work of the translator.

Just seventeen of the Amazon reviews, or 2.9%, are assigned to category F, where a short comment is made upon the translation, and it is justified. Many of the words used by reviewers which are justified are more general terms to discuss the translation. The most frequent words which are justified are 'well' and 'excellent', being used in three reviews each. The justification is always short, fewer than three sentences, as the following example, taken from a review of Kaoru Takamura's *Lady Joker*, translated by Allison Powell, demonstrates: '[T]he translation is extremely well done and it reads as colloquial American (the 1947 section sounds slightly off but I think this is deliberate to convey the difference in colloquial Japanese at that time)'

(Amazon UK 15: online). The reviewer has dedicated more thought to the translation than those allocated to category E, discussing what makes them think that the translation is 'extremely well done' and engaging with a specific part of the translation. Other words which are justified and more general in nature are overwhelmingly positive: 'award-worthy', 'beautiful', '(does) justice (to)', 'just right' and 'wonderful' are all used and justified in one review each. Only two reviewers justify a comment which is critical of the translation, describing it as 'not good' (one review) or 'poor' (one review). In the reviews in which this happens, the reviewers provide specific examples to demonstrate which parts of the translation they believe to be troublesome. In a review of *Maria Theresa: The Habsburg Empress in Her Time* by Barbara Stollberg-Rilinger, translated by Robert Savage, for instance, the reviewer gives the work four, not five, stars, 'because the translation is not good e.g., Erbprinz translated as heir prince – it should be hereditary prince' (Amazon UK 16: online). This approach, however, is slightly problematic, since it is simpler to spot a mistake than it is to appreciate the work that goes into what might be considered a 'good' translation by individual reviewers. The reviewer in question therefore may well be tarring the quality of the whole translation with the same brush based on certain individual mistakes that they have spotted; for all we know, this one translation could be damned due to the one mistake which has been picked out.

Three of the reviews assigned to category F justify a comment pertaining explicitly to how the text reads in the target language: the word 'fluent' is justified in two reviews, whilst the word 'clear' is justified in one review. One of these reviews, of *Brezhnev: The Making of a Statesman* by Susanne Schattenberg, translated by John Heath, is particularly interesting, since it begins with the assumption that 'academic often equates to dull and translated means expect stulted [sic] English' (Amazon UK 17: online). The reviewer is therefore surprised that the text 'is written in a very accessible style for the non-specialist – indeed it crackles along at a good pace' and reserves praise for translator Heath: '[H]ats off to the translator who has made an excellent job of rendering the German into fluent English' (ibid.). In this instance, it becomes clear that the only criterion for this reviewer in particular is target-language readability, as the translator receives high praise. This, however, is not a common theme amongst the reviews. The other reviewer who justifies their comment about the translation being fluent (from a review of Rainer Maria Rilke's *Duino Elegies*, translated by Vita and Edward Sackville-West) asserts that this is due to a 'lyrical quality' (Amazon UK 18: online) being maintained; however, they also admit that they do not know the original German and therefore 'can't [sic] say what might be lost in recreating a form rather than just attempting to translate text and meaning', ultimately suggesting that this translation 'might be interestingly compared with other renditions in English' (ibid.). On the other hand, just one reviewer makes a justified comment on the translation using the word 'faithful'. In this review of Stendhal's *The Red and The Black*, translated by Horace B. Samuel, the reviewer admits that the translation is 'faithful to the style of original writing', but that this makes it 'difficult to understand at times and to appreciate the ironies used by Stendhal' (Amazon UK 19: online). It would therefore seem that faithfulness is good to an extent, but only if this does not detract from the easy readability of the translation at hand.

Just three of the 573 British Amazon reviews are assigned to what we would consider the 'ideal category' G, where there is extensive engagement with the translation, or, in other words, when more than three sentences of the review are dedicated to the translation. One of these reviews, of Geetanjali Shree's *Tomb of Sand*, translated by Daisy Rockwell, is overwhelmingly positive towards the translation and even has a sub-title 'WELL, DAISY ROCKS'. This reviewer engages with the translator's foreword to try and understand the translation decisions that have been made, asserting that Rockwell tried to 'recreate the text as an English dhwani of the Hindi, seeking out wordplays, echoes, etymologies and coinages that feel Hindi-esque. Thus, there are literal translations like "their minds turned to curd". I also enjoyed the translator's own little gems like noisome' (Amazon UK 20: online). The reviewer goes on to provide more insight into Rockwell's work, stating that the 'real skill of the translator lies in judging what portions should not be translated, [but] retaining a flavour of authenticity to satisfy the Indian reader' and gives an example from the text to support the point: 'D V Paluksar is singing Raga Shree, Hari ke Charan Kamaal. His voice circles softly above the mother-daughter conversation' (ibid.). This, the reviewer says, allows the reader to perfectly visualise the scene and 'the effect would have been completely lost' (ibid.) if Rockwell had attempted to translate this differently. The extensive analysis and examples provided make it clear that the translation is not simply considered in isolation of its context.

The second review assigned to category G is a review of *Duino Elegies* by Rainer Maria Rilke, translated by Vita and Edward Sackville-West. This review begins by discussing the context of the original translation which was published in 1931 and has been out of print until recent re-publication. The reviewer claims that the translation was initially well received, mainly because it was the first and only time the verses of Rilke had appeared in English, but that it eventually turned out to be highly controversial 'not least [due to] their decision to render the cycle entirely in blank verse – only one of the ten elegies that formed the piece was originally written using this structure' (Amazon UK 21: online). The reviewer then provides their own balanced opinion of the translation, outlining the positives and negatives of the Sackville-Wests' decision to adopt this form (ibid.):

> The use of blank verse here does seem to lend this a certain Shakespearian grandeur and resonance, particularly when read aloud, but I felt the structure and ornate style also made Rilke's verses more arcane and inaccessible than they needed to be. Although they do retain some of Rilke's marvellous imagery and, to be fair, the cycle's notoriously difficult to translate into English without losing or compromising some aspect of Rilke's intense vision.

Once again, this review feels far more convincing than most of the reviews encountered on Amazon, as it demonstrates a considered and developed understanding of what is involved in the translation process, not simply basing a judgement on a mistake in the translation or solely on how well the text reads in the target language.

The final review assigned to category G is the most critical of the translation. This review of *Too Much of Life* by Clarice Lispector, translated by Margaret Jull Costa and Robin Patterson, initially contextualises the release of the new translation and attempts a comparison with a translation by Giovanni Pontiero which was released in 1992. Pontiero's translation, the reviewer argues, is 'a work of love, has a beautiful clarity, with absolutely appropriate cadences' and 'never jars' (Amazon UK 22: online). The new translation, however, 'often does. Too often one is brought up short by a thoughtless, questionable tone' and, in that respect, the reviewer considers it to be 'not that well written' (ibid.). The reviewer ultimately says that readers should 'go back to Pontiero's translation' and claims that 'Lispector's work is worth 5 stars, but not this translation' (ibid.). This review is certainly vaguer than the other reviews classified into category G, does not draw upon specific examples, and the reviewer's main issue with the translation appears to be linked to a lack of target-language readability (in other words, that the translation often 'jars'). Nonetheless, the extensive engagement is still present, and it makes the review feel much more convincing than the majority of the Amazon reviews collected.

Overall, British Amazon reviewers are not likely to engage with translation in any form; indeed, we saw that 446 of the 573 reviews, or almost 78%, have been assigned to categories A or B and do not even mention the fact of translation. In this regard, we cannot consider that these reviews promote the visibility of translation. As we have seen, however, some reviewers do engage with translation in meaningful ways and in most cases their views towards translation are overwhelmingly positive: very few of the reviews assigned to categories E, F and G are critical of translation. However, we have also ascertained that there is a notion amongst some of these non-professional reviewers that translation is almost expected to be problematic and have a negative impact on the reading experience. In some of the reviews assigned to categories C1 and C2, and to some extent a couple of reviews assigned to categories E and F (such as the one that states 'translated means expect stulted [sic] English'), reviewers feel like translation may be something to be avoided, something with which it is not easy to engage. This is reinforced by those reviewers who say that problems with a work are definitely *not* down to translation; they are still acknowledging that there is a wider belief that translation is expected to be problematic.

## *Times Literary Supplement (TLS)*

The *TLS* published 173 reviews of translations in 2022. None of the *TLS* reviews are assigned to categories A through C2, since all of them have a minimum of a mention of the translator's name in the bibliographical information of the reviews. It seems, therefore, that the *TLS* gives its reviewers systematic guidelines that the name of the translator has to appear in a given location, since it is always present in the same place directly after the name of the translated work, and before the name of the author. A total of 51 of the 173 reviews are assigned to categories D1 and D2, 20 in the former, which seems to be the *TLS*'s minimum requirement, and 31 in category D2. These are the reviews which promote the superficial visibility of translation. The reviews which are assigned to these categories are generally of non-fictional works. Only four of the twenty reviews assigned to category D1 focus on translated literature, and three of these reviews come from the *TLS*'s set of 'In Brief' reviews, a selection of shorter reviews, generally between 200 and 400 words. In a review of this length, there is less space and perhaps less of an expectation that the reviewer will engage with the translation. Nineteen of the thirty-one reviews assigned to category D2 focus on translated literature, a significantly higher proportion of reviews than those in category D1. It may well be therefore that reviewers find it more important to draw attention to the name of the translator within the main body of the text for a piece of translated literature, even when they are not wanting to engage with the translation any further. All of the reviews assigned to category D2 contain a reference to the translator in a similar manner to the following review of *The Chief Witness* by Sayragul Sauytbay, translated by Caroline Waight: 'It first appeared in German in 2023 and has now been translated into English (by Caroline Waight)' (Holdstock 2022: online).

Given the small number of reviews assigned to categories D1 and D2, this means that 122 of the reviews fit into categories E through G, categories which promote the embedded visibility of translation. The majority of these reviews fit into category E, where the reviewers provide a short, unjustified comment on the translation: almost 50% of the reviews published in the *TLS* in 2022, 85 of the 173, are assigned to this category. The kinds of words used to comment upon translation are particularly interesting. Many of these appear to be related to how much of the original text the translator has managed to retain: for instance, 'sensitive' appears six times and is therefore the most common word used to comment upon translation without further justification; 'captures' appears four times; 'conveys' four times; 'faithful' three times, 'maintains' once and 'preserves' once. These words are often used in combination with one another, as can be seen in the following review of Édouard Louis's *A Woman's Battles and Transformations*, translated by Tash Aw: 'The frequent shifts from "you" to "she" aren't always easy for a reader to follow, but they convey a woman in motion, alive, as if tracked by a restless lens. Tash Aw's sensitive translation captures the vividness of Louis's voice' (Dennis 2022: online). Whenever the word 'faithful' is used by reviewers in the *TLS*, it seems that the reviewers are pre-empting that general readers may fall back into their preconceived attitudes about translation being problematic, but are almost taking the blame away from the translator through the use of the word 'faithful'. In a review of *Violets* by Shin Kyung-sook, translated by Anton Hur, reviewer Juhea Kim says that the prose is 'distinctly unlyrical and brusque', something which has been 'reflected in Hur's faithful translation' (Kim 2022: online). Rather than evaluating the brusqueness of the prose as a negative, the reviewer tempers down what could be seen as criticism with praise for the work of the translator. Similarly, in a review of *The Child Is the Teacher* by Cristina de Stefano, translated by Gregory Conti, reviewer Caroline Moorhead reflects on the translator's decision to write the book entirely in the historical present, claiming that it 'results in slightly breathless prose'. However, this is offset by the reviewer adding that it is 'in vogue in Italy' and the 'accomplished translator, Gregory Conti, has faithfully reproduced' the style (Moorhead 2022: online). The words which are used to comment on the relationship between the source text and target text are never used to criticise the translation but rather to reflect positively on what the translator has managed to achieve.

*TLS* reviewers are slightly more likely to use words which pertain to how the translation looks or feels in the target language than they are to use the words in the previous paragraph. In this body of reviews, the word 'elegant' appears four times; 'smooth' four times; 'brisk' three times; 'readable' three times; 'crisp' twice; 'lucid' twice; 'clear' once; 'graceful' once; 'idiomatic' once; and 'stylish' once – and all of them are used to portray a positive opinion on the translation. These words are often seen in combination with one another. For instance, a review of Johann Peter

Eckermann's *Conversations with Goethe*, translated by Allan Blunden, praises the translator for his 'clear and idiomatic translation [which] will provide Eckermann's artistry with grateful new anglophone readers' (Nicholls 2022: online). Only one review published in the *TLS* in 2022 uses an unjustified comment to criticise the work of the translator. This comes in a review of *Lucky Breaks* by Yevgenia Belorusets, translated by Eugene Ostashevsky, in which the reviewer claims that the original texts were 'lacking in clarity, unresolved, whimsical' and that this was not helped in the target language 'by Eugene Ostashevsky's unidiomatic translation' (Evans 2022: online); however, no supporting analysis or examples are provided here and the quality of the translation is solely assessed by how it reads in English. Much like we saw with Amazon reviews, *TLS* reviewers see little need to further justify a positive comment on the translation.

The majority of reviews which are classified into category E include the same kinds of more general comments upon translation which we saw on Amazon, whereby it is difficult to ascertain what the reviewers are actually reflecting upon when the comments are used. The remaining words which appear without further justification, all used positively to praise the translation, are as follows:

- Words which appear four times: beautiful; excellent; skilful.
- Words which appear three times: able; fine.
- Words which appear twice: admirable; brilliant; deft.
- Words which appear once: adept; agile; alert; assonant; capable; creditable; enthusiastic; expert; exquisite; flawless; gallant; ideal; inventive; nice; playful; solid; suitable; superb; vivid; well; with appropriate formality; with great freshness; with great verve; wonderful; worthy.

These words are rather generic and, without further justification to back up how they are being used, it is difficult to know what exactly about the translation and the work of the translator they are praising.

A total of 15 of the 173 *TLS* reviews, or 8.7%, are assigned to category F, where a short comment is made on the translation, and it is justified in fewer than three sentences. It is noteworthy that all of the reviews assigned to this category focus on translated literature or translated poetry. The words used to comment on translation which reviewers feel need further justification are varied. There are five instances of words appearing with a justification which are related to the relationship between the source text and the target text: the word 'preserves' (or a similar phrase such as preserving) is used three times; 'sensitive' appears once; and 'reproduces' is used once. We also see five instances of justified comments pertaining to the look and feel of the translation in the target language: the words 'accessible', 'clean-cut', 'elegant', 'fluid' and 'readable' are justified in one review each. In this regard, it does not seem that reviewers feel any extra need to justify their comment depending on which aspect of the translation they are focussing on, but rather it is an idiosyncratic process, whereby individual reviewers will decide whether or not to expand on their comment. All of the words listed above are used to praise the work of the translator, as are the majority of the more general words which are justified and each appears once: 'capable', 'engaging', 'skilful', 'successful', 'superb', 'tour de force' and 'witty'.

Only two words are used to criticise the work of the translator – 'rushed' and 'infelicities' – but the reviewers do provide justification as to why they have come to this impression. In both cases, it is ultimately down to what the reviewers consider to be individual mistakes in the translation which detract from target-language readability. In a review of *Co-wives, Co-widows* by Adrienne Yabouza, translated by Rachael McGill, reviewer Koelb (2022: online) appreciates that the translation is 'readable', but argues that it also feels 'rushed', since there are frequent 'tics [which] include retaining many of the commas and possessive prepositions from the original French text, wreaking havoc with restrictive clauses or simply gumming up sentences ("She was the child, of the child, of an aunt of Lidou's")'. This could be framed in more positive terms, in other words faithfulness to the source text: after all, the use of the commas in a phrase like this is not entirely natural in French and presumably part of the source text author's style. However, as this detracts from the reading experience in the target language, it is judged to 'gum up' sentences. To further support this point, Miller's (2022: online) review of Elin Cullhed's *Euphoria*, translated by Jennifer Hayashida, is critical of the translation for instances of the translation not reading entirely idiomatically in English, but is framed as 'infelicities': '[T]he self-punitively perfectionist Plath might have winced at the solecistic "I returned to the thoughts of Ted and I" – and would anyone really refer to the front hall of a thatched English rectory as a "foyer"?' Ultimately, these translations are damned for not reading completely idiomatically and naturally in the target language. The only other word used in a review assigned to category F which could initially be considered to be critical of the translation is 'lost'; however, the reviewer Fox-Martens (2022: online) in her review of Irene Sola's *When I Sing, Mountains Dance*, translated by Mara Faye Lethem, admits that there is an inevitability about the loss and the translator has actually done a good job: '[S]ome subtle nuances of the culture – and the power dynamic between Spanish and Catalan – are unavoidably lost, but Lethem ensures that Sola's distinctive lyricism survives in English.'

This means that twenty-two reviews – or 12.7% of all *TLS* reviews – are assigned to category G. All of the reviews included in this category focus on translated literature or poetry, with the exception of two, both of which focus on translations of philosophical works. In one review, Hall (2022) discusses the translations of two works: *Homilies on Isaiah* by Origen, translated by Elizabeth Ann Dively Lauro, and *Homilies on the Psalms* by Origen, translated by Joseph Trigg. Hall (ibid.: online) outlines that 'translators of literary works must make significant aesthetic decisions. It is no less the case in translations of philosophical works, where a great deal of our understanding of an author can hang on the framing of their key concepts and terms.' The reviewer then discusses each translation in turn: first dealing with Dively Lauro's translation and showing how the translator 'tak[es] time to explain her translation decisions' (ibid.), with examples, and then analysing how Trigg translates, or rather transliterates, the term 'Logos', assessing the benefits and pitfalls of the translator's approach. In total, 307 of the 1,304 words in this review are dedicated to engagement with the work of the translators. The other review of a philosophical work which is assigned to category G here looks at Ludwig Wittgenstein's *Private Notebooks 1914–1916*, translated by Marjorie Perloff. The reviewer in this instance, Ground (2022: online), provides a short biography of the translator, assessing that 'her native language is, like Wittgenstein's, Austrian

German' and demonstrating how the translator has 'real presence', drawing out how Perloff's work conveys key elements of the source text:

> In Philosophical Investigations, Wittgenstein wrote of how 'words can be wrung from us – like a cry. Words can be hard to utter: those, for example, with which one renounces something, or confesses a weakness. (Words are also deeds.)'. The translation here conveys that sense of expression in a particular place and moment: 'I am like a burnt-out oven, full of slag and dung', he writes in March 1915.

This review is a total of 3,419 words, and 199 of those are dedicated to the translation and its context.

Of the twenty-two reviews assigned to category G, the majority of these are overwhelmingly positive towards the translation at hand: indeed, fifteen of the reviews discuss the challenges that the translator has faced and analyse how they have managed to overcome them successfully. As an example, in a review of Fernanda Melchor's *Paradais*, translated by Sophie Hughes, reviewer France (2022) engages with two particular elements of the novel's language – swearing and slang – and how translator Hughes has managed to render these in the target language. France (ibid.: online) claims that this 'isn't a translation that nervously aims to please all markets but one that makes use of both British and US vernacular […] to create a tone and an argot that capture Melchor's hyperlocal language'. The reviewer provides examples from Hughes's lexicon, including 'old-time endearments such as "sunshine" and "scamp", alongside more robust anglicisms like "cunt-struck" or "lard-ass"' (ibid.). France's reflection is not simply on how the text reads in the target language, as this may have led the reviewer to an entirely different opinion of the translation, but also considers how the translator attempts to reconstruct what is present in the source text.

Five of the twenty-two reviews are positive towards the translation in the main, but provide examples and further analysis to outline some of their reservations with the translator's work. In his review of *Deceit* by Yuri Felsen, translated by Bryan Karetnyk, Naiman (2022) spends 385 of the review's 2,225 words on contextualising the translation and evaluating the work of the translator. Naiman (ibid.: online) assesses that Karetnyk has 'done an excellent job of reproducing the obsessive rhythm – the difficulty of Felsen's prose' and provides examples of the way in which Karetnyk 'adds an extra touch of metaphor' in his translation; nonetheless, the reviewer also outlines his slight quibble with the translation: 'Karetnyk's anachronistic use of "gift" as a verb, which seems more of the current century than the middle of the last one.' Given that, back in 1995, Venuti asserted that the currency of language is judged to be an important part of fluency, this review is particularly interesting: the reviewer criticises the translation, precisely because the use of a phrase is too current for the context of the work.

Yet this is not the only review assigned to category G which is broadly positive yet has reservations about the translation which has nothing to do with how the translation sounds in the target language but rather which focuses on the relationship between the source text and the target text. In her review of Colette's *Chéri and the End of Chéri*, translated by Rachel Careau, Roberts (2022) compares Careau's translation to a previous translation by Senhouse. She praises Careau for the fact that she has translated in line with her ultimate goal of Americanising the novel by drawing upon words and phrases like 'cookies', 'playing hooky' and 'gotten'. Nonetheless, Careau is also criticised for the translation being rather misleading at times: for instance, Roberts (ibid.: online) picks up on the fact that Careau translates 'lingerie' as 'linen closet rather than linen room, the place where washing can be hung to dry as well as stored, a status symbol in a large house such as Lea's'. The reviewer also picks out an instance from the source text where Léa and Chéri are lying in bed in which

> Colette employs the subjunctive: 'ils attendaient l'un et l'autre, dans une immobilité respectueuse, que la foudre décroissant du plaisir se fut éloignée d'eux'. Senhouse captures this mood, if imprecisely: 'Both were waiting, concentrated and motionless, for the abating tempest of their pleasure to recede.' Careau has: 'they waited, each of them, in a respectful stillness from which the decrescent thunderstroke of pleasure had distanced them'. (ibid.)

Once more, it is the fidelity to the source text, or rather the lack thereof, which is criticised by the reviewer here, even though the translation itself has in the main been successfully Americanised. We see a similar notion in Lensing's (2022) review of two translations of Felix Salten's *Bambi*. Damion Searls's 'elegant' translation is praised for proving to be 'a more sensitive guide to the original text than Zipes' (ibid.: online). The reviewer here provides examples of 'substantial deficits' which make Zipes's translation 'unreliable':

> In addition to several instances of dropped phrases and omitted sentences, a dozen lines describing Bambi's first encounter with the old roebucks – a passage important enough to have been illustrated in the 1928 translation – disappear entirely. Elementary vocabulary is also misunderstood: 'längst', or 'long since', becomes 'at last'; 'über einen herfallen' is translated as 'fall all over' rather than 'fall upon' (attack) someone. (ibid.)

The review continues with further analysis and examples and dedicates over 300 words to the two translations. Much of the impression gained by the reviewer, particularly on Zipes's translation, comes from the relationship between the source text and target text, not just on how the translation reads in the target language.

The other two reviews which are broadly positive towards the translation but have some reservations are Scott's (2022) review of Stendhal's *Red and Black*, translated by Raymond MacKenzie, and Paloff's (2022) review of *Black Earth* by Osip Mandelstam, translated by Peter France. In the former, the translation is assessed to 'capture much of the nimbleness and humour of the original text, as well as the experience of reading it in French' (Scott 2022: online). Nevertheless, Scott (ibid.) criticises the translator, not only for the translation sometimes being 'needlessly opaque – for example, he opts for "The ambitious" as the title of one chapter, where "an ambitious man" is a much more straightforward and logical translation of "Un ambitieux"', but also for MacKenzie's updating, considered to be jarring, 'as when the haughty Marquise de la Mole berates her daughter for "acting moody"'. The translator is also criticised for occasionally losing the wit of the original: '[A] circling "épervier" (sparrowhawk), whose resemblance to an eagle prompts Julien's self-comparison to Napoleon, but whose relative smallness makes us smile – is presented simply as a hawk' (ibid.). Reviewer Scott is critical of the translator for both a lack of readability and a lack of fidelity to the original text; both criteria appear to be important for Scott. In Paloff's (2022: online) review of France's translation, on the other hand, the translator is praised for having 'done a service not just to the poet, but to the work of future translators' by 'seductive[ly] rendering many of Mandelstam's most famous and difficult poems'. However, the reviewer criticises France for often choosing to remain too faithful to the source text at the expense of how the text flows in the target language. Indeed, Paloff (ibid.) asserts that 'not all of France's efforts are pitched so evenly between sound and sense; there are a few poems that seem to shed their music as they race through the poet's formal gauntlets and fondness for abstraction (e.g. "convex recognition's happiness")'. Unlike in the previous reviews that we have discussed, in this review, it is the fact that the translation of certain poems is not entirely natural and musical in the target language which is criticised by the reviewer, despite the acknowledgement that this is down to the source text poet's 'formal gauntlets' and 'fondness for abstraction'.

Just two reviews assigned to category G are mainly critical of the translation at hand, but for entirely different reasons. In her review of Kristín Marja Baldursdóttir's *Karitas Untitled*, translated by Philip Roughton, Moss (2022) criticises the work of the translator based on how the text reads in the target language. The reviewer outlines that, in the Icelandic text, the characters speak a dated language and then asks whether, as a translator, 'one tr[ies] to replicate archaic speech, given that the relationship between early twentieth-century and modern vernacular Icelandic will be different from the English equivalents' (ibid.: online). Moss (ibid.) admits that her Icelandic is not good enough to assess

> whether various awkward expressions are original or introduced in Philip Roughton's translation, but characters dismiss each other's ideas with 'oh, pish!' and refer to inconvenient events as 'dratted'. In the opening chapters in particular there are sentence fragments, missing punctuation and oddities of phrasing, such as 'the better-offs took precedence among farmers'.

The judgement is based on how the translation reads in the target language, not on the relationship between the English text and the Icelandic original. However, the other review which is critical of the translation here, even entitled *Lost in Translation*, focusses on the manner in which the translator attempts to make the text more readable and accessible in the target language. The review of Rainer Maria Rilke's *Duino Elegies*, translated by Vita and Edward Sackville-West, first claims that the 'translation is unreliable, with many misreadings: the church ("like a post-office on Sunday") of the Tenth Elegy does not belong to the angel, but to the city and its inhabitants, for instance' (Conquer 2022: online). Conquer (ibid.) then assesses the ways in which the Sackville-Wests have attempted to make Rilke 'become an English poet' by translating into a form which was significantly different from the original German text, namely blank verse. The reviewer claims that not only does 'this give the translation an undue regularity, but it also implies a different relation to tradition than is given by Rilke's dynamic and unsettled dactylic lines [...] which echo and at points resolve into the classical elegiac distich' (ibid.). The reviewer understands where the source text sits in its own cultural and poetical context and therefore bases his assessment on the infidelity and inaccuracy of the translation, rather than on how it reads in the target language.

Overall, reviewers for the *Times Literary Supplement* actively promote the visibility of translation at both a superficial and embedded level. All of the reviews collected for this study fit into one of the categories between D1 and G, meaning that the minimum reference to translation is a mention of the translator's name in the bibliographical information, thus promoting visibility at what we have termed a superficial level. But, even more importantly, 122 of the 173 reviews fit into categories E, F or G, reviews which are seen to promote the embedded visibility of translation. It is also noteworthy that the vast majority of *TLS* reviewers are positive towards the work of the translator. Generally, if a reviewer is less positive towards any aspect of the translation, these comments are very frequently further justified with analysis and/or examples from the text, and the reviews have thus been assigned to the latter of the categories, F and G. Indeed, seven of the twenty-two reviews assigned to category G are not overwhelmingly positive towards the work of the translator and reserve some criticism for the work of the translator. However, the way in which *TLS* reviewers tend to evaluate the translation seems to be idiosyncratic: some reviewers assess the translation solely by how it reads in the target language, but many also assess fidelity to the source text. The situation therefore seems to have evolved quite considerably since previous studies into reviewing practices, and *TLS* reviewers are now evaluating translations against a range of criteria.

## *The Guardian (TG)*

A total of 102 reviews of translated works were published in 2022 by *The Guardian*. Of these reviews, five, or 4.9%, are classified into category A, where there is no reference to the act of translation at all. Two of these reviews are focussed on the translation of political works: Narges Mohammadi's *White Torture*, translated by Amir Rezanezhad, and *We Uyghurs Have No Say* by Illham Tohti, translated by Cao Yaxue, Cindy Carter and Matthew Robertson. Two of the reviews are focussed on a collection of essays: Haruki Murakami's *Novelist as a Vocation*, translated by Philip Gabriel and Ted Goossen, and Elena Ferrante's *In the Margins*, translated by Ann Goldstein. Just one of the reviews is focussed on a work about architecture, namely, Charlotte van den Broeck's *Bold Ventures*, translated by David McKay. It is interesting that all of the reviews from *TG* which are classified into category A are works of non-fiction, where the act of translation is potentially seen as less creative or even less important. It also seems that the prominence of the location of the acknowledgement of translation within the review is important in determining whether or not the fact of translation will systematically be acknowledged: whilst *TLS* reviewers systematically mention the name of the translator immediately after the title of the book and the author of the source text (seemingly based on guidelines and templates that they receive from the publication), and therefore no *TLS* reviews have been classified into category A, the first mention of the translation and/or translator often comes within the main body of the text of the review in *TG*. Whether the prominence of the location of the acknowledgement of the translation or mention of the translator is of great significance at all is debatable. However, the broadsheet in which the translator's name appears before the main body of the review achieves greater consistency in ensuring that the fact of translation is acknowledged. None of *TG* reviews make a comment on the style of the work without acknowledging the fact of translation; therefore, no reviews are assigned to category B.

Equally, none of the reviews in *TG* are classified into category C1, where the act of translation is acknowledged, but not within the main body of the text. Three reviews, or 2.9%, are classified into category C2, where the act of translation is acknowledged within the main text, but without a mention of who translated the work. In a different review of Murakami's *Novelist as a Vocation*, translated by Philip Gabriel and Ted Goossen, to the one assigned to category A, reviewer Hughes (2022: online) comments that the Japanese author's voice has 'duly been translated into scores of other languages'. The other two reviews classified into category C2 review the same work: Serhii Rudenko's *Zelensky: A Biography*, translated by Michael Naydan and Alla Parminovia. In the first of these, written by Hinsliff (2022: online), there is a passing reference to translation and the idea that 'the book was originally intended for a Ukrainian audience'; in the second review, written by Anthony (2022: online), there is a reference to the work being a 'translated book'. It is noteworthy that all of the reviews that are classified into category C2 are works of non-fiction, supporting the point that some reviewers seemingly feel less need to engage with the act of translation beyond fictional works.

The majority of *TG* reviews from 2022 are classified into categories D1 and D2; in fact, a total of 60 out of the 102 reviews are assigned to these categories, or in other words 58.8%, a significantly higher proportion than for *TLS* (just under 30%). Many of these reviews – forty-five of the sixty – are classified into category D1, where the translator's name is mentioned in the bibliographical information of the text. In thirty-three of the forty-five cases in which this is done, the reviews come from what *TG* refers to as a 'roundup' (e.g. of best translated fiction, crime and thrillers, poetry). These articles review multiple works, sometimes all of them in translation, sometimes just one in translation alongside works originally written in English, and they all mention the translator's name very clearly after the title and name of the original author in the bibliographical information. This is not, however, to say that all 'roundup' reviews are assigned to category D1; indeed, some go on to further engage with the work of the translator and are therefore classified into one of the subsequent categories. Fifteen reviews from *TG* are classified into category D2, where a passing reference to the translator is made within the main body of the text. Most of these reviews focus on literary works (ten of the fifteen), with two focussing on comics and graphic novels, one on a picture book, one on a philosophical work, and one on a biographical work.

In a clear contrast to *TLS*, from which almost half of the reviews collected were assigned to category E, just 27 of the 102 reviews collected from *TG* in 2022, or 26.5%, fit into the same category. It seems, therefore, that *TG* reviewers are either less willing to make a comment on the translation than *TLS* reviewers or are provided with editorial guidelines with different recommendations compared to their *TLS* counterparts. Nonetheless, this number of reviews still allows us to gain interesting insights into the kinds of words which are used by *TG* reviewers to comment upon the work of the translator. It is particularly noteworthy that all of the reviews assigned to category E use words to comment upon the translation which are positive in nature. The overwhelming majority of these comments are more general in nature, and it is therefore difficult to know how the reviewer is coming to their judgement on the translation. The following is a comprehensive list of the words used by *TG* reviewers to comment upon translation which are more general in nature and remain unjustified:

- Words which appear three times: beautifully.
- Words which appear twice: deft; excellent; superb.
- Words which appear once: agile; clever; convincing; lyrical; meticulous; moving; nimble; (with) brio; (with) clarity; (with) empathy.

Most of the remaining comments from reviews assigned to this category focus on how the translation looks or reads in the target language. The words 'elegant', 'lucid' and 'seamless' all appear twice, whilst 'fluent' and 'transparent' both appear once. The following extract, taken from a review of *Retrospective* by Juan Gabriel Vásquez, translated by Anne McLean, demonstrates how reviewer Harrison shares his judgement on the translator's work with a passing reference: 'And what a life story it is. Fittingly, Vásquez opens the novel (transparently translated by Anne McLean) in Barcelona, during the Spanish civil war, where Cabrera's father, Fausto, is sheltering from bombs' (Harrison 2022: online). Just one review assigned to category E could be focussing on the relationship between the source text and target text, but in this particular review of Elisa Shua Dusapin's *The Pachinko Parlour*, translated by Aneesa Higgins, it is hard to know whether this is definitely the case given the lack of further engagement: 'Sensitively translated from French by Aneesa Abbas Higgins, it won the US National Book award for translated literature' (Feeny 2022). It is difficult to know whether the reviewer's comment, 'sensitive', refers to attentive and delicate preservation of certain features of the source text or rather sensitive to the topic of the novel, immigration.

Just seven, or 5.9%, of the 106 reviews from *TG* are classified into category F, where a short comment on the translation is justified with further analysis and/or examples, but no more than three sentences of the review are dedicated to the translation. Two of these reviews are overwhelmingly positive towards the work of the translator. In a review of Ásta Fanney Sigurðardóttir's *Forevernoon*, translated by Vala Thorodds, reviewer Tamás (2022) dedicates thirty-six of the ninety-eight words written about this collection of poetry to the translation itself. Tamás (ibid.: online) outlines that Thorodds's 'potent' translation 'conveys an unusual, lyrical voice, rendering the striking imagery into mysterious and appealing English', supporting the point with examples such as 'a circular pool/full of white water (moonlight is milk for nightcats)'. Here, the reviewer is not simply looking for readability in the target language but appreciates that the translator has managed to convey the imagery of the source text with the use of an English which is unusual and mysterious. In the other positive review assigned to category F, reviewer McGuinness (2022: online) praises translator Angela Rodel for 'the skill and delicacy' of her translation of Georgi Gospodinov's *Time Shelter*. The reviewer argues that qualities present in the ST – humour, sadness, absurd situationism, tragedy, pathos and ironic observation – 'are in abundant display for the anglophone reader' thanks to the work of the translator (ibid.). McGuinness (ibid.) supports his point by providing the example of the novel's title, asserting that it 'is a neologism in Bulgarian as it is in English, a grafting from the noun "bomb shelter"'. Much like in Tamás's review, McGuiness does not solely focus on how the text reads in English but also considers the relationship between source text and target text. One of the seven reviews classified into category F is mainly positive but with some criticism of the translator. In his review of Maylis Besserie's *Yell, Sam, If You Still Can*, translated by Clíona Ní Ríordáin, Banville (2022: online) praises the translator for how the text reads in the target language, claiming that 'the book reads as if it had been written in English, with much wordplay carried over deftly and inventively from the French'. The criticism of the translator comes from the fact that the reviewer does not agree with the translation of the title of the work – 'the title is a mistake – why not The Third Age, as in the original French?' (ibid.), but this does not impact on the positive impression that the reader gets from the review about the translation.

The other four *TG* reviews assigned to category F are mainly critical of the translation at hand, and in three of the four cases, this is because the translator has not produced a text which is natural and entirely fluent in English. In his review of Mariana Enríquez's *Our Share of Night*, translated by Megan McDowell, for instance, Byers (2022: online) claims that something with the translation is 'off' and clarifies what he means with the provision of examples and further analysis: 'Is "an adult depression that collapsed him into bed" really flawless English? And what are we to think when we're told, hilariously, that in the course of learning to cook, Gaspar "ventured painstakingly into a potato pie"?' The reader of the review gets the impression that the whole translation is flawed, as the reviewer pays no attention to how the source text was written and assesses the text solely on the fact that the work has not been translated into English which is completely transparent and natural. There is a similar theme in Thomas-Corr's (2022) review of Maria Gainza's *Portrait of an Unknown Lady*, translated by Thomas Bunstead. The reviewer admits to not finding this text as 'enthralling' as *Optic Nerve*, one of Gainza's previous novels, 'not helped by a few awkwardnesses in translation (e.g. "Alfonso suddenly seemed to step off his hurtling erotic toboggan")' (ibid.: online), even though this may have been down to the translator maintaining a key stylistic feature of the original text. The final review which criticises a translation purely based on its lack of fluency claims that the translator has been 'excessively loyal' to the source text. In her review of Geetanjali Shree's *Tomb of Sand*, translated by Daisy Rockwell, Chakraborty (2022: online) asserts that there 'would be no Booker for Shree' without the work of translator Rockwell, but that the translation is 'excessively loyal to the Hindi version', a notably different evaluation to the review of the same work collected from Amazon that we analysed earlier in the chapter (which praised Rockwell for retaining 'a flavour of authenticity'). The reviewer provides examples – for instance, '"no eating, no drinking, not even touching tea to mouth" is a commonly spoken sentence in Hindi, but its literal translation into English doesn't work' – and ultimately concludes that the novel 'is strewn with such phrases, where you can hear the Hindi and the English is broken' (ibid.). It is clear to see, in all three of the reviews, that naturalness in the target language is the main criterion against which the translations are assessed.

The final review assigned to category F which is mainly critical of the work of the translator comments that the translators attempt to make the target text more accessible and natural in English than the source text was in the original language, German. In the review of *Duino Elegies* by Rainer Maria Rilke, translated by Vita and Edward Sackville-West, which forms part of a 'roundup' review of the best recent poetry, reviewer Wheatley (2022: online) first situates the translation and outlines that it has been reissued for the first time in ninety years, before analysing what 'sank' the Sackville-West's translation, namely 'their insistence on parcelling him [Rilke] into blank verse, smoothing out so much that should have been spiky'. It is the excessive naturalness of the target text which is criticised, very much in opposition to the three reviews in the previous paragraph. Wheatley (ibid.) supports his point further by adding that 'chumminess is also a factor: "Every angle is redoubtable," begins the second elegy here, as though we are dealing with a doughty old dinner-party guest rather than a supernatural emanation'. It is noteworthy to add that all of the reviews from different publications which engage meaningfully with the Sackville-West's translation of *Duino Elegies* agree that their attempt to naturalise their texts in English are excessive and not faithful enough to the original German text.

All of the reviews published by *TG* which are assigned to category E were positive towards the work of the translator, whereas the majority assigned to category F have some reservations about the translation. *TG* reviewers are therefore more likely to provide analysis and/or examples in their reviews when they have been critical of, rather than positive towards, the translation. No reviews in *TG* dedicate more than three sentences to the translation and thus none are classified into category G. This is indicative of the fact that *TG* is a general-reading publication, and its reviews are published as part of the main broadsheet newspaper rather than in any separate supplement (unlike *TLS*). On the whole, *TG* reviews are much more likely to promote the superficial visibility of translation than embedded visibility: indeed, 63 of the 102 reviews published in 2022 fit into categories C1, C2, D1 or D2 (compared to thirty-four in categories E and F, and none in category G). We have also been able to determine that *TG* reviewers more frequently base their judgement of the translation on the criterion of naturalness in the target language than their *TLS* counterparts.

## *London Review of Books (LRB)*

The *LRB* published just thirty-three reviews of translated works in 2022, a significantly lower amount than the two broadsheets, but this is hardly surprising given the relative sparsity of publication of this outlet, in other words every two weeks. None of the thirty-three reviews here fit into categories A through C2, meaning that the minimum engagement with translation that we see from *LRB* reviewers is a mention of the translator's name in the bibliographical information. More than half of the reviews collected from *LRB* (19), however, are classified into categories D1 and D2 where the translator's name is mentioned somewhere in the review, thus promoting the superficial visibility of translation. A total of fourteen of the nineteen reviews sit in category D1 where the name of the translator is only mentioned in the bibliographical information. It appears that *LRB*, much like *TLS*, reviewers systematically add the name of the translator, along with the name of the author of the review, the title of the book being reviewed and the author of the original text, to their reviews. The subject of eight of the reviews which fit into category D1 is a fictional work, whilst only six of the reviews focus on non-fictional works. It does not seem, then, as though genre has an impact on what kind of engagement the work of the translator receives. Five reviews sit in category D2 and the subject of three of these are non-fictional works. In these five instances, a passing reference is made within the text to the translator, such as in the following review of *Myself and My Aims: Writings on Art and Criticism* by Kurt Schwitters, translated by Timothy Grundy: 'His activity involved multiple, often manic collaborations, the range of which is evident in the edition of his writings, expertly selected by Megan Luke and translated by Timothy Grundy' (Foster 2022: online).

A further six of the thirty-three reviews, or 18.2%, are assigned to category E where a short comment is made on the translation without any further justification. The subject of two of these reviews is non-fictional works, and four of the reviews focus on a fictional work; once more, it appears that genre has no real impact on the extent of reviewer engagement on the work of the translator in *LRB*. Five of the six reviews assigned to this category make a positive comment on the translation. In his review of Aziz BineBine's *Tazmamart: Eighteen Years in Morocco's Secret Prison*, translated by Lulu Norman, reviewer Harding (2022: online) asserts that the translator 'has done well by BineBine's original, as Linda Coverdale did by Jelloun's', presumably, although not definitively, reflecting upon the relationship between the source text and target text. In his review of *Kapo* by Aleksandar Tišma, translated by Richard Williams, Parks (2022: online) reflects on three works by the original author – *The Book of Blam*, *The Use of Man* and *Kapo* – and comes to the conclusion that all of the works are 'superbly translated by Michael Henry Heim, Bernard Johnson and Richard Williams'; the comment is general in nature and it is difficult to know which aspect of the translation has been 'superb'. The third review classified into category E which is positive towards the work of the translator is Lennon's (2022) review of Hervé Le Tellier's *The Anomaly*, translated by Adriana Hunter. Lennon (ibid.: online) claims that Le Tellier's prose 'is beautifully efficient and capable of quiet devastation', adding that it has been 'translated (wittily) by Adriana Hunter'. It is possible to infer that the use of the word 'witty' is a judgement by the reviewer on how the text reads in the target language, rather than a comparison between the source text and target text.

Another positive comment comes from a review of two translations, *Voices of the Lost* by Hoda Barakat, translated by Jonathan Wright, and Hassan Blasim's *God 99*, translated by Marilyn Booth. Reviewer Dziadosz (2022: online) praises the work of both of the translators: Wright 'keeps the ribaldry of these moments [a particularly harrowing scene in which a workshop owner rapes his young, male employees, and the boys get revenge] alive in his English translation', whereas Marilyn Booth is assessed to have 'capture[d] the starkness of *Voices of the Lost*'. A review of Anne Serre's *The Fool and Other Moral Tales*, translated by Mark Hutchinson, is the final review to be classified into category E which praises the work of the translator: reviewer Elven (2022: online) assesses that 'Hutchinson's translations retain as far as possible the rhythms of Serre's prose', the only comment which explicitly reflects on a key aspect of the source text and how it is conveyed in the target language. Just one of the reviews which sits in category E makes a slightly critical comment towards the work of the translator. In her review of Maryse Condé's *Crossing the Mangrove* and *Waiting for the Waters to Rise*, translated by Richard Philcox, reviewer Reza (2022: online) contends that many of the translations of Condé have 'been undertaken by her husband, Richard Philcox, with a sometimes heavy hand'. It is difficult to ascertain precisely what the reviewer is reflecting upon with this comment, but 'with a sometimes heavy hand' certainly seems to refer to a lack of fluency and naturalness in the target language.

Another four reviews are assigned to category F where a short comment is made upon the translation and further justified. Once again, we see that the genre of the work does not really affect the kind of engagement that the translation receives: three of the reviews assigned to this category focus on a work of non-fiction, whilst only one focusses on a piece of fiction. It is also noteworthy that there is no pattern in what kind of comment receives further justification. One of the reviews here is overwhelmingly positive towards the work of the translator, one almost entirely balanced, with positive and critical comments, and two overwhelmingly negative. The positive review is of Marit Kapla's *Osebol: Voices from a Swedish Village*, translated by Peter Graves. In this review, Greenlaw (2022: online) outlines the way in which the original author Kapla takes a poet's approach to the work, 'attending to the rhythms of thought and breaking the natural phrase'. The reviewer engages with the work of the translator in thirty-two words of the review, asserting that Graves 'more than rises to the challenge this [the poetic approach] presents', since he 'has found a register in English – both offhand and choral – that brings the voices together without letting them merge' (ibid.). In this instance, it appears that Greenlaw is assessing the work of the translator by the relationship between the style of the source text and the target text and is not solely interested in how the translation reads in the target language. In Mitchell's (2022: online) review of *My Heart Hemmed In* by Marie Ndiaye, translated by Jordan Stump, the reviewer firstly outlines that the translator admits to initially giving up on the translation after the first few pages, as Ndiaye's sentences are 'tonally precarious, easy to make flat or overly poetic'. Mitchell (ibid.) nonetheless comes to a balanced judgement on the end product: Stump, she claims, 'doesn't always find the balance – some passages are too heavy or verbose – but on the whole he conveys the strangeness of Ndiaye's French'. Once more, it is not only the fluency of the target text being assessed but rather there is some consideration of how and why the target text is translated in a 'strange' manner to mirror how the text was written in the source language.

The final two reviews assigned to category F are, on the other hand, critical of the work of the translator, and in both instances, this is down to the fact that the reviewers have picked out what they consider to be non-subjective, real translation errors. In his review of Juan Villoro's *Horizontal Vertigo: A City Called Mexico*, translated by Alfred MacAdam, reviewer Tony Wood (2022: online) is critical that the US publisher let through what he refers to as 'translation gaffes': '[A]t one point a notary (*notario*) is rendered as "notorious" (*notorio*) and, throughout, indigenous Mexicans are bafflingly transformed into "Native Americans".' The impression the reader of this review gets is that the whole translation is flawed, and yet the reviewer only provides two examples of issues that he has found with the translation. There is a similar theme in Mars-Jones's (2022) review of Benjamin Labatut's *When We Cease to Understand the World*, translated by Adrian West. Mars-Jones (ibid.: online) asserts that the translator 'could have done better' with his translation, 'Ministry of Home Safety', adding that 'such an institution would presumably concern itself with such things as electrical insulation and the flammability of soft furnishings, potentially life or death matters but not a concern of the wartime Ministry of Home Security'. Whilst this criticism seems to be justifiable, the overriding impression the reader of the review receives from this evaluation is that the translation is entirely flawed based on one mistake, since the reviewer does not offset their comment with any praise for the work of the translator.

Four of the reviews collected from *LRB* in 2022, or 12.2%, are assigned to category G where the engagement with the translation takes up more than three lines of the review. All of the reviews offer a comparison between the source language and target language, and two even compare multiple translations of the same source text. The first review classified into category G here is Shaw's (2022) review of Susanne Wedlich's *Slime: A Natural History*, translated by Ayca Türkoğlu. In this review, Shaw (ibid.: online) argues that the translator 'deploys an impressive and viscous vocabulary' to portray the universal 'feeling of disgust that slime provokes'. The reviewer discusses the existence of the concept of slime in English and German, asserting that both languages 'have slimy words for slimy things' and providing an example from Türkoğlu's translation: frogspawn looking like 'slimy star snot' (ibid.). However, Shaw (ibid.) is also aware that 'differences in translation do exist […]. German-speaking friends tell me that *schleim* is more neutral than in English; you can tuck into a warm bowl of *Haferschleim*, for example ('oat slime', or oatmeal)'. In this instance, there is clear engagement with both the source and target languages, alongside a comparison between the two. Morrison's (2022) review of Geetanjali Shree's *Tomb of Sand*, translated by Daisy Rockwell, is similar in scope to Shaw's review. In this instance, Morrison (ibid.: online) takes a balanced approach between praise for the retention of the 'Hindi-esque effect' in the target language, but also has reservations about how the prose sounds in English:

> Rockwell reproduced a Hindi-esque effect in English with sufficient brio for *Tomb of Sand* to win this year's International Booker prize. The prose can be discomfiting: allusions are perplexing and wordplay is strained ('Their minds turned to curd: hue and cry occurred'; 'One more knot. A no, not. A know not. A knew not. A new not. A new desire'). But there are markers to sustain the narrative, and engagingly terse chapters, and the humour never lets up.

Unlike some of the previous reviews of Shree's *Tomb of Sand* which we have encountered in this chapter, reviewer Morrison (ibid.) does not only judge the text against the criterion of naturalness in the target language but also considers the relationship between the source and target languages. A review based solely on how the prose sounds in the target language may have come to an entirely different judgement on the translation as a whole.

Gooding (2022) takes a slightly different approach in his review of a new translation of Claude-Lévi Strauss's *La Pensée Sauvage* by Jeffrey Mehlman and John Leavitt. In this review, 535 of the 3,243 words are dedicated not only to the translation at hand and the relationship between the source and target languages but also to previous translations of the same text. Gooding (ibid.: online) begins with a discussion of the title of the work *La Pensée Sauvage*, critically evaluating previous translations with a comparison between the source language and target language, before judging that the 'new title is much better':

> The first English translators went for 'savage', giving the book a real facepalm of a title: The Savage Mind. The original French has the primary sense of wild or untamed thought, but it also plays on the name of the flower – *la pensée*, pansy – whose image appeared on the cover. The connection was also made through the epigraph from Hamlet that Lévi-Strauss placed in a later edition: Ophelia's 'and there is pansies, that's for thoughts'. Both pun and quotation were gentle invocations of the book's main theme: for Lévi-Strauss, human thought in all its complexity is as natural a thing as a wild flower, and *La Pensée Sauvage* tried to show how its garden grows. The play on words doesn't carry into English (this new translation has a bouquet of pansies on the cover in lieu), but calling it The Savage Mind butchered the primary sense too, suggesting the brutal and witless natives of the colonial imagination – a reversal of the book's intention. Jeffrey Mehlman and John Leavitt generously suggest that the choice of 'savage' might have been an ironic reference to the anthropological vocabulary of an earlier generation, whose theories Lévi-Strauss had set himself to overturn. Maybe, but if so it didn't come off, and in any case it was only the most obvious symptom of a deeper malaise. ' "Wild thought" and not "the thought of wild men"', Lévi-Strauss explained, to no avail. The new title is much better.

In this review, there is comprehensive engagement with how the title works in the source language, criticism of why previous translations do not do justice to the original title, along with a judgement on the title of the latest translation. However, the review does not focus solely on the title: it also engages with the 'complex prose style' and 'the breadth of references' which make things extra difficult for any translator (ibid.). There is a discussion of how previous translations were problematic: for instance, the reviewer shows how 'Lévi-Strauss didn't recognise his own book' in the 1960s translation by Needham, Wolfram and Gellner (ibid.). And this is all the more reason, according to the reviewer, that Mehlman and Leavitt's new translation is needed: '[F]inally, there is a fresh, agile English rendering of one of the 20th century's greatest, strangest and most challenging works' (ibid.).

Michael Wood's (2022) review of *The Aphorisms of Franz Kakfa*, edited by Reiner Stach and translated by Shelley Frisch, is similar in many ways to the Gooding review; in other words, it picks apart how the source language works, reserves praise for the most recent translation – Wood (ibid.: online) asserts that 'Shelley Frisch's English version keeps pace admirably' – and compares it to previous translations. The majority of the focus of the review is, much like Gooding's, on the title of the original German work, *Du bist die Aufgabe*, a quotation from the text, 'part of a larger proposition: "Du bist die Aufgabe. Kein Schüler weit und breit"' (ibid.). Wood (ibid.) claims that the translators are very close to one another in their translations of the title: Malcolm Pasley, for instance, takes an identical approach to Frisch in his translation from 1999 and translates it as 'You are the task. No pupil far and wide' (ibid.); Michael Hofmann, in his translation from 2006, has '"task" too, but adds the word "exercise", and his pupil is a student' (ibid.); and finally, Wood recalls a translation which he considers to be 'a more ordinary, less dignity-prone rendering: "You are the homework. No student anywhere near." The tone is too casual, but it does evoke more immediately the absent teacher as well as the missing student' (ibid.). Such a comparison between source and target language, as well as between multiple existing translations, is very much the exception rather than the norm. It is noteworthy to add here that, although we may have expected critical comments on the work of the translator to be justified more frequently, all of the *LRB* reviews assigned to category G are mainly positive towards the work of the translator in question.

Overall, we have been able to observe that the *LRB* reviews collected from the year 2022 do promote the visibility of translation in some regard: nineteen of the thirty-three reviews are classified into categories D1 and D2, where the act of translation is acknowledged briefly, thus promoting what we term the superficial visibility of translation; the other fourteen reviews are classified into categories E through G for reviews in which there is more extensive engagement with the work of the translator, promoting the embedded visibility of translation. In this regard, *LRB* reviews are similar to *TLS* reviews: no reviews in this publication are classified into categories A, B, C1 or C2. However, *LRB* reviewers are less likely to engage with the work of the translator at the embedded level than *TLS* reviewers, with more than half of *LRB* reviews being classified into categories D1 and D2, compared to less than a third of *TLS* reviews. Much like all of the other platforms, *LRB* reviewers much more frequently praise, rather than criticise, the work of the translator.

## Conclusions

The discoveries of this chapter are represented in Figure 1, which outlines the percentage of reviews that have been assigned to each category across the four different United Kingdom platforms.

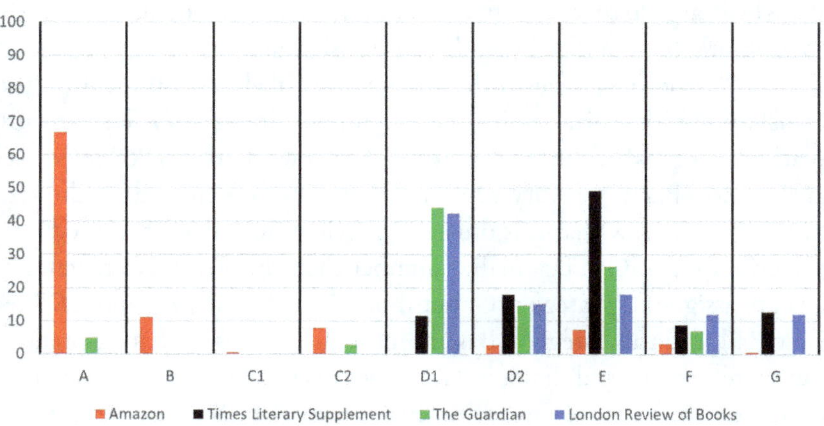


Figure 1: Percentage of reviews assigned to each category across the different UK platforms

Amazon is the clear outlier of the four platforms, with the vast majority of Amazon reviews being classified into category A where no reference is made to the fact of translation at all. Reasons have been suggested for this earlier in the chapter, but none seem more convincing than the fact that Amazon reviewers have a vast number of things that their reviews could focus on and, in reality, only a limited amount of time. The only other reviews which are classified into category A are from *TG*, which, unlike *TLS* and *LRB*, do not seem to have a systematic manner in which to mention the name of the translator. Amazon is also an outlier in terms of the number of reviewers who comment on the style of the target text without mentioning the translator; indeed, no *TLS*, *TG* or *LRB* reviewers do this. It has become clear throughout the chapter, then, that Amazon reviewers are the most likely to ensure that translation remains invisible within their reviews. On the other hand, *TG* and *LRB* reviewers are the most likely to mention the name of the translator and not engage with the work of the translator any further; more than 40% of *TG* and *LRB* reviews have been classified into category D1, where the name of the translator is only mentioned in the bibliographical information of the review and nowhere else. It has been argued therefore that *TG* and *LRB* reviewers are the most likely to promote the superficial visibility of translation.

*TLS* reviewers, meanwhile, are the most likely to comment on the translation with a brief, unjustified comment. Indeed, *TLS* is the only platform from which more than 30% of reviews do this. *LRB* reviewers are the most likely to justify a comment once it has been made (although, in practice, we saw that it is only eight reviews which are classified into categories F and G, a far smaller number than the *TLS*). No reviews in *TG* are assigned to category G, but more than 10% of *TLS* and *LRB* reviews fall into this category. Based on the discoveries of this chapter, we can therefore contend that it is *TLS* reviewers who promote the visibility of translation at a more embedded level: 70.5% of *TLS* reviews fit into categories E through G (compared to 42.4% of *LRB* reviews, 33.4% of *TG* reviews and 11.0% of Amazon reviews). Beyond the figures, there are also two particularly noteworthy trends. Firstly, the vast majority of reviewers across all four platforms have praised, rather than been critical of, the work of the translator. Particularly on the professional platforms, it is only on rare occasions that there is any form of criticism towards the translation at hand. Secondly, words relating to transparency are not used that frequently to discuss translation. Often, there is extensive and meaningful engagement with the relationship between the source text/language and the target text/language. Overall, therefore, it seems justifiable to argue that translators are now more visible in the United Kingdom in the present day, both at the superficial and embedded levels of visibility, than back in the early 2000s.

CHAPTER 4

# Reviewing in France

In Chapter 2, we saw how French reviewers engaged with the act of translation in the 2000s and 2010s: Vanderschelden (2000) discovered that the name of the translator is often mentioned in the title of a review, but that the translation is of secondary importance in the body of a review. If a comment is made, it is frequently a brief blanket judgement such as 'excellent translation'. Bush (2004) found that reviewers always include the name of the translator in the heading of the review and almost never comment on the quality of the translation. Similarly, Gray (2018) determined that only 7.04% and 4.31% of reviews in French broadsheets *Le Monde* and *Libération*, respectively, go beyond an acknowledgement of the fact of translation to comment upon the work of the translator. Previous studies have therefore painted a clear picture that French reviewers have been likely to promote what we term the superficial visibility of translation, but are loath to engage with translation at a more embedded level. But is this still the case in 2022? This is where the present chapter intervenes, demonstrating how reviewers from a general public platform (amazon.fr), two broadsheets (*Le Monde* and *Le Figaro*) and one specialised literary magazine (*Actualitté*) reviewed works in 2022. For this purpose, a total of 1,058 reviews were collected, broken down as follows: 604 from amazon.fr, 138 from *Le Monde*, 172 from *Le Figaro* and 144 from *Actualitté*. This chapter will progress much like Chapter 3: in other words, it will examine reviews from each of these platforms in turn, assessing whether French reviewers are now more willing to engage with translation at an embedded level and whether there are significant differences between reviews from the distinct types of platform.

## Amazon France

Of the 604 reviews collected from amazon.fr, 517 are assigned to category A for reviews in which there is no reference to the act of translation at all, and no comment is made upon the style of the target text. This equates to 85.6% of all French Amazon reviews. Much like British Amazon reviewers, French reviewers do not have a limit on the number of characters that they can write, but they do in reality have a limited amount of time and are not being paid or rewarded in most cases for their reviewing activity. Unsurprisingly, therefore, reviewers generally focus on one of three things in their review: the plot; the service; or an evaluation and/or recommendation of the book. The vast majority of Amazon reviews assigned to category A include some information about the plot. The following example is a complete review, just fifty-four words in length, of Michael McDowell's *Blackwater*, translated by Yoko Lacour and Hélène Charrier, and which focusses exclusively on what happens in the work. The reviewer (Amazon France 1: online) writes

> from the very first pages, you are drawn into the story, the setting and the characters: the antagonism between Mary-Love (the dominant woman of the family) and Elinor (a mysterious creature), the relationship between the whites (rich) and the blacks (servants), the superstitions, the supernatural, the presence of the rivers, etc. All of that makes this saga addictive.[1]

Yet many reviewers choose instead or additionally to focus on the service that they received from Amazon, such as the delivery time or the price and quality of the product. For instance, in this review – only thirteen words in length – of Stephen King's *Billy Summers*, translated by Jean Esch, the reviewer only discusses the service that they received and does not touch on what takes place in the novel: 'Rapid and diligent service. Careful packaging. Fast delivery and the book is top!' (Amazon France 2: online). The final thing that French Amazon reviewers tend to

1 All of the quotations in this chapter were originally written in French and have been translated by the author.

focus on, if not the translation, is their evaluation of whether a book is worth reading. An example of this comes from a review of Deon Meyer's *Cupidité*, translated by Georges Lory: 'I loved it. Simple reading. The plot is well constructed, and the author "is to the point". You do not want to put down the book. I recommend it' (Amazon France 3: online). It is also noteworthy that, despite the lack of engagement with the work of the translator, twenty-seven of the reviews assigned to category A are willing to engage with the work of other contributors to the work beyond the original author. The two groups of contributors who frequently get mentioned are illustrators and, in the case of the audiobooks, speakers. In a review of the audiobook version of Douglas Kennedy's *Les hommes ont peur de la lumière*, translated by Chloé Royer, it is noteworthy that Royer is not mentioned, but speaker François Cognard is. Not only is his name mentioned in the review, but the reviewer goes on to say (Amazon France 4: online) that Cognard 'delivers a quality interpretation, embodying the different characters to perfection'. Illustrators and speakers are very visible contributors to the final product that the reader receives, whereas the role of the translator is invisible by definition; this may be why Amazon reviewers who do not mention the translator feel more comfortable commenting upon the role of illustrators and speakers.

A total of thirty-nine of the Amazon reviews, or 6.5%, are assigned to category B where the fact of translation is not acknowledged, but the style of the target text is commented upon. This could be considered the most problematic of the categories in this study, as reviewers are actively commenting upon the work of the translator without actively acknowledging him/her. The reviews assigned to this category do one of two things, both of which are problematic: either the reviewer praises the style of the writing and the important work of the translator in contributing to the style in the target language is overlooked, or the style of writing is criticised, and the blame is attributed to the author when this could well be down to the translator. The following example, taken from a review of *Vies et mort de Lucy Loveless*, written by Laura Shepherd-Robinson and translated by Pascale Haas, demonstrates how the style of the author is praised, yet it could well be the style of the translator that the reviewer likes, as they are reading the translator's, not the author's, words. However, the translator is not mentioned once: 'One thing is for certain: I will follow this author closely because I like her style of writing a lot' (Amazon France 5: online). On the flipside, this example, taken from a review of Michael McDowell's *Blackwater*, translated by Yoko Lacour and Hélène Charrier, emphasises how the criticism of the writing style can potentially be attributed – mistakenly – to the original author: 'The style of writing lacks fluidity for me. I often stumbled over phrases. Nevertheless, this novel can be read quickly because the text is airy, and the book only has 250 pages' (Amazon France 6: online). In this review, that lack of fluidity may well be down to how the text reads in translation, but given that the reviewer has not acknowledged that this is a translated text, the reader of the review may assume that the blame for this lies with the original author.

None of the Amazon reviews collected from 2022 fit into category C1, or, in other words, none of the reviewers only acknowledge the fact of translation in the header of their review without also touching upon translation in the main body of their review. Twenty of the 604 reviews, or 3.3%, however, are assigned to category C2 for reviews in which the translation is acknowledged in the main text. This is mainly done in two ways by Amazon reviewers. The most frequent way in which reviewers assigned to this category acknowledge the fact of translation is through a phrase such as 'now translated into French' or similar. All in all, thirteen of the twenty reviews take a similar approach to this reviewer of Seo Mi-ae's *Les 30 Meilleures Façons d'assassiner son mari*, translated by Jihyun Kwon and Rémi Delmas, who comments (Amazon France 7: online) that 'translated into French for the first time here is her first book which includes several short stories on particularly disastrous pieces of life'. The remaining seven reviews assigned to category C2 give their thanks to the translator but do not provide the name of the translator anywhere in their review. The following example, taken from a review of Viola Ardone's *Le Choix*, translated by Laura Brignon, demonstrates this perfectly: '[W]hat is certain, however, is that I really appreciated the reading experience (thank you to the translator)' (Amazon France 8: online). Unlike the reviews which were assigned to category B, there is an acknowledgement here that the work has been translated and that the translator has contributed to the reading experience. In a similar vein, nine reviews give thanks to the translator, but also provide the name of the translator; they are therefore assigned to category D2. In most cases, the name of the translator is mentioned when they are well-known in the French context. For example, in a review of Ferdinand von Saar's *Le Lieutenant Burda*, translated by Jacques Le Rider, Le Rider is mentioned by the reviewer with thanks for the translation: 'Thank you to distinguished translator Jacques Le Rider for this translation and the very enlightening afterword which puts it into the context of the period' (Amazon France 9: online). No reviews, incidentally, are assigned to category D1 for reviews in which the translator's name is mentioned in the bibliographical information (since Amazon reviews do not generally provide any bibliographical information).

Overall, 16 of the 604 French Amazon reviews, or 2.6%, are assigned to category E where a short, unjustified comment is made on the translation. Ten of these sixteen comments are positive towards the work of the translator, with seven of them using rather general comments to discuss the translation: 'very well translated' appears twice; 'high-quality translation', 'meticulous translation', 'magnificently translated', 'excellent translation' and 'impeccable translation' all appear once. In these seven reviews, it is difficult to know which aspect of the translation the reviewer is referring to, whether that be how the text reads in the target language or the relationship between the source language and target language. Two of the positive reviews, however, explicitly comment on the fluidity of the target language. In a review of *Les abeilles grises*, written by Andreï Kourkov, translated by Paul Lequesne, the reviewer (Amazon France 10: online) comments that the 'fluid and lively translation contributes to the great reading pleasure', whilst another reviewer (Amazon France 11: online), in their review of Fiona Mozley's *Dernière nuit à Soho*, translated by Laetitia Devaux, thanks the translator for 'the fluid writing [which] allows us to penetrate into this universe'. The other positive review, however, comments on the relationship between the source language and target language. In a review of Chris Offutt's *Les gens des collines*, translated by Anatole Pons-Reumaux, the reviewer (Amazon France 12: online) outlines that, in the source text, 'the dialogues are tinged with local colour', and that the translator has done well to get this across in the target language: '[T]he translation has managed to capture this well, transporting us into total immersion' (ibid.).

This means that six of the sixteen reviews assigned to category E are considered to be critical of the work of the translator. Two of these reviews – one of Haruki Murakami's *Première personne du singulier*, translated by Hélène Morita, and the other of *Zone de crise* by Simon Hanselmann, translated by Fanny Soubiran – outline that there are some 'spelling mistakes' in the translation, but do not provide any more detail on what these mistakes are. Two reviews assess that the book has been 'badly translated', but again do not provide any more details on what makes the works badly translated. Despite this, one of those reviewers – of Julie Otsuka's *La Ligne de nage*, translated by Carine Chichereau – says that 'every time that I come across a translation by this translator, I will buy the original version' (Amazon France 13: online), which is a very strong comment based on what seems to be a vague impression of the translator and her work. One review (Amazon France 14: online) assesses that *Vivre avec les animaux au Moyen Âge* by Chiara Frugoni has been 'not translated excellently' by translator Lucien d'Azay and adds that 'the translator has done the absolute minimum amount of work, but there is no refining – this seems to be relatively common nowadays, I have noticed'. In this review, we can see that there is a brief comment on the translation at hand, but a quite revelatory comment into the attitude of the reviewer towards the work of translators; this attitude, however, does not appear to be widespread, only appearing explicitly in this one Amazon review. In the final review assigned to category E which is critical of the work of the translator, the reviewer admits that they are surprised that they have arrived at a critical impression, because they expected a more positive experience from the original author and the esteemed translator. The review in question (Amazon France 15: online) – of Michael Connelly's *Les ténèbres de la nuit*, translated by Robert Pépin – outlines that 'we have the impression that the first part (65% even) was not written by Connelly nor translated by Robert Pépin', because the work is 'sh**, long, confusing, with double-Dutch translations'.

The final three French Amazon reviews collected in 2022 – just 0.5% of the 604 reviews – are assigned to category F. In two of these three reviews, the work of the translator is evaluated positively, precisely because it allows a fluent reading experience in the target language. In one review of *Stöld* by Ann-Helen Laestadius, translated by Anna Postel, the reviewer

(Amazon France 16: online) comments that they would like to congratulate the translator for 'the magnificent translation work', because the target text offers 'outstanding fluidity'. Similarly, in a review of Damon Galgut's *La promesse*, translated by Hélène Papot, the reviewer (Amazon France 17: online) thanks the translator for their 'excellent translation work', once more because it allows 'a fluid and enjoyable reading experience'. The other review assigned to category F assesses the work of the translator by another criteria: how he manages to replicate one of the key elements of the source text in the target language. In this review of José Falero's *Supermarché*, translated by Hubert Tézenas, the reviewer (Amazon France 18: online) believes that the translator 'has managed to pull off a tour de force in translating and reproducing the language of the favelas, preserving the powers of persuasion of Pedro without erasing the difficulties of living in these places'. In this instance, therefore, it is the relationship between the source language and target language that matters for the reviewer, rather than how the text reads in the target language. The engagement with translation by French Amazon reviewers is never more than two sentences of the review; for this reason, none of the Amazon reviews collected in 2022 are assigned to category G.

Overall, the vast majority of French Amazon reviewers do not engage with the translation in any way. Indeed, 556 of the 604 reviews fit into either category A or category B. French Amazon reviewers can therefore be considered to not promote the visibility of translation in the main. In instances where translation is acknowledged and/or the name of the translator is mentioned, the work of the translator is appreciated and generally viewed positively as a way for a text to enter the French-speaking world. In those reviews in which a comment is made upon the translation, the comments mainly praise individual translations; only six of the reviews assigned to either category E or F are critical of the work of the translator, compared to thirteen of the reviews which praise the work of the translator. Amazon reviewers also most frequently use brief, general comments, such as 'excellent' or 'magnificent', to provide their opinion of the translation; this chimes with what Vanderschelden discovered back in 2000. We have seen, therefore, that it is difficult to establish whether translations are being assessed by how they read in the target language or by the relationship between the source language and target language.

## *Le Monde (LM)*

On the *LM* website, it is difficult to access reviews of works which have not been published in the last three months, due to a lack of systematic archiving beyond big news stories. Nonetheless, 138 reviews of works in translation were collected for the purposes of this study. None of these reviews are assigned to categories A through C2; in other words, the minimum engagement that we see from *LM* reviewers with translation is a mention of the translator's name in the bibliographical information. A total of 113 of the 138 reviews collected, or 81.9%, only mention the translator's name in the bibliographical information and are therefore assigned to category D1. *LM* reviewers may be provided with guidelines to mention the translator's name, as *LM* is the only platform in the French context where this is achieved systematically. In *LM* reviews, the name of the translator comes along with the title of the work, the name of the original author and, interestingly, the language from which the work was translated. Just over half of the reviews – sixty-seven – assigned to category D1 are part of a group article, with contributions from various reviewers on a range of works, with titles such as *Nos conseils de lecture* [our recommended books]. These reviews are generally short-form, between 150 and 250 words, and focus mainly on the context and plot of the work at hand. It is likely that reviewers do not have enough space in this kind of review to engage with the translation beyond a mention of the translator's name in the bibliographical information, and it is therefore hardly surprising that the vast majority of this kind of review are assigned to category D1. An example of what a short-form review like this focusses on can be seen in a group article entitled *Les brèves critiques de la rentrée littéraire* [brief reviews for the new publishing season]. The following review, written by Noiville (2022a: online), of *Mes fantômes et moi* by Gabriel Byrne and translated by Diane Meur, demonstrates how reviewers typically use the entirety of their brief review – in this case, all 221 words – to focus on the context of the work and what happens in the work itself, leaving just a short mention of the translator's name at the end of the review:

> He acted in nearly 80 films, works as important as *Excalibur* by John Boorman (1981) and *Usual Suspects* by Brian Singer (1995). In series as well (he is the psychotherapist in the American version of *In Therapy*, 2008–2010). However, as you read his memoir, you discover Gabriel Byrne as a words man, an author with an incisive and very certain style. With poignant sensitivity, Byrne describes his modest Irish family, his extremely shy nature, his introverted childhood, the appeal of priesthood, the bitter failures from the beginning of his life, depression, all of the 'ghosts' which have haunted him since he was born in Dublin in 1950. Particularly excellent: the pages on the healing power of fiction. Opening a book is like walking onto the stage at the beginning of a play, 'entering into a dream in which time is modified by imagination'. One is incredibly touched by this confessionary work introduced by the expression of poet Percy Shelley (1792–1822): 'Fear not for the future, weep not for the past.' An expression repeated by the mother of the little Byrne, who also really wanted to become an actress. 'Walking with Ghosts' by Gabriel Byrne, translated from English (Ireland) by Diane Meur, Sabine Wespieser, 290 p., 22 €, digital 16 €.

However, not all of the reviews which are part of a group article fit into category D1. The genre of the work under review seems to have little impact on whether the review is classified into category D1: of the 113 reviews assigned to this category, 82 are reviews of translated literature, whilst 31 are reviews of translated non-fiction.

Ten of the 138 *LM* reviews are assigned to category D2, where there is a mention of the translator's name within the main body of the review text. In this case, the genre of the work does seem to have an impact: just one of the ten reviews assigned to category D2 is a review of a non-fictional work, meaning nine are of translated literature. It appears therefore that *LM* reviewers feel that it is more necessary to draw attention to the fact that a literary work is translated in the main body of the text, potentially because of the widespread notion that this type of translation is a more creative, work-intensive process. Three of the ten reviews also come from the kind of brief review outlined earlier in this section. For instance, in a group article entitled *Les brèves critiques du « Monde des livres »* [brief reviews of *Monde des livres* (a publication that *LM* runs)], there is a short review of 235 words, written by Deshusses (2022a: online), of Helga M. Novak's *Silvatica*, translated by Laurent Cassagnau, which includes a mention of the translator in the main body of the review: '[F]irst of all, let us pay tribute to *Éditions Unes* publishing house and to the translator Laurent Cassagnau for being daring enough to engage with one of the most disregarded and yet most talented German poets of the 20th century: Helga M. Novak.' All ten of the reviews assigned to category D2 are similar in tone to this review; in other words, they all give thanks or pay tribute to the translator for bringing a text to a French-speaking audience. Given that 123 of the 138 *LM* reviews collected in 2022 are assigned to either category D1 or D2, it would be reasonable to assert that the majority of *LM* reviewers promote the superficial visibility of translation.

However, only fifteen reviews are assigned to categories E through G. Thirteen of these, or just under 10% of all reviews collected from *LM* in 2022, fit into category E where there is a short comment made upon the translation. Whether a translation is commented upon seems to be rather idiomatic: ten reviewers comment upon the translation in one review each; the only person to comment upon the translation in more than one of the reviews is Camille Laurens, an author herself, who adds a comment on the translation in three of her reviews. However, that is not to say that she does so in all of her reviews. Indeed, the other five reviews which were written by Laurens in 2022 are assigned to category D1. Whether a translation receives a comment also seems to be heavily linked to the genre of the work. Only two reviews of translated non-fictional works – *Le Livre noir des Mille et Une Nuits* by Richard Francis Burton, translated by Jean-Marie Blas de Roblès, and *L'Indonésie et la naissance du monde moderne* by Daavid Van Reybrouck, translated by Philippe Noble and Isabelle Rosselin – are assigned to category E, and both use a rather general comment to praise the work of the translators. In the former review, written by Angelier (2022: online), the reviewer praises Blas de Roblès for his 'inspired translation', whilst reviewer Noiville (2022b: online) in the latter review comments on the 'magnificent translation' of Noble and Rosselin.

The remaining eleven reviews classified into category E are therefore reviews of translated literature, and ten of these are positive towards the work of the translator. Seven of the reviews praise the translation using rather general words or phrases, making it difficult to assess what aspect of the translation is being commended, as follows: 'brilliantly translated' appears in two of the reviews, whilst 'admirable translation', 'empathetic translation', 'impeccably chiselled by the translation', 'magnificent translation' and 'subtly translated' all appear in one review each. Two of the positive reviews towards the work of the translator praise how the translation looks or feels in the target language. In a review of *Les Idéalistes* by Kristopher Jansma, translated by Sophie Troff, reviewer Leyris (2022: online) comments that 'reading the elegant translation by Sophie Troff is to be relished as a real privilege'; in the other review, written by reviewer Laurens (2022: online), of Sara Mesa's *Un amour*, translated by Delphine Valentin, Laurens comments that the novel is 'well-served by Delphine Valentin's beautiful translation'. These comments are presumably assessing how the language reads in the target language, rather than the relationship between the language of the source text and the target text. The only review classified into category E which praises the work of the translator and seemingly because the translator has managed to maintain fidelity to the source text is Deshusses's (2022b) review of Stefanie vor Schulte's *Garçon au coq noir*, translated by Nicolas Véron. Deshusses (ibid.: online) spends the majority of his review discussing the context and plot of the novel, but adds in the last paragraph that the elements of the novel have been 'very well reproduced by Nicolas Véron's translation'. Only one of the reviews classified into category E is critical of the translation: in her review of *Le Fleuve des souvenirs* by José Maria Merino, translated by Typhaine Ducellier, Singer (2022: online) claims that this novel 'is dazzling despite the awkwardness […] of its translation'. It is particularly noteworthy that the criticism appears to come from Singer's judgement on how well – or rather not – the text looks and feels in the target language, rather than a comparison of the language of the source text to that of the target text.

Just one review collected from *LM* in 2022 is assigned to category F where there is a comment on the translation with further engagement, but this engagement takes up fewer than three sentences of the review. The review in question is written by Weill (2022), a translator himself, and focusses on the translation of Johannes Reuchlin's *Les Bésicles*, translated by Hélène Feydy and Delphine Viellard. One paragraph of this 1,263-word review is dedicated to the work of the translators. Weill begins by outlining that the translators of the text have accompanied this first translation into French with a variety of materials, including a foreword from the translators. He includes a quotation from one of the translators outlining the difficulty of translating the text which, in the source language, contains both Latin and early High German: '[D]ue to the length of the sentences, the Latin periods are impossible to reproduce in French and, until fifteen days before submitting the manuscript, we were still discussing possible misinterpretations' (ibid.: online). Nonetheless, Weill (ibid.: online) ultimately concludes that 'the result, supplemented with headings and explanations, turns out to be very readable'. Once more, we see a translation essentially being assessed positively for how it reads in the target language.

Only one review is assigned to category G, where there is extensive engagement with the translation beyond three sentences. The review is written by Boutang (2022) and focusses on John Steinbeck's *Des souris et des hommes*, translated by Agnès Desarthe. The review is 857 words long in total, and only 70 words of the review are not dedicated to the translation. These seventy words provide context to the original work and outline what Steinbeck was attempting to do with the novel in English. The remainder of the review contextualises the current translation – a new translation which allows us to 'rediscover the fierce lyricism of the American author' (ibid.: online) – and compares it to a previous translation, outlining the similarities and differences between the two. For instance, Boutang (ibid.: online) argues that there are subtle differences in how Desarthe translates the text compared to the previous translation by Coindreau, and provides the example of elisions:

> Where Coindreau's version says: 'If you do not tell anybody what happened to you, we will not say anything. But if you speak and you try to get this boy fired, we will talk', Desarthe writes: 'If you don't tell anybody what happened, we won't say anything either. But if you say one single word and try t' get this boy fired, well we're gonna tell everything to everyone and you'll be the laughing stock of the ranch'.

Boutang (ibid.: online) argues that, despite the subtility of the differences, Desarthe's version does not only 'sound right, but also pays tribute to Steinbeck's meticulous work with the language, with the words of others'. In conclusion to her article, Boutang (ibid.: online) assesses that Desarthe's translation 'reads like a new and seductive interpretation of the original work and reproduces its force and power'. Ultimately, the judgement on the translation comes from the relationship between the source language and target language, not just on how the target text reads in French.

Throughout this section of the chapter, it has become clear that the majority of *LM* reviewers will do the bare minimum and only mention the name of the translator in the bibliographical information of the text or in the main text itself. Indeed, this is the approach taken by 123 of the 138 reviews collected. It seems fair to assert, therefore, that *LM* reviewers actively promote the visibility of translation at a superficial level. However, just fifteen of the reviews are classified into categories E through G which promote the visibility of the translator at an embedded level, and thirteen of these only provide a short, unjustified comment on the translation. In the main, the comments on translation are general and do not allow us to assess what precise aspect of the translation the reviewers are evaluating, but it seems that the main criterion against which *LM* reviewers assess translations is fluency and readability in the target language. Only two reviews, one assigned to category E and one assigned to category G, attempt to engage with the relationship between the source text and target text and to assess the fidelity of the translation. From this point of view, *LM* reviewers overwhelmingly prefer translators to be invisible in their work.

## *Le Figaro (LF)*

The *LF* website is easier to navigate than the *LM* website and the archives of reviews are all available and in date order, meaning that all reviews of translated works which were published in 2022 by *LF* could be collected; in total, this amounted to 172 reviews. Much like *LM*, *LF* have a relatively standard way of acknowledging that a text has been translated and by whom: there is the title of the original text, the author, the language from which the text has been translated and by whom at the end of a review. However, unlike *LM*, not all *LF* reviews mention the name of the translator: indeed, eight of the 172 reviews – or 4.6% – are assigned to category A, where there is no reference to the act of translation at all, and no comment is made on the style of the target text. The reviews in question are as follows:

- Bruno Corty's review of *Cupidité* by Deon Meyer, translated by Georges Lory;
- Paul-François Paoli's review of *Aux portes de l'Europe* by Serhii Plokhy, translated by Jacques Dalarun;
- Jacques de Saint-Victor's review of *L'Appel de la tribu* by Mario Vargas Llosa, translated by Albert Bensoussan and Daniel Lefort;
- Astrid de Larminat's review of *Jimmy Bluefeather* by Kim Heacox, translated by Marc Sigala;
- Two reviews written by Eric Neuhoff: *Un (autre) toi* by Joyce Carol Oates, translated by Christine Auche, and *La Pêche à la truite en Amérique* by Richard Brautigan, translated by Marc Chénetier;
- Two reviews written by Thierry Clermont: *Elizabeth Finch* by Julian Barnes, translated by Jean-Pierre Aoustin, and *Indépendance* by Javier Cercas, translated by Aleksandar Grujicic and Karine Louesdon.

However, it is unclear why these eight reviews do not acknowledge the fact of translation in any form. It does not appear to depend on the genre of the translated work under review: despite the fact that we have previously seen that non-fictional works tend to receive less engagement from reviewers, only one of the works in the above list – Serhii Plokhy's *Aux portes de l'Europe* – is a work of non-fiction. It also has nothing to do with the length of the review, since many shorter reviews than the ones in the list above are assigned to at least category D1 with a mention of the translator's name in the bibliographical information. And yet it does not seem to be a consistent choice of the individual reviewers in question: for instance, many of the reviews written by Eric Neuhoff and Thierry Clermont – the only two reviewers who do not acknowledge the fact of translation more than once – in 2022 are classified into categories D1 through E. A lack of acknowledgement of the translation could well mean that the reviewers were reviewing the original text, but this is not explicitly expressed and, in the bibliographical information, the title that appears is always the title of the translated text. The reasons for this lack of acknowledgement therefore remain unestablished. No reviews are assigned to category B; in other words, none of the *LF* reviews which do not acknowledge the fact of translation attempt to comment on the style of the text.

None of the *LF* reviews are assigned to category C1 either, and only one review is assigned to category C2 where the translator's name is not mentioned in the bibliographical information or the text, but the act of translation is acknowledged in the main body of the text. This is the case for Saint-Victor's (2022) review of Frank Dikötter's *Comment devenir dictateur*, translated by Omblage. The reference to the fact of translation does not thank the translator for their work, like many French Amazon reviewers did, but rather just acknowledges the fact that there is an original work, written in English: '[I]n reality, the title of the original is *How to be a dictator*: "comment être un dictateur"' (ibid.: online). Much like other *LF* reviewers who do not mention the translator's name in some of their reviews, Saint-Victor has multiple reviews assigned to category D1, so does generally mention the name of the translator. It is therefore unclear why he does not mention the translator's name in this particular review.

A similar percentage of *LF* reviews are assigned to category D1 as *LM* reviews: 86.0%, or 148 of the 172 reviews published by the outlet in 2022. All in all, twenty-four of these reviews are short-form reviews which come from group articles, such as *La selection du Figaro de livres à offrir pour Noël* [The *Figaro*'s choice of books to gift at Christmas], including reviews of multiple works and generally between 200 and 300 words long. These short-form reviews tend to focus exclusively on contextualising the original work and providing information on the plot of the text, so it is not surprising that they only mention the name of the translator in the bibliographical information. However, there are some short-form reviews from group articles which fit into our latter categories. The genre of the translated work does not seem to have an impact on whether a review will only mention the name of the translator in the bibliographical information: in fact, of the 148 reviews assigned to category D1, 42 focus on a work of non-fiction, whilst 106 reviews translated fiction.

Seven of the 172 *LF* reviews, or 4.1%, are assigned to category D2, where there is a mention of the translator's name in the main body of the text, and not just the bibliographical information. Six of these seven simply mention the translator as the person behind the work in a matter-of-fact way, as can be seen from the following example, taken from a review of *Dans les rêves* by Delmore Schwartz, translated by Daniel Bismuth. In this review, Fillon (2022: online) writes that 'some of these short stories had already been published in France under the initiative of translator Daniel Bismuth and publisher Michel Bulteau'. Just one of the reviews assigned to category D2 explicitly praises the translator for bringing the text to a French audience. In his review of *John Sherman* by William Butler Yeats, translated by Jean-Yves Masson, reviewer Palou (2022: online) comments that 'one hundred and thirty-one years after the publication of the original novel, Jean-Yves Masson has just given us the first French translation, and we would like to thank him for this'. All of the reviews assigned to category D2 focus on translated fiction; this adds weight to the argument that reviewers often find it more important to mention the translator of fiction than non-fiction in the main body of their reviews, and the potential reasons for this have already been outlined.

This leaves just eight *LF* reviews from 2022 which are classified into categories E through G, categories which promote the embedded visibility of the translator. Of these, six reviews are assigned to category E where a short, unjustified comment is made on the translation. Five of these reviews focus on a piece of translated fiction and only one on a piece of translated non-fiction (Lapaque's review of *Vivre avec les animaux au Moyen Âge* by Chiara Frugoni, translated by Lucien d'Azay). All six reviews in category E praise the work of the translator. Five of them use rather general words to comment upon the translation. In a review of *L'homme invisible* by H. G. Wells, translated by Philippe Jaworski, the only review assigned to category E which is a short-form review (278 words) written as part of a group article, reviewer Rivière praises Jaworski for the 'new and remarkable translation' (Neuhoff et al. 2022: online). Develey (2022: online), in her review of *Euphorie* by Elin Cullhed, translated by Anna Gibson, comments that the writing of Elin Cullhed is supported by 'the translation of Anna Gibson which is breathtaking'. Fernanda Melchor's *Paradaïze*, translated by Laura Alcoba, comes up for review by Clermont (2022: online), who believes that the novel is 'very well translated by the novelist Laura Alcoba'. The final two reviews which use a general comment to praise the work of the translator are written by Lapaque, the only reviewer to do this more than once: in his review of José Falero's *Supermarché*, translated by Hubert Tézenas, Lapaque (2022a: online) comments that Falero's text is 'deliciously translated from the Brazilian by Hubert Tézenas', whilst in his review of the aforementioned *Vivre avec les animaux au Moyen Âge*, he asserts that the novel has been 'marvellously translated' (Lapaque 2022b: online). It is difficult to ascertain from these comments what aspect of the translation these reviews are praising. However, in the final review classified into category E, it seems that the reviewer praises the work of the translator for maintaining one element of the source text. In a review of Hans Magnus Enzensberger's *Un bouquet d'anecdotes ou opus incertum*, translated by Bernard Lortholary, reviewer Kaddour (2022: online) comments that 'this book is a true tale of development, with a lively rhythm that Bernard Lortholary's translation is able to perfectly reproduce'. The phrase 'is able to perfectly reproduce' here hints at the fact that the reviewer has compared the source text to the target text and is able to comment on how successfully the translator has conveyed the rhythm into the target language.

Only one *LF* review is assigned to category F where there is further engagement with the translation beyond a short, unjustified comment, taking up to three sentences of the review. The review in question is written by Gras (2022) and focusses on the translation of *Dersou Ouzala* by Vladimir Arseniev, translated by Yves Gauthier. In his review, Gras compares the new translation of Gauthier to a previous translation from the 1930s and is ultimately positive towards the work of the most recent translator. He comments that 'the translator from the 1930s seemed to feel compelled to make the Tungusic native speak like a local of St. Petersburg. An aberration. Yves Gauthier has put the soul back into him: "*That's all my people think about: land, mountains, forest, all the people!*" ' (ibid.: online). From the way that Gras engages with the translation here, the reviewer appears to assess the translations against the main criterion of how they read in the target language and not necessarily on how faithful the target text is to the source text; after all, it seems that the previous translator attempted to get the linguistic difference of the Tungusic language across in his translation, and this is judged critically by the reviewer.

Similarly, just one review collected from *LF* in 2022 is assigned to category G, a review authored by *Le Figaro* Editorial, focussing on a new translation led by Jean-Pierre Lefebvre of a collection of Franz Kafka's works. Almost all of the 757-word review is dedicated to the translation and a comparison with a previous translation by Alexandre Vialatte which essentially governed the reception of Kafka in France before the publication of the new translation. The review (*Le Figaro* Editorial 2022: online) outlines that Vialatte's translations were 'sometimes wrong' and adds a quotation from the new translator Jean-Pierre Lefebvre who asserts that 'the summary of Vialatte is simple: he was a talented writer, perfectly readable, but strayed a little from the original text, even a lot'. The review actively draws attention to the fact that, despite the translation being perfectly readable, the issue with the original text is a lack of fidelity to the source text. The review then provides multiple examples of how the new translation addresses this non-fidelity to the source text: for instance, the previous translation uses the phrase '*mal fagoté*', whereas the new translation uses '*mal habillé*'. Both mean 'badly dressed', but the latter is more formal than the former, and the reviewer adds a comment that '*mal fagoté* is a spoken phrase, but it does not correspond to Kafka. He always kept this caution' (ibid.). The review therefore focusses on the correspondence between the language of the source text and that of the target text, rather than how the text reads in the target language. The main criterion against which this review assesses the translation is not fluency and readability, unlike the review assigned to category F.

Taking everything into consideration, we can assert that *LF* reviewers are similar to *LM* reviews in how they review translated works. The vast majority of the reviews have been assigned to category D1 where the reviewer only mentions the translator's name in the bibliographical information, supporting the discoveries of previous studies into French reviewing practices in the 2000s and 2010s. Fewer *LF* reviewers than *LM* reviewers engaged with the translation at the embedded level: indeed, only eight reviews, or, in other words, 4.7% of the 172 reviews published by *LF* in 2022, attempt to make a comment on the translation and are therefore assigned to categories E through G. This figure is significantly less than the almost

11% of reviews in *LM* which are assigned to these categories. Another significant difference between *LF* and *LM* reviews is that no *LM* reviews are assigned to categories A or B, whereas eight *LF* reviews are assigned to category A where there is no acknowledgement of the fact of translation in the review. It is unclear why this is the case, but it is fair to say that *LM* reviewers more systematically promote the visibility of translation than *LF* reviewers, perhaps as a result of editorial guidelines.

## *Actualitté*

*Actualitté* is an online French magazine dedicated to keeping readers up-to-date with the literary world and offering them 'an insight into what is being published: the good … and the less good, with its own personal touch' (*Actualitté* Editorial 2023: online). In 2022, it published a whole host of reviews of recently published works – from young adult, through comics and manga, to essays – and 144 of these reviews focussed on works which had been translated into French. Just one review, of *Fille A* by Abigail Dean, translated by Jean Esch, does not make any reference to the act of translation at all and does not provide a comment on the style of the target text, therefore being assigned to category A. Similarly, one review makes no reference to the act of translation at all, but this time does comment upon the style of the target text. In this review, written by an anonymous bookseller as part of *Actualitté*'s *Parole de Libraires* – translated literally 'Words of Booksellers' – series, the translators of Michael McDowell's Blackwater Book 1, Yoko Lacour and Hélène Charrier, are not mentioned, but the reviewer does comment on the style of the target text: '[T]hanks to his fluid and clear writing, […] McDowell leads the reader on a journey with no return' (Parole de Libraires 2022: online). This review is therefore assigned to category B, as the style of the target text is commented upon without an acknowledge of the fact of translation. The review assigned to category A is also written by an anonymous bookseller as part of the *Parole de Libraires* series. These reviews are not written by the regular professional *Actualitté* reviewers and are perhaps therefore more comparable to the French Amazon reviews. Sixteen of the 144 reviews published by *Actualitté* in 2022 are authored by booksellers, and none of the reviews are assigned to a category beyond D2, providing further indication that non-professional reviewers are less likely to engage with translation beyond a mention of the name of the translator. None of the *Actualitté* reviews are assigned to categories C1 or C2, meaning that the remaining 142 reviews at least mention the name of the translator and are therefore assigned to categories D1 through G.

A total of 101 – or 70% – of the 144 collected reviews fit into category D1, where there is the minimum mention of the translator's name in the bibliographical information. *Actualitté*, much like *LM* and *LF*, have a systematic manner for mentioning the translator's name in all but the two aforementioned reviews. What is particularly noteworthy, however, is that it requires a lot of scrolling down the page past a whole range of adverts before actually reaching the bibliographical information, meaning that there is a quite significant difference between the *Actualitté* reviews assigned to categories D1 and D2: the likelihood of readers scrolling down past adverts to reach the bibliographical information seems less likely on a website such as *Actualitté* than the more accessible bibliographical information on the *LM* and *LF* websites, whereas if the name of the translator is mentioned in the main body of the text, it is practically impossible to miss.

There is not any pattern with regard to the types of review that are assigned to category D1. Firstly, it is not idiosyncratic; in other words, there are no *Actualitté* reviewers who wrote reviews in 2022 which are exclusively assigned to category D1. Secondly, it does not depend on the length of the review. Both short-form reviews, between 100 and 200 words long, which likely have less space to engage with translation, and long-form reviews, more than 1,000 words long, are assigned to this category. Thirdly, it does not depend on the genre of the work being reviewed, either: 40 of the 101 reviews assigned to this category focus on a work of translated non-fiction, and 61 focus on translated literature. Ultimately, whether a reviewer includes more than just a mention of the translator's name in the bibliographical information is decided on a case-by-case basis depending on the individual work being reviewed. Many of the reviews assigned to category D1 which focus on the translation of manga, a comic or a picture book do find space within the main body of the review to comment on the work of the illustrator, but not the translator. An example of this comes from a review written by Nicolas Ancion (2022a) of Timothy Snyder's *De la tyrannie. Vingt leçons du XXe siècle*, translated by Pierre-Emannuel Dauzat and illustrated by Nora Krug. There is no mention of the translator beyond his name appearing in the bibliographical information; however, the illustrator gets a whole paragraph dedicated to their work:

> The version put into pictures by Nora Krug is less a comic strip than an illustrated essay, but the contributions of the colours, designs, collages and reworked photographs to the book are undeniable. On each occasion, the illustrator manages to find sufficiently strong visuals both to mitigate the harsh content of the text and to shine a light, through images, on the validity of what is written in the text. (ibid.)

Since the work of the illustrator is quite literally visible, or, in other words, that you can see it in the book, and the images do not change from the source text to the target text, it appears that there is more of a steer for *Actualitté* reviewers to engage with the illustrations. Translation is visible on the page in the target text, but not in the same literal way: the reader is not inherently conscious of the work of the translator, and this may well be the reason behind the lack of engagement with the work of the translator in these specific reviews.

Out of the 144 *Actualitté* reviews collected, 29, or 20.1%, are assigned to category D2 where the name of the translator is mentioned within the main body of the text. Whether the reviewer gets mentioned in the main body of the text does not seem to depend on the length of the review or the genre of the work being reviewed. However, there is some idiosyncrasy on the part of some reviewers who almost always include the name of the reviewer within the main body of their reviews, but do not comment on the translation itself. For instance, Fasseur published three articles in 2022, each of which gives a round-up of recently published translations, chosen by various contributors, with three different reviews in each article. All nine of Fasseur's reviews provide the name of the translator in the main body of the text but never comment on the translation at hand. For instance, in her review of the *All Free !* by Terubo Aono, translated by François Boulanger, Fasseur (2022: online) introduces the work with the following comment: 'And to start with, *All Free !* by Terubo Aono (trans. François Boulanger) which is making its debut this month with Mangetsu publishing house, because "after all, judo which wins … is not always the judo that we like"'. The reviews assigned to this category draw significantly more attention to the name of the translator than those reviews which are classified into category D1 for which there is a lot of scrolling to get to the bibliographical information of the review.

Just nine of the 144 reviews – or 6.3% – are assigned to category E where the reviewer makes a short unjustified comment on the translation. In all instances, the work of the translator is praised by the reviewer. Bouhadjera is one of three reviewers to have two reviews classified into category E, both times using a general comment. In a review of *Les chevaux de feu* by Mykhaïlo Kotsioubynsky, translated by Jean-Claude Marcadé, Bouhadjera (2022a: online) comments that '*Les chevaux de feu* was published in French as part of the L'Âge d'Homme Slav Classics collection in 2001, in a virtuoso translation by Jean-Claude Marcadé'. There is a similarly positive review written by Bouhadjera (2022b: online) towards the work of translator Pierre Guglielmina for his translation of Jack Kerouac's *Anges de la Désolation*: 'a novel of freedom, of style (thanks for the formidable translation by Pierre Guglielmina) which transports us to the heart of the Beat Generation'. Lucie Ancion, a regular reviewer for *Actualitté,* has most of her reviews assigned to category D1, but two of her reviews are classified into category E. The first of these is a review of Yukinobu Tatsu's *Dandadan Tome 1*, translated by Sylvain Chollet, in which Lucie Ancion (2022a: online) makes a general comment that 'the dialogue is not found wanting: thanks to the fresh and incisive translation by Sylvain Chollet, it is fun and quirky'. In her other review assigned to category E, however, it seems that Lucie Ancion (2022b) has compared the translation to the original work. The review focusses on Shûji Takeya's *The Chilling Dead*, translated by Sarah Boivineau, and outlines that the text has been translated 'with care, allowing us to benefit from the creativity of the original work' (ibid.: online). It is unclear what creativity has been transmitted in the translation, but the comment implies that Ancion has read the source text and is not judging Boivineau's work from the target text alone.

Ancion is not the only reviewer who believes the translator has translated 'with care': Costantini, another reviewer to have written two reviews which are assigned to category E, also uses this phrase to praise the work of the translator in her review of Alex Pheby's *Mordew*, translated by Claro. In this review, Costantini (2022a: online) criticises parts of the content of the work – 'the plethora of information tends to weigh down the narrative and slow down every event' – but praises the work of the translator: '[O]n the flip side, the author's prose – translated with care by Claro – is pleasing on a number of levels.' Much like Ancion's review, the reviewer has seemingly read the source text and compared the language of the translation to the original work. In her other review to be assigned to category E, Costantini (2022b) assesses the translation by how it reads in the target language and potentially by how the target text matches up to the source text. The review, of Elizabeth Buchan's *Le musée des promesses brisées*, translated by Typhaine Ducellier, contains a comment that the translation should be 'commended for its elegance and appropriateness' (ibid.: online). 'Elegance' is surely a comment on how the text reads in French; 'appropriateness' is a more complicated word to interpret in the review, as it can have multiple meanings, but Costantini may be commenting on the relationship between the source text and target text with the use of this word. As she does not provide justification for her comment, however, it is difficult to be sure.

The other three reviews assigned to category E are equally positive towards the work of the translator. Le Roy (2022: online), in her review of *Espions en Révolution* by Joel Richard, translated by Bernard Frumer, makes a comment criticising some of the content of the work, but praising the work of the translator: 'The translation by Bernard Frumer seems excellent, but we regret that this is an altogether approximate and succinct biography of Beaumarchais.' The use of the word 'seems' tends to imply that Le Roy has not compared the source text to the target text. We can infer, therefore, that her believing the translation to be 'excellent' is a judgement on how it reads in the target language. Mimiche (2022a: online), in a review of Haruki Marukami's *L'étrange bibliothèque*, translated by Hélène Morita, comments on the style of the writing and attributes its success to translator Morita: 'This book is a page-turner, can be read too quickly, progressing at the pace of a frenzied short story, of which the incisive and rapid writing produced by Hélène Morita, the translator, makes a large contribution to the quality of the work.' This, once more, is an assessment of how the text reads in the target language, rather than a comparison between the source text and the target text. The final review assigned to category E is particularly interesting, since the main editor of *Actualitté*, Nicolas Ancion, openly acknowledges that the magazine does not engage with the work of the translator enough before adding a comment on the work of the translator. In his review of *Nettoyage à sec* by Joris Mertens, translated by Maurice Lomré, Nicolas Ancion (2022b: online) finishes his review with 'NB: we do not mention it enough, but the translation from the Dutch is very successful and it is thanks to the pen of Maurice Lomré.' The comment in Ancion's review is rather general; it remains unclear what aspect of the translation has been 'successful'.

Just three, or 2.1%, of the 144 reviews collected from *Actualitté* in 2022 are assigned to category F which is a short, justified comment of no more than three sentences made on the translation. Lucie Ancion (2022c: online), in her review of Tatsuki Fujimoto's *17–21*, translated by Sébastien Ludmann, praises the 'marvellous' work of the translator in translating the work into French without losing anything from the original text: 'Once again, Sébastien Ludmann has done a marvellous translation job on Fujimoto's texts and gives them to us without losing anything their original bite.' Much like in one of her reviews which was assigned to category E, Ancion has seemingly compared the translation to the source text and came to her evaluation on the basis of this comparison. Costantini's (2022c) review of David Joy's *Nos vies en flammes*, translated by Fabrice Pointeau, is similar to the Ancion review, since it praises the translator for not changing or misrepresenting the content of the original text; however, this review introduces the notion that the translator should be praised for hiding the act of translation from the reader. Costantini (ibid.: online), therefore, argues that the translator succeeds in 'this masterful mission of shadowing the original pen without ever misrepresenting it, whilst hiding any trace of the act of translation for the reader'. This review is particularly telling, because it reveals what reviewer Costantini believes translators should be trying to achieve in their work – accuracy and fluency – and gives weight to the idea that her use of 'appropriateness' in her review of

*Le musée des promesses brisées*, assigned to category E, is indeed a comment upon how the translator has managed to achieve accuracy in the translation to the source text.

The final review assigned to category F is written by Mimiche (2022b). In a review of László Krasznahorkai's *Le Dernier Loup*, translated by Joëlle Dufeuilly, the reviewer begins by arguing that the original author's stylistic choice – of writing in long sentences and with 'a certain musicality' – makes things difficult for the translator, before adding that the translator has done a magnificent job in dealing with it:

> And even if I think that the monumental task imposed on the translator by László Krasznohorkai's stylistic choices was insurmountable and did not fully allow her to translate the perhaps untranslatable convolutions in this very unusual writing format, even if I think that the result is less breathtaking than what I previously admired about Pierre Demarty's *Mort aux Girafes*, the reformulation of this work through the means of translation is a feat that deserves a lot of admiration. (ibid.: online)

The reviewer has compared the translation to the original text and has a clear understanding of the challenges that the translator faced. The assessment of the work of the translator may well have been different had the reviewer only judged the translation on how fluently it reads in the target language. All three reviews assigned to category F therefore appear to take the relationship between source text and target text into consideration in some regard in their assessment of the translation. No reviews, incidentally, are assigned to category G.

Overall, almost all of the *Actualitté* reviews collected in the year 2022 do the bare minimum of mentioning the translator's name in the bibliographical information. Just two reviews do not acknowledge the fact of translation at all; however, these reviews are not written by *Actualitté*'s regular, professional reviewers, but rather by booksellers who have been invited to contribute to an individual series. Over 90% of *Actualitté* reviews are classified into categories D1 or D2, meaning that we can assert that reviews in this specialist literary magazine most frequently promote the visibility of translation at a superficial level. However, it is more difficult to find the bibliographical information on the *Actualitté* website than, for instance, the *LM* and *LF* websites. Just twelve reviews of the 144 published in 2022 are assigned to categories E and F, and therefore *Actualitté* reviews are not considered to promote the embedded visibility of translation, supported by that review written by the editor, Nicolas Ancion, who acknowledges that the magazine does not engage with the work of the translator enough. All of the reviews which are assigned to categories E and F praise the work of the translator, and many of the reviewers appear to have assessed the relationship between the source language and target language. Unlike other French platforms, it seems that readability in the target language is not the main criterion against which *Actualitté* reviewers assess translation.

## Conclusions

The findings of this chapter are displayed in Figure 2. It shows the percentage of reviews assigned to each category across the four different French platforms.

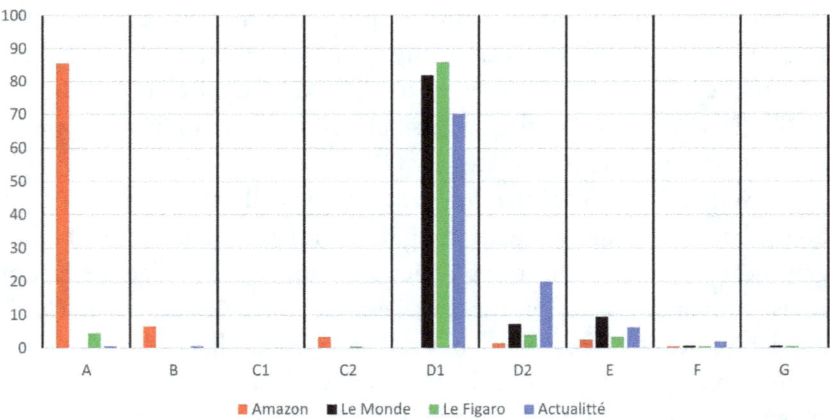


Figure 2: Percentage of reviews assigned to each category across the different French platforms

French Amazon reviews are the major outlier of the four platforms, as the vast majority of these reviews are classified into categories A and B, whereas *LM*, *LF* and *Actualitté* very rarely have reviews classified into these categories, if at all. Amazon is therefore the platform upon which translation frequently remains the most invisible, and the reasons for this have been outlined earlier in the chapter. What is also startling from Figure 2 is the percentage of reviews which are classified into categories D1 and D2 across the other three platforms: at least 90% of reviews collected from *LM*, *LF* and *Actualitté* are assigned to one of these two categories where there is only a brief mention of the translator's name in the bibliographical information or within the main body of the text. It is therefore considered that these platforms are rather systematic at promoting the visibility of translation at the superficial level.

However, a completely different picture emerges when we consider the embedded visibility of translation. None of the outlets have more than 10% of their reviews assigned to category E. The platform which most frequently comments on the translation with a brief, unjustified comment is *LM* and, even then, only 9.4% of its reviews did this. This discovery becomes even more emphasised when we consider categories F and G. The bars in Figure 2 are almost not visible in those categories for any of the outlets: the largest percentage of reviews assigned to category F come from *Actualitté*, with just 2.1% of its reviews assigned to this category, whereas the largest percentage of reviews assigned to category G come from *LM*, with 0.7% of its reviews assigned to this category (in reality, just one review). French reviewers are therefore loath to comment on the translation to any great extent. The chapter thus supports the findings of Vanderschelden (2000), Bush (2004) and Gray (2018): in other words, French reviewers almost always mention the name of the translator (with the exception of Amazon reviewers), but very rarely engage with translation in any deeper way in their reviews.

CHAPTER 5

# Reviewing in Germany

Back in 2009, Lanschützer examined reviews from three German-speaking publications, *Die Presse* (Austria), *Neue Zürcher Zeitung* (Switzerland) and *Die Zeit* (Germany), and discovered that only one review in each newspaper did not engage with translation in any regard at all; the majority of reviews in all three newspapers either name the translator in the bibliographical information, add a remark in the text that they are reviewing a translation, or use a brief blanket comment, such as 'congenial' or 'bumpy', to judge a translation; and, finally, very few reviews in these publications engage with the translation beyond an initial comment or compare the original text and the translation at hand or two different translations. Lanschützer (ibid.) also found that fluency is much revered by reviewers in Germany and that a translation which reads as though it was originally written in German will always be evaluated positively by reviewers. It is in this context that the present chapter comes in: it will show how reviewers from a popular platform – amazon.de –, two broadsheets/cultural supplements – *Süddeutsche Zeitung* and *Der Spiegel* – and one specialised literary magazine – *Literaturkritik* – review works in translation in the year 2022. For this purpose, a total of 1,898 reviews were collected: 1,469 from amazon.de; 233 from *Süddeutsche Zeitung*; 43 from *Der Spiegel*; and 153 from *Literaturkritik*. This chapter therefore provides a comprehensive insight into how German reviewers discuss translation by examining the reviews collected from each platform in turn and assessing whether the reviewers engage with the work of the translator and, if they do, what form this engagement takes.

## Amazon Germany

Of the 1,469 reviews collected from amazon.de, 1,167, or 79.4%, are assigned to category A, for reviews in which there is no reference to the act of translation at all, and no comment is made upon the style of the target text. This mirrors what we saw in the British and French chapters, and the reasons for this may be the same: in other words, Amazon reviewers will, in reality, have a limited amount of time to write these reviews and are generally not being paid for this activity. The reviewers overwhelmingly focus on one of three things. The plot line of the work at hand is the most common thing that Amazon reviewers comment upon. For instance, in a review of Ian McEwan's *Lektionen*, translated by Bernhard Robben, the reviewer (Amazon Germany 1: online) spends roughly 70% of the review discussing what happens in the novel, including the following lines:

> The author tells the story of the life of a human being. The ups and downs, love, wounds, missed opportunities. But also what happens in the world during this person's life, be it the Cuban Missile Crisis, Chernobyl, the fall of the Berlin Wall, the pandemic and climate change. And so we accompany the protagonist Roland through his long life.[1]

However, German Amazon reviewers are also likely to include an overall opinion of the work at hand. Just over 50% of the reviews assigned to category A provide an opinion on the work, beyond the number of stars that Amazon invites every reviewer to award. For instance, in a review of Florence Aubenas' *Er ist keiner von uns*, translated by André Hansen, the reviewer writes that the book has a great cover, but 'unfortunately I did not like this book at all. Such a shame' (Amazon Germany 2: online). German Amazon reviewers may in addition include a comment on the service received from Amazon: just under 20% of the Amazon reviews assigned to category A include a section on the service they received, and some even dedicate their whole review to the service. Such is the case

1 All of the quotations in this chapter were originally written in German and have been translated by the author.

in a review of Jean Malaquais' *Planet ohne Visum*, translated by Nadine Püschel, in which the reviewer (Amazon Germany 3: online) comments that 'the delivery came late and the paperback book cover was damaged, because the very bulky novel was put into packaging which was not big enough'.

In a good number of the reviews assigned to category A, it is somewhat noticeable that reviewers are willing to engage with the work of other parties beyond the original author, but not the translator. For instance, in forty-nine of the Amazon reviews assigned to category A, there is a comment on the work of the illustrator, but not on the work of the translator. A good example of this is a review of an illustrated guide to China, written by Giulia Ziggiotti, illustrated by Sabrina Ferrero and translated by Barbara Neeb and Katharina Schmidt. At the end of this review, the reviewer (Amazon Germany 4: online) writes:

> In particular, I would like to highlight the beautiful illustration of the book by illustrator Sabrina Ferrero. It is just a bit of a shame that her name is not on the cover of the book, but rather only briefly mentioned on the last page, given that the guide comes to life through the images.

The work of the illustrator is entirely visible, or, in other words, the reader can see what work the illustrator has undertaken. On the other hand, the work of the translator is, in the main, invisible to the average German reader. It is therefore noteworthy that German Amazon reviewers are willing to comment on the work of parties who are inherently visible rather than invisible. It is also noteworthy that the reviewer asks for the illustrator's name to appear on the cover of the work when that is often what translators also demand (incidentally, the Amazon webpage for this work includes the names of the original author and the illustrators, but not the name of the translators).

A total of 136 of the 1,469 reviews are assigned to category B, for reviews in which there is no reference to the act of translation at all, but comments are made about the style of the target text. This accounts for 9.3% of all German Amazon reviews collected from the year 2022. Out of the 136 reviews which comment upon the style of the target text without acknowledging the translation, 109 praise the writing style. This can be considered problematic because it undervalues the work of the translator in reconstructing the style of the original text in the target language. A review of Katie Katimura's *Initimitäten*, translated by Kathrin Razum, effectively demonstrates how this works in practice. Translator Razum receives no praise for her work, despite the reviewer assessing that the writing style is fluent (Amazon Germany 5: online): 'Katie Katimura's writing style is fluent with a good pace and the right perspective.' On the flipside, however, twenty-seven of the reviews which do not acknowledge the translation but comment on the style of the target text criticise the writing style. This could be considered even more problematic from the point of view of the original author, as it could be the style of the translator which should be criticised; in other words, the writing style of the author is assessed, despite the fact that the writing style is not entirely theirs. In a review of Fernando Aramburu's *Die Mauersegler*, translated by Willi Zurbrüggen, for instance, the lack of fluency in writing is attributed to the author of the original text when it could well be down to translator Zurbrüggen (Amazon Germany 6: online): 'On the one hand, the book reads well. No incredibly long sentences, very few parentheses which would make the reading experience more difficult. But, on the other hand, the book also does not read fluently.' Whether praise for or criticism of the writing style, the reviews assigned to this category appear to be the most problematic, as the translator either does not receive praise if the writing style is assessed positively or criticism if the style is judged negatively.

None of the Amazon reviews are assigned to category C1. However, 65 of the 1,469 reviews are assigned to category C2, for reviews in which there is no mention of the translator's name, but the act of translation is acknowledged within the main text. All in all, fifty-nine of the reviews assigned to this category simply acknowledge the fact that the text has been translated into German without mentioning the name of the translator. This is the case for a review of Anna Burns' *Amelia*, translated by Anna-Nina Kroll, for example, in which the reviewer simply provides some contextual information for the translation, including the title of the original work and when it was originally written (Amazon Germany 7: online): 'Her debut novel – "No Bones" in the original – from the year 2001 has now been translated for the German-speaking world.' However, the remaining six reviews seemingly only mention the fact that the book has been translated as a potential justification for them to assess that the writing of the work is poor. A review of *Das Zuhause* by Emanuele Coccia, translated by Andreas Thomsen, is representative of the other five reviews: the reviewer (Amazon Germany 8: online) assesses that the book is 'very difficult to read' and immediately adds that this 'could obviously be down to the translation'. Much like we saw amongst British Amazon reviewers, then, it is noticeable that there is a notion amongst some German Amazon reviewers that translation may ultimately diminish the quality of the reading experience. It is not widespread – indeed, only six reviewers do this from the 1,469 Amazon reviews – but there must be a driving force behind these six reviewers feeling the necessity to add this comment to their reviews.

For the same reason that no reviews were assigned to category C1, no reviews are assigned to category D1, either. However, 36 of the 1,469 Amazon reviews, or 2.5%, are assigned to category D2, for reviews in which there is a mention of the translator's name within the main text of the review. In all of these reviews, the reviewers are simply stating a fact – who has translated the text – and are not similar to some of the reviews in category C2 in this regard; in other words, they do not only mention the name of the translator as a justification for a poor reading experience. For instance, a reviewer of Hannah Gold's *Der letzte Bär*, translated by Sylke Hachmeister, adds a comment at the end of the review (Amazon Germany 9: online), clarifying that 'the book, which takes almost five hours to read in full, was translated from English by Sylke Hachmeister'.

More frequently, however, if a German Amazon reviewer mentions the translator's name, they provide a comment on the work of the translator as well. As a result, 48 of the German Amazon reviews, or 3.3% of the 1,469 reviews in total, are assigned to category E where a short, unjustified comment is made on the translation. The majority of these comments praise the work of the translator: indeed thirty-seven of the forty-eight reviews are overwhelmingly positive towards the translation. A large number of words and expressions are used to praise the work of the translator, as follows:

- Appearing six times: good translation.
- Appearing three times: excellently translated; wonderfully translated.

- Appearing twice: outstanding translation; great translation; congenial translation; translated very successfully.
- Appearing once: pleasant translation; impressively translated; reliable translation; fantastic translation; masterful translation; smooth translation; hats off for the translation; skilful translation; perfect translation; correct translation; translated appropriately; translation leaves nothing to be desired; translation reads well; translation is on point; translation transmits the right vibe; comprehensible translation; wonderfully translated.

Many of the comments on the work of the translator are rather general in nature and it is difficult to know which aspect of the translation is being praised. Only a few of these expressions make it explicitly obvious which aspect of the translation is being referred to: for instance, 'smooth translation' and 'translation reads well' are clearly comments on how the translation reads in the target language, and not on the relationship between the source text and target text. However, comments on translation never reference fluency explicitly by using words such as 'fluent'.

This means that eleven of the reviews which are assigned to category E are critical of the work of the translator in their comments. Just two expressions appear in two separate reviews, 'incorrect translation' and 'bad translation', with other words and expressions appearing in one review each: 'something got lost in translation'; 'something snags in the translation'; 'erroneous translation'; 'bumpy translation'; 'not particularly successful translation'; 'problematic translation'; and 'senseless translation'. In these instances, it seems slightly more evident what the comments are referring to without extra analysis being provided. Phrases like 'incorrect translation' and 'erroneous translation' appear to imply that the translation is not an accurate representation of the original text, whereas expressions such as 'bumpy translation' and 'something snags in the translation' seem to be comments on the reading experience in the target language. In other words, criticism aimed at the work of the translator by German Amazon reviewers is not only based on how the text reads in the target language but also on how the text has been transferred from the source language to target language.

A total of 16 of the 1,469 reviews, or just 1.1%, are assigned to category F where a short comment is made on the translation and is justified with further analysis, but this takes up fewer than three sentences of the review. Unlike the reviews assigned to category E, there are fewer reviews assigned to category F which praise the work of the translator: just six of the sixteen reviews assigned to this category are positive towards the translation at hand. Two of these reviews focus on Gulraiz Sharif's *Ey, hör mal*, translated by Sarah Onkels and Meike Blatzheim. In the first of these reviews, the reviewer (Amazon Germany 10: online) makes a comment on the extraordinary writing style of Sharif and immediately adds that the translators deserve a huge amount of praise, because, although it would not have been an easy task to achieve, 'the way they have captured Mahmoud's deep-rooted slang, distinctive wit and childlike outlook is truly magnificent'. The second reviewer of this work (Amazon Germany 11: online) agrees with the previous reviewer, claiming that the translation is 'great', since 'youth language can be really embarrassing (or better: cringeworthy) when it is intended to appear "crass and stable"; but here it is so authentic'.

The other four reviews assigned to category F which praise the work of the translator are of four different translated works. The first is a review of Lauren Groff's *Matrix*, translated by Stefanie Jacobs. In this review, the reviewer (Amazon Germany 12: online) praises Jacobs for her 'quite excellent' translation, and it appears to be because the target text is fluent and pleasant to read in German: 'Despite the very sophisticated and full-bodied language, you just fly through the pages, it does not grate at any point and the text has its very own sound. A big compliment to the translator!' Ursel Allenstein's translation of Tove Ditlevsen's *Gesichter* is praised for a similar reason, in other words, because the text is great to read in German. The reviewer (Amazon Germany 13: online) judges that Allenstein has 'once again translated the novel excellently into German', precisely because 'there is a great flow to the reading experience which is a delight linguistically, while being clear and understandable'. The remaining two reviews which praise the work of the translator and provide a justification are less about how the target text reads and more about how the translator has managed to replicate certain aspects of the source text. In a review of Andrej Kurkow's *Samson and Nadjeschda*, the reviewer (Amazon Germany 14: online) assesses that translators Johanna Marx and Sabine Grebing have produced a 'sensitive translation', since they have 'retained the typical Russian narrative style which is particularly evident in the dialogues'. Similarly, translator Ulrich Blumenbach gets praised for his 'sensational translation' of Joshua Cohen's *Witz* (Amazon Germany 15: online). The reviewer assesses the translation to be sensational because it retains the 'ambiguities and word inventions [...] and proves in its effortlessness that Blumenbach is one of the best German-speaking translations' (ibid.: online). German Amazon reviewers are therefore not just basing their praise for the work of the translator on how the text reads in German, but are assessing the translation against other criteria as well.

Ten of the sixteen comments assigned to category F, therefore, are critical of the work of the translator. However, five of these ten critical comments come from reviews of the same work: a collection of fables published by Chronicle Books, *Keltische Märchen: Zauberhafte Märchen und Geschichten aus Irland, Schottland, der Bretagne und Wales*, translated by Ulrich Magin. All of the reviews here criticise errors or slips in the translation which affect understanding and the reading experience. One reviewer (Amazon Germany 16: online) claims that 'while reading, one stumbles over clumsy expressions again and again which have an effect on the comprehensibility of the texts'; another reviewer (Amazon Germany 17: online) feels that there are too many uncommon words in the translation, such as 'Kirmes' [parish fair] and 'scheel' [a colloquial word for suspicious], which 'bothered me when reading'; a third review (Amazon Germany 18: online) asserts that there are a number of 'slips' in the translation and that, in some areas of the text, 'the transitions do not make any sense at all and I was occasionally confused about the expressions'; the fourth review (Amazon Germany 19: online) blames the 'many translation mistakes' for the frequent 'gaps in logic', adding that 'this clearly spoils the reading pleasure'; and the final review (Amazon Germany 20: online) does not understand how there can be so many translation mistakes, given that 'many sentences either make little or no sense, or the words are misspelled or sometimes chosen too modernly, so that it is not quite appropriate'. In all of these reviews, there is a clear notion that the translation has interfered with the reading experience in the target language.

Two reviews of Liao Yiwu's *Wuhan* are also critical towards the work of translators, Hans Peter Hoffmann and Brigitte Höhenrieder – and both for the same reason that the text reads poorly in the target language. In the first review, the reviewer (Amazon Germany 21: online) refers to the translation as an 'insult', because it 'reads as though the text has been translated word-for-word by Google'; the second reviewer (Amazon Germany 22: online) takes a very similar view to the first reviewer, asserting that the translation 'seems strangely literal, almost as if done with a machine'. This reviewer (ibid.: online) does at least acknowledge that 'you can see what is meant and what is probably there in the original', but concludes that 'what it turns into is not German'. Two reviewers take umbrage with the use of different forms of the German language by the translators in their reviews: the use of a pseudo-colloquial language in Anna Burns' *Amelia*, translated by Anna-Nina Kroll, and the use of youth language in Candice Carty-Williams' *People Person*, translated by Henriette Zeltner-Shane. In the former, the reviewer (Amazon Germany 23: online) finds Kroll's pseudo-colloquial language to be 'unsuitable', since the language 'certainly has a completely different quality than the juxtaposition of Irish slang and written English that I assume is present in the original text'. In the latter, the reviewer (Amazon Germany 24: online) assesses Zeltner-Shane's translation to be 'alienating', due to the fact the reader has to grapple with features of youth language, such as 'neologisms that are often derived from the English language (e.g. sus for suspect)'. The final review to be assigned to category F is of Catherine Belton's *Putins Netz*: in this review, the reviewer (Amazon Germany 25: online) criticises translators Elisabeth Schmalen and Johanna Wais, because 'there are several grammar and spelling mistakes in this book' and 'the meaning does not come over so well here and there'. In the main, however, the majority of the reviews assigned to category F which are critical of the work of the translator(s) are based on how well (or rather not) the text reads in the target language.

Just one Amazon review is assigned to category G, for reviews in which there is extensive engagement with the translation beyond three sentences of the review. This review is of the aforementioned *Amelia* by Anna Burns and takes a similar stance to the review of this work assigned to category F. In other words, the reviewer (Amazon Germany 26: online) is critical of the fact that the translator, Anna Nina-Kroll, attempts to use a pseudo-colloquial language in German to mirror the presumed slang-like language of the original text:

> In any case, it should still be considered that the novel is most likely presented in a significantly different way in English. In the German version, we have a standard German narrative voice and characters who often shorten the language in a pseudo-colloquial way ('was hastn?', 'wer bistn du' etc.). I strongly assume that the original English is locally Irish and socially coloured. Of course, this is difficult to translate, and this variant is probably the best, apart from the option of simply leaving some things in English. But it still reads a bit forced. Whereas, in the original, local colour probably strengthens the atmosphere, pseudo-standard-colloquial language in German is rather detrimental to the atmosphere.

Unlike the review assigned to category F, however, there is an acknowledgement here that the translator faced an extremely difficult challenge and that, short of leaving some sections in English, they have made a valiant effort to get the language across in German, but the solution is not particularly effective.

Overall, the majority of German Amazon reviews do not engage with translation in any way: 1,303 are assigned to either category A or B. This equates to 88.7% of the 1,469 Amazon reviews collected from the year 2022. This is not entirely surprising, since Amazon reviewers will, in all likelihood, have limited time to write their review and are unlikely to be in a position to judge a translation in any meaningful way. When translation is mentioned in some capacity, most of the remaining reviews are assigned into categories C2 and D2. Just eighty-three – or 5.7% – of all Amazon reviews fit into categories E, F and G where there is a minimum of a brief blanket comment on the translation. Of those reviews which fit into category E, most reviewers praise the work of the translator; the majority of reviews which fit into categories F and G, however, are critical of the translation. German Amazon reviewers therefore find it more necessary to justify their comments if they are critical towards the work of the translator. In addition to this, we have also discovered that many of the German Amazon reviewers who comment on translation do not simply judge a translation against the criteria of fluency and naturalness in the target language; rather, they also frequently attempt to assess the relationship between the source language and target language and to understand what the translator has tried to achieve in their work. All in all, though, translation remains mainly invisible in German Amazon reviews.

## *Süddeutsche Zeitung (SDZ)*

A total of 233 reviews of translated works were published by *SDZ* in the year 2022. Of those, 221 reviews are assigned to categories D1 and above; in other words, the minimum reference made to translation is a mention of the translator's name in the bibliographical information. In fact, *SDZ* reviews seem to have a relatively systematic way of acknowledging the name of the translator. The bibliographical information generally comes after a picture of the book and includes the author of the original work, the German title, the language from which the text has been translated and then the name of the translator(s). It is somewhat surprising therefore that twelve reviews from *SDZ* are assigned to categories A through C2. Ten of these, or 4.3% of all *SDZ* reviews collected from the year 2022, are classified into category A, as these reviews make no reference to the act of translation at all, and no comment is made upon the style of the target text. It is difficult to establish why these ten reviews do not at least mention the name of the translator. It is not idiosyncratic: indeed, each of the ten reviews is written by a different reviewer. Seven of these ten reviewers (Bovermann, Heidenreich, Knoben, Minkmar, Pollatschek, Spiekermann and Wennerscheid) wrote at least one more review each in 2022, and all of those reviews are assigned to category D1 or above. Mönninger and Winkels only wrote one review each in 2022, so it is difficult to ascertain whether it is their 'go-to' practice to not mention the name of the translator. El Ouassil is the only reviewer for *SDZ* who wrote more than one review in 2022 and does not mention the name of the translator in either; her other review is assigned to category C2. It also does not appear to depend on the length of the review. Indeed, many of the reviews assigned to category D1 are short-form reviews which form part of a group article and still mention the name of the translator (none of the reviews assigned to category A are one of these short-form reviews).

It may be that it ultimately comes down to the genre of the work being reviewed. Of the ten reviews assigned to category A, seven focus on a non-fictional work, two a comic and only one a work of fiction (Tove Ditlevsen's *Gesichter*, translated by Ursel Allenstein). This adds weight to the idea, developed over the previous two chapters, that reviewers are potentially less interested in the work of the translator for works of non-fiction than they are for works of fiction, and that this type of translation is seen as less creative and a more straightforward process.

None of the *SDZ* reviews are assigned to categories B or C1, but two reviews are classified into category C2; in other words, these reviews acknowledge the act of translation within the main body of the text, but the name of the translator remains unmentioned in the review or the bibliographical information. The first of these reviews is written by El Ouassil (2022: online) and focusses on Bruno Latour's non-fictional work *Zur Entstehung einer ökologischen Klasse: Ein Memorandum*, translated by Bernd Schwibs. The only reference to the act of translation comes early in the review when El Ouassil (ibid.: online) is providing some context for the work being published:

> 'A spectre is haunting Europe and the rest of the world: ecologism!' claims Bruno Latour's new memorandum which he published with the Danish sociologist in the original language at the start of this year and which now, a few weeks after Latour passed away, appears in German translation.

In the bibliographical information, however, the name of the translator is not mentioned. Despite the fact that it is the same format of bibliographical information, we only see Latour's name, the title of the German text and the name of the publishing house. The second review to be assigned to category C2 comes from a group article entitled *Bücher des Monats August* [Books of the Month August], written by a group of *SDZ* authors. This article contains six short-form reviews, each between 100 and 150 words long. One of the reviews focusses on Salman Rushdie's *Die Satanischen Verse*, translated by an anonymous translator, and includes links to other articles, one of which draws attention to the fact that this work is translated from German: 'You can read the background here, about the German translation here, and about the political function of the Fatwa here' (SDZ Autorinnen und Autoren 2022a: online). It may be because the translator of this text is anonymous that there is no mention of translation in the bibliographical information.

The vast majority of *SDZ* reviews published in 2022 fit into category D1; indeed, 148 of the 233 reviews, or 63.5%, only mention the name of the translator in the bibliographical information of the review and are thus assigned to this category. Forty-one of these 148 reviews are short-form reviews, generally between 75 and 200 words long, taken from group articles. It may be due to a lack of space that the name of the translator is mentioned, but there is no further engagement with the translation. These group articles bring together a variety of newly published works and provide quick insights, mainly into the content of the work. A representative example of this is a review of Serhij Zhadan's *Himmel über Charkiw*, translated by Stöhr and Durkot, taken from a group article written by SDZ authors entitled *Bücher des Monats Oktober* [Books of the Month October]. This is the complete review, 110 words in length, including the bibliographical information:

> Since the start of the Russian war of aggression, Serhij Zhadan has been writing a diary on his Facebook page. His posts from the first five months have been published as a war diary under the title 'Himmel über Charkiw': the best thing to read about the current situation in Ukraine, because it is not only about observations of the present. Zhadan organises donations on Facebook, writes obituaries for fallen artists and speaks to the people around him with courage. Zhadan is not only the most important Ukrainian writer of his generation, but also a community worker.
>
> Serhij Zhadan: Himmel über Charkiw. Nachrichten vom Überleben im Krieg. From the Ukrainian by Sabine Stöhr and Jurij Durkot. Suhrkamp, Berlin 2022. 239 pages, 20 Euros. (SDZ Autorinnen und Autoren 2022b: online)

In this type of review, there are no comments on anything but the content of the work, and certainly nothing about the work of the translator. This review is standard for works of this length. Indeed, none of the short-form reviews taken from a group article are assigned to categories E through G.

A total of fourteen reviews are assigned to category D2, for reviews in which there is also a mention of the translator's name within the main body of the review text. Twelve of the fourteen reviews which fit into this category are of literary works, and the other two focus on non-fictional works. It appears, therefore, that *SDZ* reviewers feel more obliged to draw attention to the name of the translator in the main body of the text when a literary work is being discussed. In all fourteen reviews, the mention of the translator's name comes early on in the review, generally when the reviewer is contextualising the work at hand. For instance, in her review of Anna Burns' novel *Amelia*, translated by Anna-Nina Kroll, reviewer Wilke (2022a: online) introduces the novel, outlining that it is Burns' debut, before mentioning the name of the person who translated the text: 'Now, Anna Burns' debut, the novel "Amelia" first published in the year 2001, is available in German, once again translated by Anna-Nina Kroll.' The fact that the translator's name is mentioned within the main body of these fourteen reviews arguably brings more prominence to the translator, as, in those reviews assigned to category D1, the reader may easily skim over the bibliographical information. Altogether, 164 of the 233 *SDZ* reviews, or 70.4%, fit into categories C2, D1 and D2, so the majority of *SDZ* reviews are considered to promote the superficial visibility of translation.

On the other hand, 59 – or 25.3% – of the 233 reviews are assigned to categories E through G, meaning that they are seen to promote the embedded visibility of translation; in other words, these reviews go beyond a brief acknowledgement of translation or mention of the translator's name to add a comment on the translator's work. A total of thirty-six of those fifty-nine reviews make a short, unjustified comment on the translation and are therefore assigned to category E. In all, thirty-four of these reviews praise the work of the translator, drawing upon the following words and phrases:

- Appearing three times: excellent translation.
- Appearing twice: brilliantly translated; translated into lively German; congenial translation; energetically translated; appropriately translated; transferred into German without loss.
- Appearing once: retained all nuances; sensitively translated; elegant translation; fabulously translated; sensitive translation; successful translation; brilliantly transferred; good translation; transferred into elastic German; skilful translation; masterfully translated; delicately translated; thrillingly translated; suitable translation;

> diligently translated; transferred into German in a stylistically assured manner; translation retains the tone; translation did not do the book any harm; expertly transferred into German.

The majority of these comments are general in nature and, as the reviewers provide no further justification for their comments, it is difficult to know to which aspect of the translation the reviewers are referring. Some of the comments hint at fluency and readability in German – for instance, 'translated into lively German' – but explicit comments such as 'fluent' and 'easy to read' never appear in these reviews. On the flipside, it appears that some reviewers are assessing the relationship between the source text and the target text: for instance, two reviewers use the phrase 'transferred into German without loss', hinting at the fact that they have compared the target text to the source text. Just two reviews assigned to category E are critical of the work of the translator. In her review of Claudio Magris' *Gekrümmte Zeit in Krems*, reviewer Maidt-Zinke (2022: online) claims that Anna Leube's translation 'could have done with more time spent on it in certain places', but does not outline what about the translation has made her come to this conclusion. On the other hand, Weber (2022: online), in his review of Pierre Charbonnier's *Überfluss und Freiheit: Eine ökologische Geschichte der politischen Ideen*, is initially critical of the original author's 'tortuous style' and is critical of translator Andrea Hemminger as she was not able to 'iron it out'; this comment feels particularly questionable without further justification, given that it is not usually considered the translator's job to do this.

A total of eighteen reviews make a comment on the translation and provide a further justification in fewer than three sentences of the review, and therefore these reviews are assigned to category F; this accounts for 7.7% of all *SDZ* reviews collected from the year 2022. Nine of these reviews are overwhelmingly positive towards the work of the translator. In almost all of these reviews, the reviewers praise the translator(s) for their ability to transfer a key element of the source text into the target language. Three of the reviews praise the translator for managing to reproduce a specific type of language in German – the language of the harbour district, a rugged mountain language and street language, respectively: in her review of Jean Malaquais' *Planet ohne Visum*, Wilke (2022b: online) claims that translator Nadine Püschel 'is a significant factor' behind the fact that 'one has the impression in German, too, of having the social conditions of the harbour district on the tip of one's tongue and in one's nose'; in a review of Irene Solà's *Singe ich, tanzen die Berge*, Janker (2022: online) claims that the effect of the novel in German 'is thanks to Petra Zickmann's translation', since she has 'carefully lifted the sound of this often rugged mountain language from Catalan into German and happily preserved its astringency'; and, finally, Welle (2022: online), reviewing Gulraiz Sharif's *Ey hör mal!*, claims that translators Meike Blatzheim and Sarah Onkels deserve praise, as they have 'transferred its blunt sound of the street into an appropriate German'.

Six of the positive reviews reserve praise for the work of the translator in reproducing the style or a specific feature of the writing of the original text. Schmidt (2022: online), in her review of Ilya Kaminsky's *Republik der Taubheit*, calls translator Anja Kampmann a 'masterful lyricist' and claims that she has done a great job keeping the contrasts of the text high, despite the fact that 'in German, with its convoluted syntax, such profound simplicity is hard to achieve'. Albath (2022: online), reviewing Stefano Massini's *Die Lehman Brothers*, praises translator Annette Kopetzky for managing to 'recreate the oscillation between terse description, laconism, rhythmised literal speech, biblical pathos and sombre wit in German'. Thomas Gunkel's 'intensive' translation of Stewart O'Nan's *Ocean State* is praised by reviewer Bleutge (2022a: online) for having 'repeatedly found plausible equivalents for the language of the characters: "bitch" and "stupid cow" are amongst the more harmless terms'. In another review written by Bleutge (2022b: online), translator Cornelius Hell is adjuged to have 'in particular superbly reproduced Venclova's rhythm, playing with metres and changing the speed of verse' and found 'very beautiful solutions for those rhymes with which Venclova, the poet of memory, concludes his volume' in his translation of *Variation über das Thema Erwachen*. In a similar review, Müller (2022a: online), reviewing Gary Shteyngart's *Landpartie*, thanks translator Nikolaus Stingl for his work in ensuring that 'Shteyngart's light tone, complete with fanned-out punchline register, is preserved in German'. The final review which appears to praise the work of the translator based on a comparison between the source text and the target text is Steinfeld's review of Andrea Giovene's *Die Autobiographie des Giuliano di Sansevero*. In this review, Steinfeld (2022a: online) praises translator Moshe Kahn for producing a German text which 'is not inferior to the Italian original in terms of liveliness and richness of relationship, no matter how much the subordinate clauses pile up'. None of the reviews assigned to category F which praise the work of the translator, therefore, judge the translation against fluency and readability alone; there is always a comparison between the source language and target language.

Three of the reviews assigned to category F are generally positive towards the work of the translator, but also have reservations about the final product. In his review of Mariana Enriquez's *Unser Teil der Nacht*, Ebel (2022: online) assesses that the translators Silke Kleemann and Inka Marter have 'preserved the sparkle of this text in German', but is critical that they sometimes use out-dated terms, such as 'studying people', when the modern term would be 'students'; Ebel (ibid.: online) even adds that he is happy that the translators 'do not turn workers into "working people" '. The remaining two reviews are broadly positive towards the work of the translator; however, the reviewers also acknowledge that something is lost from the original text. Lisa Kögeböhn's translation of Adam Silvera's *More Happy Than Not* is evaluated to not be as cool as the English text by reviewer Holger Moos (2022: online), since the original is stylistically 'authentic', something which the German text does not quite achieve: '[I]t is difficult to judge whether the German translation can do this: for example, when a "dude-liker" is described as an "Auf-Typen-Steher", a lot of things sound cooler in English.' Similarly, Cornelius Reiber's translation of Maggie Nelson's *Freiheit: Vier Variationen über Zuwendung und Zwang* is adjuged by reviewer Shaller (2022: online) to be 'fleet-footed', but the reviewer questions 'whether the American culture war can really be transferred to Germany so easily'. He ultimately concludes that, in the translation, 'many of the examples mentioned will be unfamiliar to a local audience' (ibid.: online).

The final six reviews assigned to category F are critical of the work of the translator(s). Three of these appear to be a judgement on how the text reads in German alone. In his review of Julia Donaldson and Axel Scheffler's *Die Rüpelbande*, Mach (2022: online) considers that 'the rhymes are bumpy and the translation from English [by Salah Naoura] hobbles along here and there, especially at the point when the witch wants to conjure away the cloth'. Similarly, Brigitte Höhenrieder and Hans Peter Hoffmann's translation of Liao Yiwu's *Wuhan* is assessed by reviewer Spengler (2022: online) to be too close to the Chinese original, supported by examples from the translation, such as 'auf Granit beißen' [bite on granite]: 'Since the translators consistently gave me the impression that I was looking into the Chinese original while reading, the examples caused unnecessary irritation.' The most telling review, however, is Stephan's review of Joshua Cohen's novel *Witz*: Stephan (2022a: online) claims that 'rarely is the presence of a translator as palpable as that of Ulrich Blumenbach' – and he assesses this to be negative, as the book 'is overrun by internal rhymes [and] the assonances sound like "clinking clunkers" ' (ibid.: online). All three reviews base their criticism of the translation on the key criteria of (a lack of) fluency and readability.

However, the remaining three reviews which fit into category F are critical of the translator for losing an aspect of the original text. In two of these reviews, this is to do with the title. In his review of Emanuele Coccia's *Das Zuhause*, Steinfeld (2022b: online) criticises the translator Andreas Thomsen for the fact that 'the "Happy" is gone' from the title and explains that this is problematic due to its significance in the rest of the work; similarly, Stephan (2022b: online), in his review of Hernán Díaz's *Treue*, is critical of translator Hannes Meyer's German title of the work, since 'in English, the novel is called "Trust", which on the one hand can mean literal trust and on the other hand an association of several companies. In the German title, the semantic play, which basically anticipates the plot of the whole novel, is unfortunately lost.' The final review assigned to category F is von Bitter's review of Pierre Loti's *Ramuntcho*. In this review, von Bitter (2022: online) is critical of Holger Fock and Sabine Müller's translation, because he believes that, when one reads the original, one 'discovers from the very first lines a persistent verse metre, like a song that pulls you along as you read'; however, he claims that in the German translation 'not only is the linguistic rhythm with syntax and emphasis different, but some words also lose their euphony' (ibid.: online). Fluency and readability are therefore not the only criteria for all *SDZ* reviewers; indeed, a comparison of the source text to the target text is evident in many of the reviews assigned to category F.

Five *SDZ* reviews are assigned to category G, or just over 2% of the 233 reviews collected from the year 2022. Three of the five reviews praise what the translator has achieved. In her review of Mary Ruefle's *Mein Privatbesitz*, reviewer Wilke (2022c: online) claims that translator Esther Kinsky has done a magnificent job in the translation of a text which is packed full of poetic creativity. Wilke (ibid.: online) provides a number of examples to support her points with regard to how Kinsky manages to retain that creativity in her translation:

> 'Earth-moving machines' and not 'heavy equipment' dig up the ground where Ruefle, with her anthropological interest, observes how the dead are treated analogously to rubbish, wrapped in 'burial boxes' and not in 'coffins'. All these small but significant shifts in perception through linguistic deviations. And then there are the particles, conjunctions and adverbs: how definitive an 'and' in Kinsky's translation sounds in Ruefle's prose piece 'Glück gehabt' when it ends the round of contradictory conjunctions with 'but': 'but that didn't happen (…) and when I woke up, I was naked like a baby and alone and afraid'.

Compared to those reviews assigned to category E, and even to category F, this review feels more convincing, given that there is a clear comparison between the source text and target text, and the reviewer engages with an array of examples to support the praise she attributes to translator Kinsky. Similarly, in a review of her translation of Andrea Tompa's *Omertà*, translator Terézia Mora is praised for managing to retain a key feature of the source text – its polyphonic nature – in German. Reviewer Müller (2022b: online) claims that Mora has ensured that 'the four voices of this idiosyncratic, exemplary novel about the establishment of a repressive regime in the European provinces can now also be heard in German'. Müller provides some contextual information about the translator, with the fact that she herself grew up in a multilingual world being of particular importance, and outlines how the translator adds an index to the German text with the terms and place names of the original. The reviewer (ibid.: online) finishes by saying that the translation 'brings the tonality of the protagonists into German, including the older layers of language'. The praise for the work of the translator in this review is once more based on the relationship between the source text and the target text. The final review in category G which is overwhelmingly positive towards the work of the translator is Magenau's review of Ted Hughes' *Wodwo: Ausgewählte Gedichte*. In his review, Magenau (2022: online) adjudges translator Jan Wagner's work to be 'extraordinarily successful', precisely because 'in German, he always remains very close to the original, as can be easily observed in the bilingual edition – the original on the left, the translation on the right'. Magenau (ibid.: online) asserts that 'Wagner preserves Hughes' brittle, acerbic tone without adding, softening or omitting anything'. Again, it is the comparison between the source text and the target text which allows the reviewer to come to this conclusion, not just an evaluation of how the text reads in German.

One of the reviews assigned to category G is generally positive towards the translation at hand, but still has some reservations. In his review of new translations of a selection of Roald Dahl's classic novels, reviewer Menden (2022: online) acknowledges that the translators Sabine Ludwig, Emma Ludwig and Andreas Steinhöfel had their work cut out, since they faced the big challenge of translating 'the linguistic inventions and onomatopoeic names'. Menden (ibid.: online) claims that, on a positive note, 'the new translations published so far read pleasantly snappy'; however, the reviewer (ibid.: online) has reservations about some of the translation solutions that the translators have come up with, including the following example from the translation of *Der fantastische Mister Fox*:

> 'Churgle' is how the foxes in 'The Fantastic Mister Fox' react at the thought of a chicken feast – a portmanteau of 'chuckle' and 'gurgle'. Steinhöfel decides on 'gackern', to cluck, which makes a nice connection to the chickens being eaten. But why not, for example, 'kirgeln'? Sometimes one would have wished for a little more courage with the translation of neologisms.

In this instance, the praise is reserved for how the text reads in German – 'pleasantly snappy' – and it is the creativity of the translation which is questioned in the reproduction of neologisms in the German text.

The final review assigned to category G is solely critical of the work of the translator. Indeed, reviewing Rachel Kushner's *Harte Leute*, reviewer

Häntzschel (2022: online) claims that the translator Bettina Abarbanell 'almost wilfully keeps steering Kushner's artful, laconic texts off course'. He provides a number of examples, including the translation of 'car' as 'Pkw' [passenger car], despite the fact that a passionate car lover would not refer to it as this, and the word 'Communities' being translated problematically to 'Kommunen' [communes] and 'Gemeinden' [municipalities] (ibid.: online). However, the biggest issue that Häntzschel (ibid.: online) has with the translation is that Abarbanell translates 'downtown' as 'Innenstadt' [city centre], when downtown in New York 'refers, as we know, to southern Manhattan and the cultural scene there which Kushner enters as a 16-year-old in a wonderful passage'. It appears, therefore, that Häntzschel has compared elements of the translation to the source text, and his ultimately critical evaluation of the translation is based on the relationship between the source and target texts, rather than just on how the text reads in German.

All in all, we have seen that the vast majority of *SDZ* reviews collected from the year 2022 promote the superficial visibility of translation: indeed, 164 of the 233 *SDZ* reviews fit into categories C1 through D2 which acknowledge the fact of translation in some regard or mention the translator's name. Ten reviews do not acknowledge the fact of translation and are therefore assigned to category A. The reason for the translation not being acknowledged in these reviews seems to be down to the genre of the work; it was therefore suggested that reviews of non-fictional works for *SDZ* are less likely to include a mention of the translator. The remaining fifty-nine reviews are classified into categories E through G and are therefore considered to promote the embedded visibility of the translator. Most of these reviews are overwhelmingly positive towards the work of the translator; indeed, forty-eight of the fifty-nine reviews assigned to these categories have nothing but praise for the work of the translator. We have also seen from the reviews assigned to categories F and G in particular that *SDZ* reviewers in the main do not simply assess the work of the translator against the assumed dominant criteria of fluency and readability, but rather frequently base their judgement on the relationship between the source and target texts; this is an especially significant development based on the findings of previous studies in this field.

## *Der Spiegel (DS)*

In 2022, *DS* published a significantly lower number of reviews of translated works than *SDZ* – 43 compared to 233. The smaller figures for *DS* are accounted for by the fact that *DS* is a weekly magazine rather than a daily publication like *SDZ*. None of the forty-three reviews of translated works published by *DS* are assigned to categories A through C2; in other words, the minimum reference to translation in each of the reviews is a mention of the translator's name in the bibliographical information of the review. *DS* reviews are very systematic in how they mention the name of the translator: at the end of each of the reviews, there is a picture of the work, followed by the original author's name, the title of the work, the name of the translator, the name of the publishing house, and the number of pages (often in a different order, but always with the same information). A total of thirty-eight, or 88.3%, of the forty-three reviews are assigned to category D1 for reviews in which there is a mention of the translator's name in the bibliographical information and no more. Ten of the thirty-eight reviews are short-form reviews which are part of a group article, entitled, for instance, *Aktuelle Kinder- und Jugendbücher* [Current Childrens' and Young People Books], and generally give reviewers between 100 and 200 words to engage with the work at hand. The lack of space is perhaps therefore the reason why reviewers do not engage with translation in any significant way in these reviews. The following complete short-form review comes from a group article entitled *Ukrainische Krimis* [Ukrainian crime novels] and focusses on Andrej Kurkow's *Graue Bienen*, translated by Sabine Grebing and Johanna Marx. The review is 113 words long in total and is dedicated purely to what the novel is about and some contextual information about the author Kurkow:

> In Spring, Sergej sets off with his colonies on an adventurous journey to the West so that his bees can once again collect their nectar in peaceful surroundings: 'So that the honey does not taste of war as well.' Author Kurkow ('Penguins Don't Freeze') is Ukrainian, writes in Russian and, in his 2019 novel, sketches the allegory of a dystopian reality in which the 'uninvolved' must somehow get by. Always on guard against the prevailing authorities, always looking for a quiet place. Sergej never

> feels like a refugee. He is with his colonies – a serving member of their humming, peaceful state.
>
> Andrej Kurkow. Graue Bienen: Roman. Publisher: Diogenes. Number of pages: 448. Translation by: Sabine Grebing and Johanna Marx. (DS Autorinnen und Autoren 2022: online)

In such reviews, the reviewers have a limited amount of space and prioritise what they consider to be really essential information for their readers. There is also something idiosyncratic about whether *DS* reviewers only mention the name of the translator and no more. For instance, Anja Rützel and Enrico Ippolito both published three reviews of translated works in 2022 and in each review only mention the name of the translator in the bibliographical information.

Just one review published in *DS* is assigned to category D2, where the reviewer in question, Xaver von Cranach, goes beyond a mention of the translator in the bibliographical information and adds the translator's name within the main body of the review text without commenting on the performance of the translator. In his review of *Das andere Mädchen* by Annie Ernaux, translated by Sonja Finck, von Cranach (2022: online) provides an introduction to the author and her increasing success in Germany: 'For years, Suhrkamp-Verlag has been publishing her old books in new translations by Sonja Finck, usually in small volumes, and her readership grows in Germany with each new book.' Xaver von Cranach, incidentally, wrote five reviews of translated works in 2022; four of these fit into category D1 and one into category D2, adding weight to the argument that whether *DS* reviewers go beyond a mention of the translator's name appears to be idiosyncratic. Overall, thirty-nine of the forty-three reviews of translated works published by *DS* in 2022, or 90.7%, fit into categories D1 and D2, so these reviews are considered to promote the superficial visibility of translation.

However, *DS* reviews much less frequently promote the embedded visibility of translation; indeed only four *DS* reviews published in 2022 fit into categories E through G where there is further engagement with translation in the review beyond a mention of the translator's name. Two of the four reviews are assigned to category E, for reviews in which there is a short, unjustified comment made on the translation. This makes up

4.7% of all *DS* reviews. One of these reviews is positive towards the work of the translator; the other is somewhat more critical. In her review of Candice Carty-Williams' *People Person*, translated by Henriette Zeltner-Shane, reviewer Stegelmann (2022: online) praises the translator for producing a sensitive translation which allows Carty-Williams's text to work in German: 'Carty-Williams deals with a lot of relevant topics in "People Person". She does so in clear, modern language and with lively dialogue that also works in German thanks to her sensitive translator Henriette Zeltner-Shane.' The praise for the work of the translator appears to be for maintaining the style of language from the source text to the target text. However, the same cannot be said for Voigt's (2022: online) review of Vendela Vida's *Die Gezeiten gehören uns*, translated by Monika Baark, as the reviewer assesses the title of the work in German to be not entirely idiomatic: ' "Die Gezeiten gehören uns" is the title of her book in German, a somewhat unwieldy title for this clever book.'

The final two reviews published by *DS* in 2022 are assigned to category F, as the reviewers make a comment on the translation and justify this comment with further analysis and/or examples; however, they do not spend more than three lines of the review discussing the translation. Much like the two reviews assigned to category E, one review praises and one review is critical of the work of the translator. The former, written by Menasse, focusses on the translation of Yasmina Reza's *Serge* by Hinrich Schmidt-Henkel and Frank Heibert. Reviewer Menasse (2022: online) refers to Schmidt-Henkel and Heibert's translation as 'fabulous', since the translation has taken Reza's original text and 'conjures up a compelling, idiomatic German out of it'. In this review, Menasse's assessment of the translation appears to be guided by the fact that ultimately the text is idiomatic and reads well in German, rather than a consideration of the source text and target text. Müntefering's (2022: online) review of Zhou Haohui's *18/4 – Der Hauptmann und der Mörder*, translated by Julian Haefs, is similar in this regard: this time, though, Müntefering is critical of the translator's work, precisely because the text is the opposite of idiomatic in places. Müntefering (ibid.: online) begins his section on the translation by stating that 'in places, the translation seems bumpy and clumsy, full of language clichés, superfluous adjectives and small mistakes'. Nonetheless, he does admit that the translator should not be blamed for this, since Haefs did not translate from the Chinese original, but rather from the American version:

> [These are] weaknesses that may be at least partly due to the fact that Julian Haefs did not translate from the Chinese original, but used the US version published in 2018 as a basis – a publishing practice that is unfortunately all too common among Asian authors from the Japanese Haruki Murakami before his books become bestsellers in Germany, to the Korean Kim Un-su. (ibid.: online)

Regardless of the fact that Müntefering attempts to mitigate his assertion that the translation seems 'bumpy' and 'clumsy' by outlining that this is probably due to the text being indirectly translated, both *DS* reviews assigned to category F ultimately judge the translation against the criterion of idiomaticity. No *DS* reviews published in 2022 are assigned to category G; in other words, no reviewers engaged with the translation for more than three lines of the review.

To summarise, all *DS* reviews in 2022 mentioned the name of the translator systematically and therefore all reviews promoted the superficial visibility of translation as a bare minimum. Thirty-nine of the forty-three collected reviews fit into categories D1 and D2, so 90.7% of the reviews only promote the superficial visibility of translation or, in other words, only mention the name of the translator within the bibliographical information or the main body of the text. As we have seen throughout this section of the chapter, *DS* reviews are far less frequently assigned to categories E through G and therefore cannot be considered to promote the embedded visibility of translation on the whole. Just two reviews made a short unjustified comment on the translation and were assigned to category E, and another two reviews made a justified comment on the translation in fewer than three lines and thus were assigned to category F. The two reviews which fit into category F both judge the translation against the criteria of readability and idiomaticity: indeed, praise is attributed to the work of the translator for conjuring up a 'compelling' and 'idiomatic' German translation, whilst criticism for the work of the translator in the other review is due to the target text being 'bumpy' and 'clumsy'.

## *Literaturkritik (LK)*

A total of 153 reviews of translated works were published by *LK* in 2022, a far greater number of reviews than *DS* published, even though *LK* is only published monthly. *LK* does have a section in each of its magazines for foreign-language literature, so reviews of translated works are guaranteed to get a space in the magazine on a monthly basis. As a general rule, *LK* reviews mention the name of the translator in the bibliographical information of the review as a bare minimum: indeed, 151, or 98.6%, of the 153 reviews do this. Reviewers for this publication generally include a picture of the German book cover, the author's name and title, followed by the line 'from the [source language] by' and then the name of the translator. However, two *LK* reviews collected in the year 2022 do not mention the name of the translator and fit into categories A through C2. One review is assigned to category A – Seiler's (2022: online) review of Michel Houellebecq's novel *Vernichten*, translated by Stephan Kleiner and Bernd Wilczek – as the reviewer does not acknowledge that translation has taken place at all within the review. The reasons behind Seiler not mentioning the name of the translator remain unclear: Houellebecq's *Vernichten* is a novel and it seems more commonplace for translators of non-fictional works not to get a mention in reviews; the review is of a rather standard length for *LK* reviews, standing at 857 words long; and it is not idiosyncratic, as Seiler wrote six reviews for *LK* in 2022, and the rest of the reviews mention the name of the translator in the bibliographical information and are thus assigned to category D1. In this instance, then, it may be a simple oversight. None of the reviews are assigned to categories B or C1, but one review acknowledges the act of translation within the main body of the review text without mentioning the name of the translator and is therefore assigned to category C2. The review in question is Lentz's (2022: online) review of Eva Tind's *Ursprung*, translated by Ursel Allenstein. Allenstein is not mentioned within the text or the bibliographical information; however, Lentz (ibid.: online) ends her review with the line '*Ursprung* is the first book of the Danish author to be published in German and was nominated for the DR Novel Prize.' This is the only review to be published in *LK* by Lentz in 2022, so it is difficult to know whether this is something idiosyncratic or whether it is an oversight by the reviewer not to mention Allenstein.

Of the 151 reviews which mention the translator's name, 93 only mention the translator's name in the bibliographical information of the review and are therefore classified into category D1. Unsurprisingly, these reviews focus mainly on the content of the work itself and provide contextualisation about the author or the backdrop for the work. It is difficult to spot any clear trends in terms of which reviews only mention the name of the translator. The majority of the reviews, eighty-nine of the ninety-three, are of translated literature, but this is hardly surprising given that *LK* is mainly an outlet for reviewing literature and there are only a couple of reviews of non-fictional works published each month. There are none of the kinds of group articles with short-form reviews which are published in *SDZ* and *DS*: the average *LK* review is between 600 and 1,000 words long, so it is not a lack of space that accounts for there being no further engagement with the translation in *LK*. There may therefore be something idiosyncratic about whether a reviewer goes beyond a mention of the translator's name in the bibliographical information. A number of reviewers for *LK* wrote more than one review in 2022 and all of their reviews are classified into category D1: ten reviews written by Karsten Hermann; four reviews each by Monika Grosche and Walter Delabar; three reviews each by Oliver Pfohlmann and Stefanie Steible; and two reviews each by Johann Holzner, Jochen Vogt and Georg Patzer. These reviewers may not be comfortable commenting on the translation and hence only include a mention of the translator's name in the bibliographical information to the review.

In addition to the ninety-three reviews classified into category D1, thirteen reviews mention the name of the translator in the main text of the review and are thus assigned to category D2. In these reviews, the mention of the translator is done factually by the reviewers, such as by acknowledging that the text has been translated into German by a certain translator. An example of this comes in a review of Toril Brekke's *Ein rostiger Klang von Freiheit*, translated by Gabriele Haefs. In this review, reviewer Helmes (2022: online) begins the second paragraph of his review by stating that 'now, in the translation of her translator Gabriele Haefs, we have another novel, *Ein rostiger Klang von Freiheit* (published in the original under the title *Klangen av friheit*), which is markedly multi-faceted and teeming with various themes and issues'. All other twelve reviews assigned to this category mention the name of the translator in the main body of the text in a similar manner. Incidentally, Günter Helmes is the only reviewer who wrote more than one review in 2022 to be assigned to category D2 and, in fact, both reviews that he published in 2022 are assigned to this category. Nine of the reviews assigned to this category focus on a piece of translated literature; four focus on a piece of non-fiction. It has previously been suggested that German reviewers very rarely acknowledge the name of a translator of non-fiction within the main body of the text, so it is particularly noteworthy that *LK* reviewers go against the general trend. Overall, a total of 107 of the 153 reviews, or 70.0%, fit into categories C1 through D2, categories which are seen to promote the superficial visibility of translation. *LK* reviews therefore do this to a similar extent as *SDZ* reviews (70.4% of *SDZ*'s reviews were assigned to categories C1 through D2).

The remaining forty-five reviews published by *LK* in 2022 are therefore considered to promote the embedded visibility of translation; in other words, they at least make a short comment on the work of the translator and are assigned to categories E through G. Just over half of these, twenty-five, fit into category E. All but one of the reviews praises the work of the translator with an unjustified comment. The following words and expressions are used to positively evaluate the translation:

- Three times: excellent translation.
- Twice: sensitively translated; fluent translation; successful translation; brilliantly translated into German; excellently translated into German.
- Once: smooth translation; excellent translation; translated into elegant German; congenial translation; thanks to the translation; translation which reads very well in German; analogously translated; translation is a delight; translation leaves nothing to be desired; translation makes a flawless contribution; wonderful translation.

Like other publications, the majority of these comments are general in nature, and it is difficult to assess the criteria against which the reviewers are judging the translation. However, many of the words and expressions used to praise the work of the translator, such as 'fluent', 'smooth' and 'reads very well', are related to the idea of idiomaticity, and it appears therefore that the reviewers are ultimately basing their judgement on how the text reads in the target language. Nonetheless, there are also some expressions which seem to hint that the reviewer has assessed the relationship between the source text and target text, such as 'sensitive'; without further justification of the comments, though, it is difficult to know whether this is definitely the case. There is just one comment in a review classified into category E which is considered to be critical of the work of the translator. In his review of N. K. Jemisin's *Die Wächterinnen von New York*, translated by Bejamin Mildner, Löchel (2022a: online) asserts that the original author 'makes use of the different slangs spoken in the city districts', but that this 'has not been reproduced in the German translation'. Ultimately, in this instance, it appears to be an assessment of the relationship between the source language and target language which allows Löchel to come to this conclusion.

All in all, 13 of the 153 reviews published by *LK*, or 8.5%, are classified into category F. Unlike those reviews assigned to category E which in the main praised the work of the translator, there is a balance between reviews which praise the translation and those which criticise the translation if they are assigned to category F. Indeed, only four of the thirteen reviews in this category are overwhelmingly positive towards the work of the translator. Three of the four reviews praise the translator for managing to retain a certain aspect of the source text in their translation. In his review of Fiston Mwanza Mujila's *Tanz der Teufel*, translated by Katharina Meyer and Lena Müller, reviewer Mazenauer (2022: online) claims that the two translators deserve 'great credit' since they have 'found an accurate equivalent in German for the jazzy, upbeat language to which the author attaches particular importance, an equivalent which, in keeping with the original, sounds at times vulgar and groovy, at times pensive and sad'. Similarly, translator Sabine Gisin is praised by reviewer Rönsch (2022a: online) in his review of Kjersti Rorgemoen's *Hoffnung and Fest*, since 'nothing is lost' in the translation. Rönsch (ibid.: online) adds that the translator manages to replicate the style of the original and provides specific examples of how this works in practice: '[A] word invention such as "winddurchzogen" is just as impressive as the virtuoso use of rare and almost extinct words such as "brünzlig" and "vor sich hin pfurren".' Another review which praises the translator for managing to retain an aspect of the original, in this case in spite of losing another aspect of the source text, focusses on the translation of Pier Paolo Pasolini's *Nach meinem Tod zu veröffentlichen. Späte Gedichte*. In this review, reviewer Sammet (2022: online) praises translator Theresia Prammer for managing to retain 'the sensual, the desirous nature' of the original text, despite the fact that she 'does not translate the rhymes'. The final review assigned to category F which is overwhelmingly positive towards the work of the translator is another review written by Rönsch (2022b: online), this time of Fang Fang's *Wütendes Feuer*, translated by Michael Kahn-Ackermann. In this particular review, Rönsch (ibid.: online) praises the translator for changing the place name from Fenghuangyuan to Phöenixdamm and claims that 'with further similar references and with concise footnotes on historical and other contexts, the book is immensely easy to read'. This is the only review assigned to category F which praises the translation and seems to assess it by the criterion of reader-friendliness in the target language, rather than the relationship between the source language and target language.

Five of the reviews assigned to this category praise the work of the translator in the main, but have some reservations as well. Two of these reviews praise the translation in general, but criticise the choice of title. Rönsch (2022c: online), in his review of Liz Nugent's *Auf der Lauer liegen*, praises translator Kathrin Razum for her 'successful' translation, but criticises the choice of title, since 'the English "Lying in Wait" also refers to the body of Annie Doyle buried in the garden – mortal remains are hardly "auf der Lauer" [on the lookout]'. Similarly, Amend-Söchting (2022a: online), in her review of Jean-Philippe Toussaint's *Die Gefühle*, assesses that 'Joachim Unseld's translation is as excellent as ever and reads almost like the French original'; however, she also wonders why the title is not simply *Gefühle* without the definite article *Die*, since this title 'would be much more in keeping with the generic definite article in French, "Les émotions" [Emotions], and likewise underline the level of abstraction at which these are negotiated'. Both reviewers' criticisms of the title of the work they are reviewing seem entirely justifiable, but this does not influence their assessment of the translation as a whole.

Two other reviews assigned to category F praise the work of the translator in general, but criticise the choice of language in the target text at times. In a review of Radka Denemarková's *Stunden aus Blei*, translated by Eva Profousová, reviewer Strebel (2022: online) believes that the translator has 'translated confidently into German'; nonetheless, he claims that this makes it all the more painful 'when the term "Studierenden" [students] is used with little linguistic sensitivity. The present participle does not replace the plural'.[2] Translator Georg Deggerich is praised by reviewer Rönsch (2022d: online) – this reviewer is particularly likely to engage with translation beyond a mention of the translator's name – in a review of Graeme Macrae Burnet's *Fallstudie* for his 'convincing' translation. However, it is an aspect of the target language with which Rönsch (ibid.: online) takes issue: 'But if the writer often finds herself neither "hausbacken" [homely] nor pretty enough for a flirt, one wonders whether "hausbacken" is really the contrast to "hübsch" [pretty].' These two reviewers take issue with what they consider to be linguistic issues in the target language, but they do not let this taint their judgement of the translation as a whole. The final review assigned to category F which has reservations about, but is generally positive towards, the translation is Gebhardt's (2022a: online) review of Seiko Ito's *Das Romanverbot ist nur zu begrüßen*, translated by Jürgen Stalph. In this review, Gebhardt (ibid.: online) praises Stalph for managing to translate 'the text's mannerisms into German with meticulous care', but is critical of the fact that 'not all the allusions or the author's numerous self-references are apparent to the reader'. *LK* reviewers frequently praise the translator for not losing anything in translation, so it is particularly noteworthy that this is reinforced by a review such as Gebhardt's which has reservations about the translation, precisely because it does lose an aspect of the source text. In other words, the reservations about the translation do not come solely from an assessment of how the translation reads in the target language, but rather of the relationship between source text and target text.

2 The expected plural form here would be 'Studenten'.

The remaining four *LK* reviews assigned to category F are only critical of the work of the translator in their comments. The first review, written by Augart (2022: online) and focussing on Sefi Atta's *Ein sonderbarer Immigrant*, translated by Simone Jakob, is critical of the title of the work in translation, since 'the English title *The bad immigrant* is more accurate, because Lukmon neither tries to assimilate nor does he change his biography or return to Nigeria. Rather, he goes his own way, slowly and with much criticism'. The German title, on the other hand, *ein sonderbarer Immigrant* means something more like 'a strange immigrant', which, Augart (ibid.: online) argues, is not a true reflection of Lukmon's character. Two of the reviews which are critical of the work of the translator focus on a specific aspect of the language and how it works – or rather how it does not – in the target text. In a review of Kodo Nishimura's *Der Mönch in High Heels. Du darfst sein, wer du bist*, translated by Judith Elze, reviewer Gebhardt (2022b: online) argues that 'probably due to the German translation from English, there is a latent disparity in the text', since 'different types of jargon clash'. What becomes evident from this review is that there has been no comparison between the source text and target text, otherwise the word 'probably' would not have been included in the review. In other words, the reviewer is presuming that the translation is at fault for the disparity in the text, even though she cannot be sure. The other review which comments on an aspect of the language is Mohr's (2022b: online) review of Guillermo Arriaga's *Das Feuer retten*, translated by Matthias Strobel: in this review, Mohr (ibid.: online) asserts that, despite the translator attempting to replicate the 'suburban slang from Mexico City', 'we could have done without sentences like "ihr Becken begann zu beben" [her pelvis began to quiver] or "im menstruierenden Einklang zu tanzen lockte die animalischste Seite unserer Weiblichkeit hervor" [dancing in menstrual unison drew out the most animalistic side of our femininity]'.

The final review assigned to category F which is critical of the work of the translator is particularly noteworthy because it explicitly refers to a lack of fluency in the target language. In the review, reviewer Gebhardt (2022c: online), who most frequently engages with translation at an embedded level for *LK* along with Rainer Rönsch, is critical of translator Nora Bartels for her translation of Riku Onda's *Die Aosawa-Morde*, because 'in some places, a cumbersome sentence structure still based on the Japanese original is distracting, in others there is an accumulation of awkward word repetitions'. Gebhardt (ibid.: online) concludes that 'a final proofreading by the publisher's editing team would certainly have produced a more fluent German translation'. The assumption is that fluency is the criterion against which editing teams should be assessing translations and, despite the fact that Gebhardt assesses Bartels' translation to be 'based on the Japanese original', this ultimately disrupts the reading experience – as Gebhardt puts it, 'distracts' – and is therefore judged negatively. Nonetheless, this review seems to be the exception rather than the norm in *LK*: many *LK* reviews assigned to category F reflect on the relationship between the source language and target language, and do not solely base their assessment of the translation on how fluently it reads in the target language.

The final seven reviews collected from *LK* in 2022 engage with the translation for more than three lines and are therefore assigned to category G; this accounts for 4.5% of the 153 *LK* reviews collected. Four of the seven reviews are overwhelmingly positive towards the work of the translator, and all of their assessments incorporate a comparison between the source language and target language, although for different reasons. In her review of Amelie Nothomb's *Ambivalenz*, translated by Brigitte Große, reviewer Amend-Söchting (2022b: online) dedicates just over 200 words to the translation itself, but spends most of those words praising Große's 'clever' decision to translate the French title *Les prénoms épicènes* [Epicene first names] – which could be rendered as 'Geschlechtsneutrale Namen' [gender-neutral names], a move which Amend-Söchting believes would have been 'meaningless' – into *Ambivalenz* [ambivalence], since 'basic figures of logic and perception emerge [in the book], especially ambivalence'. Rainer Rönsch (2022e: online) spends 147 words of his review of Abi Palmer's *Sanatorium*, translated by Astrid Köhler and Henrike Schmidt, discussing the 'ideal' work that the translators have undertaken, not only accompanying the translation with 'a knowledgeable and insightful epilogue' but also managing to ensure that their translation is 'minimally invasive'. Rönsch (ibid.: online) clarifies what he means by this phrase, adding that 'one reads with interest how thoughtfully the potential conflict between linguistic stigmatisation of disabled people and the glossing over disability are dealt with'. Rönsch (ibid. online) ultimately concludes that the translators have not deviated from the author's contentious language, 'which is to be welcomed without reservation'.

The other two reviews to be assigned to category G which are overwhelmingly positive towards the work of the translator focus on the translation of poetry – and are written by the same reviewer. In a review of three works by Sophia de Mello Breyner Andresen, translated by Sarita Brandt, reviewer Mengeringhaus (2022a: online) claims that the translations into German 'show Sarita Brandt to be an excellent poetry translator who finds plausible solutions even for strict stanzaic forms and rhyme sequences'. Mengeringhaus (ibid.: online) provides a sample of the translation and provides further analysis, asserting that Brandt 'not only swaps the rhyme scheme, she also subtly grinds the consonance'; nonetheless, the reviewer does not criticise Brandt for this but rather claims that 'these liberties are not only legitimate in the translation of poetry, but indispensable'. In total, Mengeringhaus spends 165 words of his review engaging in a deeper manner with Brandt's translation. The idea that translators of poetry can take more liberties is also present in Mengeringhaus's (2022b: online) another review of a poetic work, this time of Al Berto's *Ein Dasein aus Papier*, translated by Michael Kegler. Mengeringhaus (ibid.: online) praises translator Kegler, as he 'succeeds in finding a specific sound without forcing himself to copy the tonality of Portuguese; German would not have so many "a"s and "o"s to offer'. The reviewer also praises that the book is bilingual, as 'the juxtaposition of source and target language alone makes many decisions transparent' (ibid.: online).

One review assigned to category G is mainly positive towards the work of the translator, but also has some reservations. In his review of Andrea Tompa's *Omertà*, translated by Terézia Mora, Horváth (2022: online) believes that Tompa's power of language can only 'come into its own through Terézia Mora's first-class translation', especially in one of the character's monologues where the language is 'partly rural-peasant, partly coarse'. Nonetheless, Horváth (ibid.: online) is critical of the fact that the translation contains 'a few blunders', particularly in instances when 'the communist newspaper Scânteia is mistakenly referred to as a Hungarian paper or the river "Alt" is translated as "Alter"'. In this instance, the criticism of the translation comes solely from actual inaccuracies that the reviewer picks out, and praise is granted for the fact that the translator has managed to replicate the powerful language of the original text. Another review assigned to category G is mainly critical of the work of the translator, but for a similar reason to Horváth's review; in other words, the reviewer finds some inaccuracies in the translation through a comparison between the source text and the target text. In the review, written by Rolf Löchel (2022b: online), of Lucy Delap's *So sieht Feminismus aus: Die Geschichte einer globalen Bewegung*, translated by Alexandra Hölscher, the translator is criticised for the translation of certain phrases, but also individual words:

> The statement 'She had been briefly married at thirteen, then had two children with another man, only to be widowed, leaving her with a baby and a toddler', which also refers to the 19th century Brazilian Nisia Floresta Brasileira Augusta, is translated by Hölscher as follows: 'She was briefly married at thirteen, then had two children with another man, only to be widowed, leaving her with a baby and a toddler.' Thus the woman becomes a widow through the death of a man to whom she was not married. But Hölscher's translation of individual words is also occasionally questionable. For examples, when she refers to the original Canadian slut walks, she does not speak about 'slut marches', as expected, but to a 'hooker march' and emphasises '"slut" means hooker'.

In this review, the criticisms that Löchel makes of the translation are based on a comparison between the source text and target text and his assessment of the lack of equivalence between the two; much like all of the reviews assigned to category G so far, the assessment of the reviewer is not based on how fluent or readable the translation is in German.

The final *LK* review assigned to category G is Klappstein's (2022: online) review of Dante Alighieri's *Commedia*, translated by Bernhard Christ. This review sits alone, as Klappstein (ibid.: online) does not appear to assess the work of the translator, concluding that 'whether Christ's translation can prove itself is therefore a matter for the readers to decide'. The review itself is more of a presentation of how, factually, the text has been translated. For instance, Klappstein (ibid.: online) outlines:

> Unlike Köhler's translation of the Divine Comedy, Christ brings the newly translated text "pure", i.e. only the continuous text in German, supplemented by footnotes. 'Continuous text' is to be taken literally here: although there are paragraphs

> that typographically divide the cantos of the Commedia, little of Dante's original is therefore preserved, and so it is not recognisable that it was originally a poem in tercets. Readers are thus given the impression that they are reading a historical prose novel.

Nonetheless, Klappstein (ibid.: online) does not criticise Christ's approach, instead choosing to present to his reader the translations produced by Köhler and Christ and demonstrating that the two translators ultimately had very different intentions with their translations: Köhler adheres strictly to the stanza structure of the original, whilst Christ 'clears up the grammatical structure and explains the research-historical background'. Engagement with two different translations of the same text in this review frames the translation for the reader and allows them to form their own informed judgement of the text, yet such practice is not commonplace amongst vast majority of German reviewers.

Overall, we have seen that the vast majority of *LK* reviewers will at least mention the name of the translator in the bibliographical information. Just two reviewers did not do this and the potential reasons for this have been outlined. 70.0% of all *LK* reviews are assigned to categories C1 through D2 and are therefore considered to promote the superficial visibility of translation; in other words, they acknowledge that the text has been translated in some manner, but do not engage further with the work of the translator. Forty-five of the 153 reviews – or 29.4% – fit into categories E through G where there is further engagement with the work of the translator, with a minimum of a short, unjustified comment on the translation. The reviews in these categories are therefore seen to promote the embedded visibility of translation. Twenty-one of the reviews are assigned to categories F and G, the two categories where we see the most extensive engagement with translation in the reviews. When considered as a whole, the majority of *LK* reviews assigned to these latter categories do appear to consider the relationship between the source language and target language, and do not make a judgement on the translation based on how it reads in the target language alone. However, there are still a few reviewers, particularly in category E, who solely assess the translation against the criteria of readability and fluency.

## Conclusions

The discoveries of this fifth chapter are displayed in Figure 3 which outlines the percentage of reviews assigned to each category across the four German platforms.

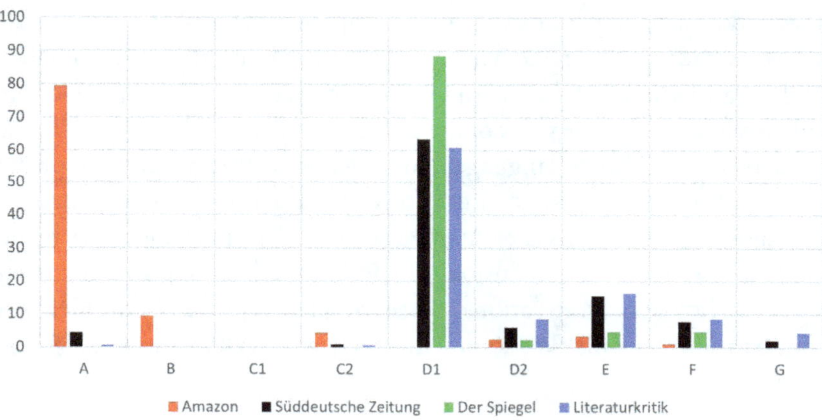


Figure 3: Percentage of reviews assigned to each category across the different German platforms

For the third chapter in a row, Amazon is the clear outlier, as the vast majority of Amazon reviews are classified into categories A and B. It is in Amazon reviews once more, therefore, that translation most frequently remains invisible. On the flipside to this, we see that most of the reviews published in *SDZ*, *DS* and *LK* are assigned to category D1 for reviews in which there is only a mention of the translator's name in the bibliographical information. *DS* reviews in particular are extremely likely to only do this, with almost 90% of its reviews assigned to this category. This platform can therefore be seen to be consistent at promoting the superficial visibility of translation. The other two publications, *SDZ* and *LK*, stand out in Figure 3 when we consider which platforms do the most to promote the embedded visibility of translation. Both publications have over 25% of their reviews assigned to categories E through G, meaning more than one in every four reviews in these publications at least provide a short, unjustified comment on the work of the translator. Furthermore, more than 10% of all reviews in these publications are assigned to either category F or G.

Despite fluency and readability being mentioned in a small number of German reviews as key criteria against which a translation has been judged, this chapter has also shown that German reviewers, particularly those who engage with translation on a deeper level and whose reviews are assigned to category F or G, tend to compare aspects of the source text to the target text before arriving at an informed opinion on the quality of the translation. In other words, the vast majority of German reviewers will not solely judge the work of the translator against the criterion of how it reads in the German language. Nonetheless, a large proportion of the comments in reviews assigned to category E are more general in nature, not allowing us to assess the criteria against which translations are being judged. Therefore, the conclusions of Lanschützer's 2009 paper in this respect still hold true: translations are still frequently judged in the German context using brief blanket comments, such as *kongenial* and *holprig*.

CHAPTER 6

# Reviewing the invisible: An entirely Anglo-American phenomenon?

Upon reading Lawrence Venuti's seminal work, *The Translator's Invisibility*, it became clear that the American scholar is extremely critical of the way in which both British and American reviewers engage with translation, ultimately claiming that the invisibility of the translator is a typically Anglo-American phenomenon. However, other critics have taken a more synchronic approach to the issue of the visibility of translation in reviews. Anthony Pym, for instance, questions why visibility is considered to be 'radically English' by Venuti and compares English reviews to reviews from other European and non-European countries, concluding that 'this kind of comparative analysis upsets [...] the assumed Englishness of invisibility' (Pym 1996: 170). It has been suggested by scholars, therefore, that the invisibility of translation in reviews is now not purely restricted to the British and American contexts, but also observable in reviews published by other countries, particularly those in the rest of Western Europe. In this closing chapter, *Reviewing the (In)visible*, such claims are assessed, by examining the extent to which translation remains invisible in British reviews compared to French and German reviews. In essence, Chapters 3, 4 and 5 have provided in-depth insight into the situation in each of the countries, drawing upon specific examples and analysing how reviewers engage with translation, if at all; this sixth and final chapter will draw out the similarities and differences between the findings of each of those chapters, allowing us to determine whether the invisibility of translation is more observable in British reviews or whether French and German reviewers are just as likely to keep translation invisible.

At this point in the chapter, it is important to remind ourselves what is meant by invisibility in the framework of this study. As discussed back in Chapter 2, the analysis here only focuses on one element of extra-textual (in)visibility, neglecting other forms of visibility: textual and para-textual (in)visibility. Extra-textual visibility has been broken down into two categories for the purposes of this project: 'superficial' and 'embedded' extra-textual visibility. Superficial extra-textual visibility has been defined as the acknowledgment of the fact of translation or a mention of the translator, and any reviews which are seen to promote the superficial visibility of translation have been assigned to categories C1 through D2.[1] Embedded extra-textual visibility, on the other hand, has been defined as any engagement from reviewers with the work of the translator in the body of the review, from a short unjustified comment on the translation to extensive engagement with the work of the translator. Any reviews which have been assigned to categories E through G are therefore considered to promote the embedded extra-textual visibility of translation. This distinction will be particularly important for the present chapter, as we will observe what percentage of reviews across each of our countries and platforms are assigned to each category, allowing us to determine whether there are any significant similarities and differences in terms of how the visibility of translation is promoted in the United Kingdom, France and Germany. This chapter will progress by comparing each type of platform – Amazon; broadsheets/cultural supplements; and specialised literary magazines – across the three countries to assess which of the countries' reviewers are the most consistent at promoting the superficial and embedded visibility of translation, before linking the findings to the wider sociocultural context of translation in those countries.

1 If a text is assigned to categories A or B, they do not promote the visibility of translation in any way.

## Amazon reviews

Figure 4 demonstrates the percentage of reviews from amazon.co.uk, amazon.fr, amazon.de which are classified into each of the assessment categories.

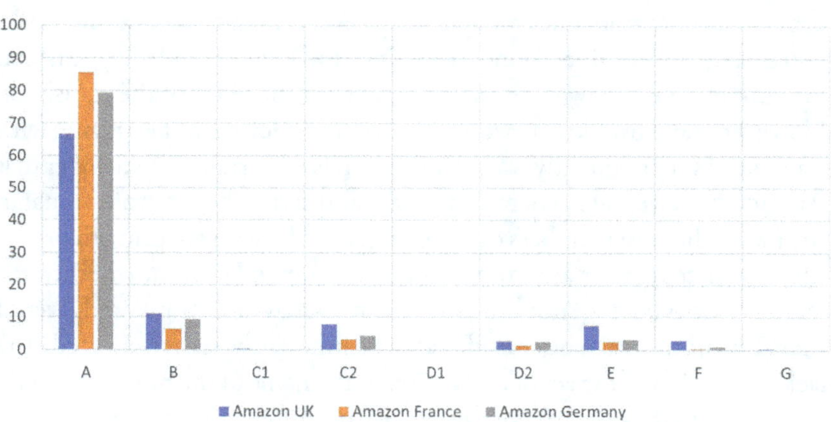


Figure 4: Percentage of reviews assigned to each category across amazon.co.uk, amazon.fr, amazon.de

As can be seen in Figure 4, Amazon users across all three countries do not very frequently promote the visibility of translation and translators at any level in their reviews. A total of 77.9% of British Amazon reviews, 92.1% of French Amazon reviews and 88.7% of German Amazon reviews are assigned to categories A and B, meaning that, in these reviews, there is no mention of the act of translation whatsoever. We could argue that this confirms the complacency shown towards translation and translators, as outlined by Venuti, and that translation is generally considered to have a 'second-order status' (Venuti 1995: 7), not worthy of discussion in reviews by the general public. Nonetheless, the lack of mention of the fact of translation in customer reviews could well be down to the fact that the translator is almost systematically named by the three Amazon sites included in this corpus straight after the name of the author in the bibliographical details of the book. Given that the reviews for the translated work appear on the same Amazon page as the bibliographical details of the book, reviewers may feel little need to re-mention the name of the translator in their reviews. Amazon users may also simply be following the community guidelines that Amazon provide for their reviewers in terms of what to include in a review: 'include the "why", be specific, not too short, not too long [and] be sincere' (Amazon 2022: online). Nowhere does Amazon provide specific guidelines for reviewing general literature, let alone works in translation. The official guidance of 'not too long' provided by Amazon may discourage reviewers from engaging with the work of the translator. However, the most likely reason for Amazon reviewers not engaging with translation very frequently is a lack of time. It is important to remember that Amazon reviewers are generally not paid and certainly not professional in the main; they are members of the general public who are using their free time to write reviews and to provide a recommendation of whether the work is worth buying, not how well the work has been translated, even if these two notions can be considered to be inherently interconnected. The lack of mention of the act of translation or the name of the translator could also be due to the fact that Amazon reviewers simply do not know who the translator is or, worse, that they do not even know that they are reading a translated work. It is difficult to determine which of these justifications is the most accurate without further research; however, the results of this study clearly demonstrate that Amazon reviewers are the least consistent set of reviewers at promoting the visibility of translators at a superficial and embedded level.

Nonetheless, it quickly becomes clear in Figure 4 that, of the different country's Amazon reviews included in this study, British Amazon users most frequently promote both the superficial and embedded visibility of translation – and by some distance. 11.2% of British Amazon reviews are assigned to categories C1 through D2, seen to promote the superficial visibility of translation, compared to just 4.8% of French Amazon reviews and 6.9% of German reviews. A similar picture emerges when the reviews assigned to categories E through G are considered: 11% of British Amazon reviews are assigned to these categories, compared to 3.1% of French Amazon reviews and 4.5% of German Amazon reviews. These are rather significant differences at both levels of visibility and seemingly point to the fact that the British public are more aware of the status of a book as a translation or are at least more willing than their French and German counterparts to engage with the work of the translator. French reviewers engage with the translation least frequently and therefore ensure that translation remains invisible in their reviews.

## Broadsheets/cultural supplement reviews

Figure 5 outlines the percentage of reviews from the British (*Times Literary Supplement – TLS* and *The Guardian – TG*), French (*Le Monde – LM* and *Le Figaro – LF*) and German (*Süddeutsche Zeitung – SDZ* and *Der Spiegel – DS*) mainstream publications which are classified into each of the assessment categories.

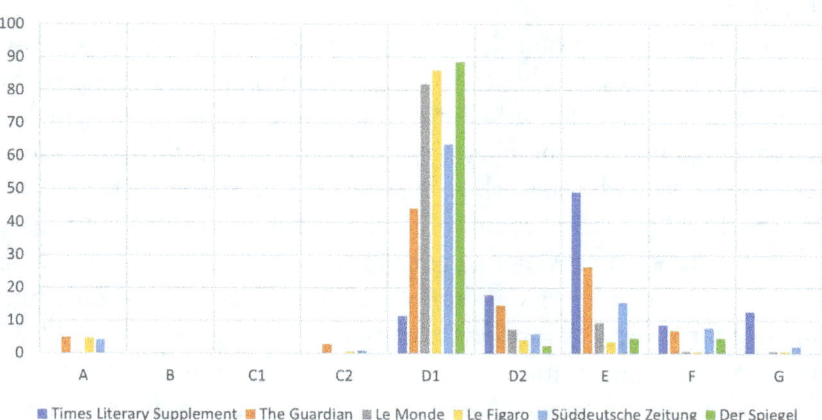


Figure 5: Percentage of reviews assigned to each category across the broadsheets/ cultural supplements

The broadsheets and/or cultural supplements from all three cultural contexts included in this study are relatively systematic when it comes to at least acknowledging the fact that a piece of work has been translated: indeed, all but 4.9% of reviews in *TG*, 4.6% of reviews in *LF* and 4.3% of reviews in *SDZ* have been assigned to category C2 or above. In this regard, we can consider that the vast majority of the mainstream publication reviews promote the superficial visibility of translation. As can be seen in Figure 5, all of the French and German mainstream publications included in the study have at least 70% of their reviews assigned to categories C1 through D2: 89.2% of *LM* reviews; 90.7% of *LF* reviews; 70.4% of *SDZ* reviews; and 90.9% of *DS* reviews. This means that these publications are particularly effective at promoting the superficial visibility of translation, but not the embedded visibility of translation; in other words, they acknowledge that the text has been translated or mention the name of the translator somewhere within or outside the main body of the review, but do not engage with the work of the translator any further. These percentage figures stand out as being particularly noteworthy when we compare them to the British mainstream publications: *TLS* has 29.5% of its reviews assigned to categories C1 through D2, whilst *TG* has 61.7% of its reviews to these same categories.

This ultimately means that, of the mainstream publications in this study, it is the British publications which most frequently promote the embedded visibility of translation. 70.5% of *TLS* reviews are assigned to categories E through G, meaning more than seven in ten of this publication's reviews engage with the work of the translator in some regard. In addition to this, *TLS* is also the only broadsheet/cultural supplement to have more than 10% of its reviews assigned to category G, meaning that, in at least one in every ten reviews of translation, the reviewer dedicates a minimum of three lines of the review to engaging with the translation. *TLS* is one of only two publications in the whole study to do this so frequently, along with *London Review of Books*. 33.4% of *TG* reviews are assigned to categories E through G, meaning that more than one in three *TG* reviews engage with the work of the translator. The *TG* percentage figure may pale in comparison to the *TLS* figure, but it is nonetheless much greater than the French and German mainstream publications included in the study: only 10.8% of *LM* reviews, 4.7% of *LF* reviews, 25.3% of *SDZ* reviews and 9.4% of *DS* reviews are assigned to the three categories which are considered to promote embedded visibility. As far as the broadsheets and/or cultural supplements are concerned, then, at least 95% of reviews in all of the publications in this study are assigned to categories C1 or above; all of the publications are therefore extremely consistent in promoting at least the superficial visibility of translation, particularly when compared to how frequently Amazon reviewers do this. However, there are significant differences between how the publications promote the embedded visibility of translation. It is once more British reviewers who do this most systematically and French reviewers who are most loath to engage with the work of the translator. This shows significant parallels with the discoveries from the corpus of Amazon reviews.

## Specialised literary magazine reviews

Figure 6 below shows the percentage of reviews from the British (*London Review of Books* – *LRB*), French (*Actualitté*) and German (*Literaturkritik* – *LK*) specialised literary magazines to be assigned to each of the assessment categories.

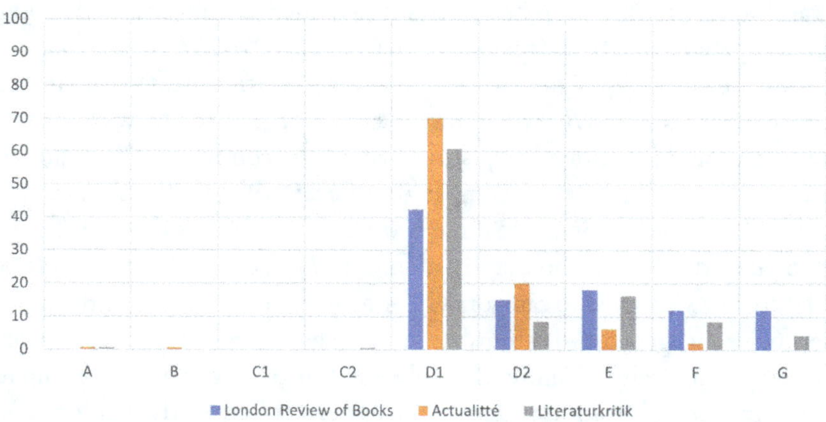


Figure 6: Percentage of reviews assigned to each category across the specialised literary magazines

Much like the reviews collected from the broadsheets/cultural supplements, the vast majority of the reviews taken from the three specialised literary magazines are assigned to at least category D1. None of the reviews published in *LRB* fit into categories A through C2; 1.4% of *Actualitté* reviews and 1.4% of *LK* reviews fit into these categories. From this point of view, the specialised literary magazines are considered to be the type of publication included in this study which most frequently promote the superficial visibility of translation across the three countries. There are also parallels between the findings for the mainstream publications and for the specialised literary magazines in this regard. More than 70% of reviews in the French and German specialised literary magazines (90.2% of *Actualitté* reviews and exactly 70% of *LK* reviews) fit into categories C1 through D2, meaning that at least seven in ten reviews in these publications acknowledge the fact of translation or mention the name of the translator, but do not engage with the work of the translator beyond this. This is compared to 57.6% of reviews in *LRB* which are assigned to these categories. It seems fair to assert, therefore, that the French and German specialised literary magazines are the most consistent at only promoting the superficial visibility of translation and no more.

On the flipside, it is once more the British publication included in this study which is most consistent at promoting the embedded visibility of translation. 42.4% of all *LRB* reviews are assigned to categories E through G, compared to 8.4% of *Actualitté* reviews and 29.3% of *LK* reviews. 24.2% of *LRB* reviews are assigned to categories F and G; this means that almost one in every four *LRB* reviews includes a comment on the work of the translator and additionally a justification of the comment. This figure is particularly significant when compared to the 2.1% of *Actualitté* reviews and 13% of *LK* reviews assigned to these two categories. *LRB* is also one of only two platforms in the whole study, alongside *TLS*, to have more than 10% of its reviews assigned to category G, for reviews in which there is the most extensive engagement with translation. Once again, the British publication most systematically promotes the embedded visibility of translation and it is the French publication which does this most infrequently. This pattern has therefore been evident across all types of publication included in this study. The remainder of this chapter will draw upon the wider sociocultural context of translation in the three countries in an attempt to understand why this might be the case.

## British reviews – An example to be followed?

Keeping the findings of Bush, Fawcett, Johnson and Venuti et al. in mind, we may have expected the British reviews to be the least consistent at commenting upon the work of the translator. However, British reviewers, at least for the publications included in this study, are the most systematic at promoting the embedded visibility of translation in their reviews, certainly compared to their French and German counterparts. We have discovered that this is the case across all types of publication included in the study: 70.5% of *TLS* reviews, 42.4% of *LRB* reviews, 33.4% of *TG* reviews and even 11% of British Amazon reviews have been assigned to categories for reviews in which there is some form of engagement with the work of the translator. On the basis of the findings of this study, we might assert that the notion of invisibility can now be more productively used to describe the situation of translators in reviewing practices in other Western European countries rather than in the United Kingdom. This suggestion of course implies a need for a significant redefinition of Venuti's initial term 'invisibility' which he used to 'describe the translator's situation and activity in contemporary *British* [my italics] and American cultures' (Venuti 1995: 1). However, it is also important to note that such a redefinition of invisibility based on the findings of the present study would be based around reviewing practices alone; further research into other areas of the translator's (in)visibility would be required to give us greater justification for a completely different take on the notion of invisibility.

Why though, based on this study of reviewing practices, does the United Kingdom seem more consistent than two of its Western European counterparts in promoting the visibility of translation? On a simplistic level, there now seems to be a wider understanding in the United Kingdom of what translation entails than there was when Venuti was writing *The*

*Translator's Invisibility* for the first time back in 1995. One of the fascinating things that my research uncovered for this book is the promotion of translation through other articles, rather than simply reviews, in British mainstream publications. The *TLS*, for instance, has frequently published articles about translation outside of its normal reviews, focussing rather on the art of translation and the invaluable work that translators undertake. The following, for example, is taken from an article published in *TLS* (Bie Brahic 2015: online), discussing the release of a new book and the task that translators face when translating literature:

> Some theorists have likened translation to a palimpsest in which the original text, though erased, glimmers through the translated one like Archimedes' theorems. And Umberto Eco, in his exploration of the myriad ways translation's sleight of hand is accomplished, *Dire quasi la stessa cosa* (2003), called translation the art of 'saying almost the same thing', but doubted people would agree on the meaning of the 'same' or 'say', or even about the existence of a textual 'thing in itself' that survives translation. And the extreme case: Borges's fictional author Pierre Menard who realized many a frustrated translator's dream when he rewrote *Don Quixote* in exactly the same words as the original.

Such discussion in a publication which is intended to be read by a general rather than specialised audience moves notions which are prevalent and widely debated in the field of translation studies into a more public domain; it contributes to the development of a wider understanding of what the translation process entails and moves us away from the common belief that translation is a simple transfer from source language to target language, therefore raising awareness of the work of the translator. As well as promoting the work of the translator in this manner, the publication also sponsors prizes for translators within its wider goal of demonstrating that 'there is plenty of excellent translated fiction available' (Tahourdin 2015: online) in an attempt to work against the fact, reminiscent of what Venuti says in *The Translator's Invisibility*, that 'it is rare, after all, to see a translated literary novel in the bestseller lists at all, let alone in the top five' (ibid.: online). The *TLS* regularly reports on the winners of such prizes. It is therefore no surprise that this publication is the most consistent platform in this study at promoting the embedded visibility of the translator by some distance.

However, it is not only the *TLS* which contributes to the promotion of the work of translators; indeed, *TG* has also more recently been publishing a handful of articles relating to the role of the translator and the importance of translated fiction. Daniel Hahn, translator and staunch advocate of the importance of translation, was commissioned by *TG* in 2018 to write a series of articles on various aspects of translation. One such article, published in March 2018, focusses on the need for visibility for translators, reflected in the title *Translators are the vanguard of literary change: we need better recognition*. Hahn not only explains how literary translation is a difficult profession to break into and discusses the skills that a literary translator requires but also asserts that working with a wider range of translators is beneficial for publishers and for the literary market in general, as new translators often lead the market to new authors as well. He reflects on the fact that more than half of the books submitted for the prestigious TA first translation prize are debuts for their translators as well as English-language debuts for their authors, 'showing that translators are in the vanguard of literary change' (Hahn 2018: online). He hopes that such translation prizes raise the status of translation by 'make[ing] a statement about what should be valued, and what we need more of' (ibid.: online). This ultimately echoes what Venuti hoped would be achieved moving forward from the publication of *The Translator's Invisibility*.

*TG* has also sporadically published articles over the past ten years about what translation means and how important translators are in the reception of foreign literature. The perfect embodiment of this is an editorial piece that was published back in November 2018, entitled *The Guardian view on translation: an interpretative and creative act*. The article considers the more than sixty prominent translations of Homer's *Odyssey* from various perspectives and asserts that 'translation is always an interpretation: an act of creation that also, paradoxically, demands a fierce loyalty to the original text' (*The Guardian* Editorial 2018: online). This further challenges the widespread notion that translation is a simple transfer from the source language to target language and gets the reader to reflect on the role of the translator. The conclusion of the article claims that

> we must cherish our translators for these shy acts of creation, these loyal betrayals (to translate is to betray, the saying goes, itself a translation of the Italian *traduttore*

> *traditore*). Translators are our guides into other times and territories. They encourage us to leave our own literary shores and to consider other ways of living, other ways of thinking. They can usher into our midst other means of expression, other forms. The literature of one place, of one language, may be reshaped by confrontations with texts from elsewhere. (ibid.: online)

Notions which are familiar in translation studies and reflected in frameworks such as Venuti's foreignisation ('encourage us to leave our own literary shores') and Even-Zohar's polysystems theory ('literature [...] may be reshaped by confrontations with texts from elsewhere') are now being expressed by authors in British mainstream publications such as *TG* and thus made more accessible to a wider audience of readers. With this in mind, it is not surprising that the reviews from British publications engage more frequently with the work of the translator than perhaps they did twenty or thirty years ago.

At this point, it would be remiss to not examine the work which has been undertaken in the United Kingdom by various different literary translation networks and associations. In a 2017 interview with Chantal Wright, Maureen Freely discusses how she became the Chair of the Translators' Association in 2010 at a time when the promotion of the profession of translation was almost non-existent. However, she worked with various people of the Translators' Association in order to begin a 'revolution' in the way that translation is considered by the general public; these people included 'a representative from the British Centre for Literary Translation [... Amanda Hopkinson]; there was Alexandra Büchler from Literature Across Frontiers; there was translator Danny Hahn who had just won the Foreign Fiction Prize, and translator Ros Schwarz' (Wright and Freely 2017: 102). Freely outlines how the board came up with various different ideas to promote translation – a Literary Translation Centre at the London Book Fair, starting a mentoring system, using Arts Council funding, setting up translation weeks, forging connections with various different organisations, like English PEN, the Foreign Fiction Prize and Boyd Donking, described by Freely as 'one of the great champions of world literature in translation' (ibid.: 103). Many of these initiatives are still running. A brief look at the report from a recent Translators' Association AGM in 2020 gives a good sense of the work that is still ongoing in the promotion of translation (Society of Authors 2020: online): online events, most recently a panel, chaired by Daniel Hahn and with Arunava Sinha, a translator of Bengali literature; Daniel Hahn receiving an OBE for services to literature; annual translation prizes administered by the Society of Authors, presented at a ceremony at the British Library; Sebald lecture, in collaboration with the British Centre for Literary Translation, given in 2020 by David Bellos, entitled 'The Myths and Mysteries of Literary Translation' (an event which received 1700 advance registrations); and the British Centre for Literary Translation Summer School, with more applications than ever in 2020.

These are just some of the activities carried out by the Translators' Association, but there have been many more. A special mention must be reserved for the work that goes into planning events for International Translation Day and the London Book Fair, two key dates in the diary which have great significance for the promotion of translation, particularly in the United Kingdom. International Translation Day is precisely that, an *international* day: on 24 May 2017, the UN's General Assembly 'adopted resolution 71/288 on the role of language professionals in connecting nations and fostering peace, understanding and development, and declared 30 September as International Translation Day' (United Nations 2017: online). It may therefore seem odd to reserve special praise for this date in the context of justification for translators being more visible in the United Kingdom alone. However, the reason for including it here is that the efforts of British associations to promote the day go far beyond many of their European counterparts, particularly those in France and Germany. For example, every 30 September, English PEN hosts 'a programme of talks, workshops and networking opportunities for literary translators' (English PEN 2020: online), with the 2022 two-day programme including lectures and workshops on the post-pandemic profession and community; what translators want from publishers and vice versa; pitching to publishers; career progression; pitching and connecting with editors; rights, royalties, pay and visibility; and the power of the bookseller (English PEN 2022: online). Beyond English PEN, the Translators' Association highlights authors and their translators with various translation prizes (translators working with Swedish, German, French, Spanish and Arabic), and they have also launched the campaign #CelebrateYourTranslator, aiming to 'highlight the important relationship between author and translator and the vital work translators do in providing greater access to books and literature and engaging more readers across the world' (Society of Authors 2020: online).

The London Book Fair is another extremely important, annual date in the diary for the promotion of translation in the United Kingdom; it welcomes 25,000 publishing professionals every year to 'learn, network, and kick off their years in business' and considers itself to be the 'global marketplace for rights negotiation and the sale and distribution of content across print, audio, TV, film and digital channels' (The London Book Fair 2023: online). The entire publishing industry is represented: from the giant houses to the smallest independents, there are 'publishers of blockbuster novels and academic texts, and the producers of children's books and graphic novels' (ibid.: online). Importantly for the status and promotion of translation, in 2010, the London Book Fair launched the Literary Translation Centre as 'a feature area that would enable publishers and translators to come together, network and attend a variety of seminars on literary translation to further this art throughout the UK' (English PEN 2011: online). The Centre is partnered with a whole host of supporting organisations: Arts Council England Literature Department, British Centre for Literary Translation, British Council Literature Department, The Calouste Gulbenkian Foundation, English PEN Writers in Translation Programme, Free Word, Literature Across Frontiers, the Translators' Association, Wales Literature Exchange and Words Without Borders.

Each year, the Literary Translation Centre seminar programme 'covers a rich range of current subjects. Discover international literary landscapes such as the Middle East, China and Japan; learn about children's literature in translation; get ideas about funding both in the United Kingdom and Europe and find out how digital publishing may affect literary translation' (ibid.: online). One of the Directors at The London Book Fair, Jack Thomas, believes that a core role of the fair is to champion the art of translation and it therefore aims to create channels for dialogues between writers, publishers and the book industry. In his words, as a 'vital lynchpin in any cross-cultural exchange, translation has never been more important' (The London Book Fair Hub 2019: online). The prominence of translation at The London Book Fair, along with all of the work carried out by translation associations and organisations in the British context, has been an influential driving force in the way that translations are perceived, assessed and evaluated. The continuing work of translation associations and organisations has therefore been invaluable in the promotion of translation as a profession and as an art form.

Another reason which could explain why the British reviews are more consistent than French and German reviews at promoting the visibility of translation at an embedded level is that reviews of translations have been discussed in much greater detail in the United Kingdom in the 2000s and 2010s – both in academic contexts, as discussed back in Chapter 2, but also in non-academic contexts. For instance, we have seen the development of campaigns and series which are accessible to a wider range of readers to promote the visibility of translators, particularly over the last ten years. A good example of this is the #NametheTranslator campaign, which has been rather productive at promoting the visibility of translation and translators on social media platforms, in particular Twitter. This is a campaign which was started by Helen Wang, former committee member of the Translators' Association, to 'ensure that the contribution of translators is recognised' and in response to 'a tendency amongst reviewers and marketers of translated works to omit the name of the translator' (Society of Authors 2018: online). In addition to this, series such as *Reviewing Translations* by Words Without Borders have thrust the issue into the public limelight and seem to have had a significant impact on public understanding of translation. All in all, there has been much activity related to the promotion of the visibility of translation across a wide range of channels in the United Kingdom over the last ten to fifteen years, and this appears to have had a major impact on the way in which translated works are reviewed.

## German reviews – A disconnect between theory and practice?

Across each of the platform categories, German reviews are very good at promoting the superficial visibility of translation (with the exception of Amazon), but did not promote the embedded visibility of translation as systematically as the British reviews: indeed, no more than 30% of reviews collected from any of the German publications included in this study are assigned to categories E through G. This is broadly in line with what Lanschützer discovered back in 2010 (with almost 25% of *Die Zeit* reviews being assigned to similar categories), so German reviews are roughly as consistent at promoting the embedded visibility of translation as they were ten to fifteen years ago. Reviews of translated works in Germany are written and published in a cultural context in which 'Übersetzungswissenschaft' – or translation studies – has long occupied a role of particular importance. Indeed, as Kittel and Poltermann point out, German scholars, such as Katharina Reiss, Christiane Nord and Werner Koller, have 'been amongst the most active in the field of translation studies and have produced a very large and influential body of literature on the subject', ultimately leading not only to individual publications but also to 'a number of journals and book series devoted to the field of translation studies' (Kittel and Poltermann in Baker 2009: 418). Germany has also been home to two member societies of FIT (*Fédération Internationale des Traducteurs* – International Federation of Translators), the *Bundesverband der Dolmetscher und Übersetzer* [Federal Association of Interpreters and Translators] and the *Verband deutschsprachiger Übersetzer literarischer und wissenschaftlicher Werke* [Association of German-speaking Translators of Literary and Academic Works], for a long period of time, with the former established in 1955 and the latter in 1954. The country has also seen the development of various university courses, both undergraduate and postgraduate, dedicated to translation and/or interpreting, as well as the foundation of a European-wide translation body, the *Europäisches Übersetzer-Kollegium* [European Translator College]. The importance of translation and its study is therefore deep-rooted in German society and culture, so it is not entirely surprising that German reviews are extremely systematic at promoting the superficial visibility of translation.

But why do German reviews appear to give less prominence to translation and translators, at least at the embedded level of visibility, than British reviews? Is there a disconnect between what is happening in the academic world and the practical world? Lanschützer (2010) does not engage in any great detail with the reasons behind German reviews not consistently promoting the visibility of translation at the embedded level. She does, however, point out the problematic nature of reviewing translations in Germany, due to a lack of accepted model for offering critique and opinion. She (ibid.: 160, my translation) believes:

> While there is a consensus in translation studies that a translation criticism model with transparent, preferably uniform evaluation principles is necessary, especially with regard to literary criticism, there is at the same time a failure to discuss which criteria should form the basis of a review of a translation that can be described as successful and what a practical set of instruments for the criticism of literary translations might look like.

This is a compelling argument advanced by Lanschützer; however, as we saw back in Chapter 1, there is no real consensus in the British context either as to how reviewers should assess or engage with a translation, and yet the embedded visibility of translation is still promoted far more frequently in reviews collected from the British publications.

Is the lack of embedded visibility, then, down to a general complacency in Germany towards translation and translators? That is the view taken by German author, Isabel Bogdan (2012: online), who believes that it is not only reviews in Germany which often neglect to understand the work of the translator, but also readers, booksellers and publishers. She asserts that the fact that, 'between the foreign-language author and the German audience, someone else has put a considerable amount of work and expertise into a book is still too often overlooked – by readers, booksellers, publishing house staff and reviewers alike' (ibid.: online, my translation). Volker Heydt (2016: online), German EU official, believes that the problem starts with publishers, way before the translated book gets into the hands of sellers, readers and reviewers. He sees the lack of acknowledgement of translators on the front cover of books as the real problem, ultimately masking the importance of the work that goes into the translation. He therefore asks:

> The translator is always mentioned on the cover of the book (as well as on any jacket) and not only in the book. When the reader then picks up a book and sees author

> and translator presented practically as a tandem, he/she takes note of both of them. (ibid.: online, my translation)

The fact that translators are not mentioned on the front cover of a book is potentially a problem with German copyright law which states that 'the German title of a translation should always be accompanied by the translator's name, for example in the bibliographical information of a translated book' (Verband deutschsprachiger Übersetzer literarischer und wissenschaftlicher Werke 2018: online, my translation). The problem is that readers do not know the name of the translator, because 'it is all too often in the small print' (Bogdan 2012: online, my translation). The lack of prominence assigned to the name of the translator appears therefore to be symptomatic of a complacency to the work of the translator, seen as a simple or unimportant role. The fact that the visibility of translation is not promoted at an embedded level very frequently in German reviews is therefore perhaps to be expected.

## French reviews – A long way to go?

Across each of the platforms included in this study, French reviews are far less consistent than the British and German reviews at promoting the embedded visibility of translation: indeed, only 10.8% of *LM* reviews, 4.7% of *LF* reviews, 3.1% of Amazon reviews and 2.1% of *Actualitté* reviews are assigned to categories E through G. Only *LM* reviewers therefore comment on the work of the translator in some way in more than one in ten reviews, and 87% of these are assigned to category E for reviews in which there is only a short, blanket judgement on the translation. It can be concluded therefore that promoting the visibility of translation is not such a pressing issue in France as it is in the United Kingdom in particular. But why do French reviewers seem less inclined than British reviewers to engage with the work of the translator on an embedded level? Previous research has indicated that France is a country which is extremely open to and welcoming of foreign literature in translation. Indeed, foreign literature is still popular in France, with sales demonstrating that translated literature occupies a significant share of the French literary market: 15.3% of books published in France in 2018 were translations (Observatoire de l'économie du livre 2020: online). The ATLF (*Association des traducteurs littéraires de langue française* – Association of French Literary Translators) frequently organises translation events, albeit nowhere near as many as the number organised by British associations, with the most important being *Les assises de la traduction en Arles* [Translation Proceedings in Arles], held every year, and which 'are part of the European Commission's actions to promote language professions; they highlight in particular the economic, social and cultural issues involved in translation and interpreting' (Ministère de la Culture 2014: online, my translation). Furthermore, the layout of French bookshops gives us great insight into the importance and visibility of foreign literature, particularly when compared to British bookshops, for instance. As Vanderschelden (2000: 282) asserts, comparing the layout of French and British bookshops can be revealing, since

> whereas the norm in Britain is to arrange 'literature' or 'fiction' alphabetically by author surname, regardless of the country of origin, in France a clear separation between French and foreign literature can be observed. The British arrangement seems to encourage the invisibility of translations, whilst the French pattern highlights the presence of foreign and, consequently, translated literature.

Nonetheless, the way that foreign literature is presented to audiences in bookshops in France could be considered to be segregationist, rather than inclusive, as Vanderschelden also acknowledges.

Given the relative popularity of translated literature in France, it feels rather surprising that reviewers do not engage with the work of the translator on an embedded level more frequently. But there are other sociocultural factors to take into consideration which may account for this discrepancy. Firstly, as argued by Boisseau (2016: online, my translation), translation studies, in an academic context, 'is a poorly organised discipline'. *La traductologie* – or translation studies – 'has not quite won its spurs in France, as it is not one of the 77 disciplines listed by the National Council of Universities' (Lavault-Olléon 2018: online, my translation). Secondly, in France, there is no concrete legislation to rule over the translation profession, thus allowing practically anybody to call themselves a translator and leading to the profession itself becoming devalued. Indeed, as a blog on the website of the Translation Masters course at the University of Lille written by Ries (2018: online, my translation) details, 'anyone can become a translator overnight', resulting in a status quo in which 'translation is still too frequently perceived to be a task which is not very difficult', the consequences of which 'can damage the reputation of the whole profession'. This echoes what Sirviö (2006: 4, my translation) asserts about reviews entertaining 'the simplistic view held by people that a translation is simply a direct transfer from one language to another where, contrary to reality, the personal choices of a translator do not have an impact'.

The translation profession is, nonetheless, equally unregulated across Europe, and particularly in the United Kingdom: a report by the European Commission found that 'the generic activity of translators appears to not qualify as a "regulated profession" in terms of Professional Qualifications Directive (2005/36/EC), [as] no one can stop an unqualified person from working a translator, except as under a 2007 law in Slovakia' (European Commission 2012: online). The United Kingdom does not have a system of sworn, or certified, translators accredited by a particular body either, and even the UK Government, on its website, claims that all you really need is the ability to speak two languages and 'perhaps' a qualification. Nonetheless, it seems that the work of translation associations in the United Kingdom has been hugely impactful on the visibility of translators amongst the general public. In France, where the promotion of translation has not happened on the same scale, in combination with the lack of regulation of the profession, the work of the translator is perceived as a simple profession; this goes some way to explaining why French reviewers are the group of reviewers who least frequently engage with translation on an embedded level. An article in *La Croix* succinctly sums up the general feeling towards translation in France, noting that the profession is still vastly undervalued in France and the media in particular still have a long way to go in promoting awareness of the work of the translator:

> It is the lack of recognition that undermines part of the profession. The media, in particular, still have some way to go, as they do not always mention the authors of

> the translations. 'In the print media, we don't have the space; on the radio, we don't have time, even if we do find it to thank the producer, the technician, the trainee …', says Olivier Mannoni. (Ferney 2015: online, my translation)

To add to this point, Vanderschelden (2000: 282) also claims that, whilst foreign literature may well be visible and appreciated in France, 'translation and translators are generally absent from the public's consciousness', since 'the French clearly retain a perception of literature, and of foreign literature in particular, which rests upon the strong image of the Author as a writer with a personal history who writes about his or her own experience, using personal themes and artistic talent'. In other words, the role of the translator is ultimately not considered to be as important by the vast majority of readers. The role of the translator therefore needs to be entirely re-evaluated in French society before there will likely be any change to the situation in which translators are largely invisible at this embedded level in reviews across all of the platforms.

Nonetheless, it does appear more recently that there is a growing awareness in France that engaging with the work of the translator should be actively promoted, but it has not quite fully taken hold yet. An article published by Alice Develey (2019: online) in *LF*, for example, entitled *Pourquoi nous avons encore besoin de traducteurs* [Why we still need translators], is similar to some of the articles published around the same time period in *TLS* and *TG*. In the article, Develey (ibid.: online, my translation) speaks to translator Jörn Cambreleng and outlines that translation is a complex process, which involves 'moving a text from one literature to another, trying to recreate in his/her own language the unique relationship an author has with the language in which he or she writes. In other words, it means reproducing what we call the style.' Develey (ibid.) ultimately concludes that the work of translators 'is a mainstay in the publishing industry'. The publication of such an article in a general-reading publication can only be seen positively in the context of attempting to promote the difficult and challenging work that translators undertake. In addition, in one of the reviews collected from *Actualitté* in 2022, reviewer Nicolas Ancion acknowledges that the magazine does not engage with the work of the translator enough and will strive to do this more in the future (Ancion,

N. 2022b). The findings of this study point towards the fact that it is in French reviews where translators remain most invisible, and yet it feels as though the next five to ten years may be a turning point in France for the acknowledgement and recognition of the role that translators play in bringing works to a French-speaking audience.

# Conclusion

> 'Invisibility' is the term that I will use to describe the translator's situation and activity in contemporary Anglo-American culture. It refers to two mutually determining phenomena: one is an illusionistic effect of discourse, of the translator's own manipulation of English; the other is the practice of reading and evaluating translations that has long prevailed in the United Kingdom and the United States, among other cultures, both English and foreign-language.
>
> – Lawrence Venuti (1995: 1)

The opening chapter of Lawrence Venuti's seminal work, *The Translator's Invisibility*, and more particularly the above quotation, provided the inspiration for this book. The question of the (in)visibility of the translator has been present throughout each of the chapters as we have examined how frequently and in which ways reviewers engage with the work of the translator. Indeed, the overarching purpose of this study of reviews has been to determine to what extent translators are visible in contemporary Britain, France and Germany. This concluding chapter will reflect on the main discoveries of the book, outlining to what extent translation and translators are visible in reviewing practices in our three countries, thus focussing on one aspect of what Venuti defines as the translator's *situation*. However, it also disentangles the very notion of invisibility, building upon the discoveries of this study and aiming at a redefinition of the concept. The conclusion will not only demonstrate precisely how this book has contributed to our understanding of visibility in translation studies but will also outline the limitations of the study by identifying the many other aspects of the notion which have not been discussed and require future research. The closing section of this concluding chapter will discuss the moral and ethical ramifications of the translator's (in)visibility and ask a crucial question: to what extent should we even want translators to be visible?

## Is translation invisible in reviews? Main discoveries of the book

With the exception of reviews on Amazon, the vast majority of which do not acknowledge the fact of translation in any regard, it would be hard to make a case that translators are invisible in reviews of translation. Indeed, across the three countries included in this study, at least 95% of reviews from each of the publications were assigned to categories C1 through G. This means that translation is at least acknowledged in at least nineteen of every twenty reviews published in the mainstream publications and specialised literary magazines. The majority of reviews from the broadsheets/cultural supplements and literary magazines across the study fit into categories C1 through D2; in other words, they only acknowledge the translation or mention the name of the translator somewhere in the reviews. This is the case for 29.5% of *TLS* reviews, 61.7% of *TG* reviews and 57.6% of *LRB* reviews in the British context; 89.2% of *LM* reviews, 90.6% of *LF* reviews and 90.2% of *Actualitté* reviews in the French context; and 70.4% of *SDZ* reviews, 90.9% of *DS* reviews and 70% of *LK* reviews in the German context. *TLS* stands out here as being the only publication which has fewer than 50% of its reviews being assigned to these categories (with more than 70% of its reviews being assigned to categories E through G). In the main, though, all of the publications in this study, with the exception of Amazon, can be considered to promote the superficial visibility of translation as a bare minimum.

British reviews are the most consistent, however, at promoting the embedded visibility of translation; in other words, they are the reviews included in the study most likely to engage with the work of the translator and be classified into categories E through G. This is the case for 70.5% of *TLS* reviews, 33.4% of *TG* reviews and 42.4% of *LRB* reviews. When compared to the French and German percentages, these figures are particularly noteworthy: 10.8% of *LM* reviews, 4.7% of *LF* reviews and 8.4% of *Actualitté* reviews are assigned to categories E through G in the French context, whilst 25.3% of *SDZ* reviews, 9.4% of *DS* reviews and 29.3% of *LK* reviews are classified into the same categories in the German context.

It was therefore argued in Chapter 6 that British reviewers are the most systematic at making translation and translators visible at an embedded level within their reviews, whereas French and German reviewers more frequently promote the visibility of translation at a rather more superficial level. Nonetheless, given how much almost all of the reviews in this study at least acknowledge the fact of translation or mention the name of the translator, it has become clear throughout that translators are not entirely invisible in any of the publications or platforms except Amazon.

## Reviewing the invisible – Towards a redefinition of invisibility and the translator's 'situation'

Venuti uses the term invisibility to 'describe the translator's *situation* and *activity* in contemporary Anglo-American culture' (Venuti 1995: 1, my emphasis). What Venuti is referring to, however, are two completely different phenomena: the *activity* of the translator is, as the American scholar outlines, the translator's own manipulation of the target language; the *situation* of the translator, on the other hand, refers initially to the practice of reading and evaluating translations in line with what he considered to be the widely accepted criterion of fluency. Nevertheless, in Chapter 1 of *The Translator's Invisibility*, it becomes clear that Venuti is also incorporating notions around authorship, copyright, contracts and the status of translation generally (issues such as what people believe about translation as a profession, how publishers treat translation, the number of translated works published in the United Kingdom/United States compared to other countries, etc.) into his notion of invisibility. However, the discoveries of this study, despite only being limited to reviewing practices in three cultural contexts, demonstrate the somewhat problematic nature of the bundling of these notions into one argument based around the concept of invisibility. It may well be the case that translators translate in a fluent manner, both enacting and masking the way in which they are made to be invisible, and therefore their *activity* does contribute to their own invisibility to some extent (although it would be difficult to be sure of whether this is the case without further research into the activities of real-life translators). In addition to this, it would be hard to argue against the points that Venuti makes about the translator having a problematic existence in terms of authorship, copyright and contracts. Copyright law still does not 'define a space for the translator's authorship that is equal to, or in any way restricts, the foreign author's rights' (ibid.: 9), and despite improvements in contracts since the late 1990s for translators, including being granted access to royalties, it remains 'difficult for a freelance translator to make a living solely from translating' (ibid.: 12). Nonetheless, it appears extremely problematic to mix these issues with other aspects of the translator's *situation*, such as how translations are received by general readers and professionals.

Indeed, there may well be fewer translated works published in the United Kingdom than in France and Germany, but this does not necessarily mean that the British translator is any less visible in more general terms than his/her French or German counterpart. This is why it has been important to break down visibility within the reviews into superficial and embedded visibility, as this has provided a much more nuanced approach to and a better understanding of the concept of visibility in practice. The findings of the present study, particularly in the British context, have pointed towards reviewers acknowledging the translator relatively frequently, and often going further than this to engage with the work of the translator in more depth. It would therefore be difficult to argue that translators are still invisible in this regard. The quotation by Venuti introduced in the epigraph to this book, in other words that 'a translated text […] is judged acceptable by most […] reviewers […] when it reads fluently' (ibid.: 1), also needs some updating; ultimately, fluency is no longer the only criterion against which translations are being assessed. What Venuti did in *The Translator's Invisibility* back in 1995 should, of course, not be understated: he brought the real-life issues that translators were facing to the fore in translation studies. Nonetheless, this study has also demonstrated that it is problematic to use the notion of invisibility as an umbrella term for all of the arguments that Venuti incorporates into it to support his general contention about translators enjoying a 'shadowy existence'. Moving forward, it is important to further break down the concept of visibility into sub-categories: naturally, a starting point in this process would be to completely divide the notions of the translator's *activity* and the translator's *situation*, rather than grouping them together under the umbrella of visibility. This would allow us to determine whether it is the translators themselves who most contribute to their own invisibility, or whether indeed it is groups such as readers, reviewers and publishers who conceal the fact of translation. These two sub-categories could also be further divided, as it is not a simple case, for instance, of saying that everything that the translator does in their translation work contributes to his/her own invisibility; there may be very precise elements of a translator's work which do this, but not their whole *activity*. Attempting to group all of these notions under the umbrella of visibility provides an ultimately inaccurate representation of the more complex existence of the translator and translation, particularly in Western Europe.

## Disentangling the invisible – Sub-categories of visibility and scope for future research

The present study has only focussed on one aspect of visibility, and more particularly of the translator's *situation*, namely how translations are reviewed by the general public and professionals. There has been a significant development in the situation of the translator in this regard, with reviewers now more likely than in the past to acknowledge the fact of translation and to engage with the work of the translator. Nonetheless, it would not be possible to claim that translators are now more visible as a whole, since visibility is a multi-faceted notion which attempts to cover various areas of both the translator's *activity* and *situation*. The studies of the visibility of translation and translators have thus far only provided us with an incomplete insight into how visible translators really are, as some aspects of the translator's *activity* and *situation* remain vastly under-researched. A more comprehensive examination of these notions would allow us to understand in more detail at what level translation and/or translators are visible or not and would be more productive than the currently accepted wide-ranging umbrella of visibility. As such, rather than aiming to engage with invisibility as an entire concept, it seems prudent for future research to focus on specific elements of the translator's *activity* and *situation*. Future projects could take inspiration from this book and focus in-depth on just one aspect of the *activity* or *situation* of the translator and the discoveries of such projects could then be analysed in conjunction to determine at what levels translation and translators are visible.

Future research may therefore focus on aspects of the translator's *activity*, such as:

- comparing source texts and target texts to determine to what extent the translator has made efforts to ensure readability by, as Venuti (1995: 1) outlines, 'adhering to current usage, maintaining continuous syntax, and fixing a precise meaning'. The aim of this would be to ascertain whether readability continues to be the main priority of individual translators in the translation process;
- determining whether there are any trends in how translators translate as a whole in the modern day and assessing to what extent fluency is cherished amongst translators;
- rather than attempting to identify a trend towards certain translation approaches across all forms of fiction and non-fiction, it would be interesting to initially break this down into two separate categories of fiction and non-fiction, and then genres within those categories. We could then identify whether translators adopt different approaches to different genres;
- or, as suggested by Munday (2012: 231), interviewing translators about their strategies and/or researching 'what the translators say they are doing, their correspondence with the authors and the different drafts of a translation if available'. Learning first-hand from real-life translators what they are hoping to achieve and what kind of work they have put into their translations would provide a comprehensive insight into their own activity and, more importantly, their own understanding of their activity.

Nonetheless, it would be remiss to neglect the importance of the translator's *situation* as well. Future research into the translator's *situation* could include:

- examining reviews from different publications in the same three countries as those analysed for the current study, or expanding the framework of the project to other countries to determine to what extent reviewers engage with translation. Investigating editorial policies and finding out about the backgrounds of the reviewers themselves would be an extra dimension to this field of research in the future;
- quantitatively assessing how many books are translated and sold, which ones are chosen to be translated and into which languages, and whether/how trends have varied over time. This is another area of research suggested by Munday (ibid.) and would provide crucial insights into how translation is considered and valued across different countries;
- analysing translator's contracts and the legal status assigned to them. Are there, for example, stipulations that the translator's name has to appear on the cover of translated literature? What rights do translators have to their own work? This links to another area of research which Venuti discusses in *The Translator's Invisibility*, namely copyright;
- scrutinising what Martin de Haan (2011: online) refers to as the 'cultural visibility' of the translator. As the European Council of Literary Translators' Associations (CEATL) has already begun to do, it would be productive to examine whether it is general practice to invite translators to press conferences, book presentations, readings, discussions and talks, and if not, why not? Quantitative research could also focus here on the percentage of launches of translations at which the translator is present compared to the percentage of launches of books written in the original language at which the author is present;
- attempting, as de Haan (ibid.: online) also suggests, to determine the importance and success of public events organised around translation, as well as translation organisations. For example, do the public actually engage at all with International Translation Day, celebrated

every year on 30 September? What kind of events take place in a wide variety of countries? This would point towards how visible translation and translators are beyond the actual translated works;

- determining what each of the parties in the translation process wants from a translation – from readers, through publishers, to the translators themselves. This could be done through focus groups, interviewing publishers and editors to see what their aims are in publishing a translation, finding out what instructions are regularly provided to translators, and more. We could also ask the question of whether increased visibility of the translator is something that is desirable for all parties, and if not, analyse in greater depth whether this is a problem or not.

These are just some of the potential areas of research that scholars could pursue in the future, but there are of course many more. The scope for research within this sub-field of translation studies demonstrates the complexity of the notion of the visibility of translation. Before justifiable comments about the overarching visibility of translators in certain cultures and contexts are made, there must first be an in-depth understanding of both the *activity* and *situation* of the translator in all of their facets. A more nuanced understanding of these areas, which currently remain vastly under-researched, would put us in a better-informed position to gauge what kind of existence translation and translators enjoy. Nonetheless, even if further research into these areas demonstrated that translators do remain invisible in contemporary Anglo-American cultures, should this be considered as a necessarily bad thing? Invisibility has always been looked upon as undesirable and unreasonable within translation studies, but invisibility may have some benefits as well.

## Debunking the invisible – Is invisibility really *that* bad?

In *The Translator's Invisibility*, Lawrence Venuti proposes his 'call to action' to counter the invisibility of the translator. He asserts that contemporary translators could and perhaps even should 'introduce discursive variations [into their work], experimenting with archaism, slang, literary allusion and convention to call attention to the secondary status of the translation and signal the linguistic and cultural differences of the foreign text' (Venuti 1995: 310–11), thus attempting to challenge readers' pre-conceptions of what a translator is and what their work entails. At no point in his seminal work, however, does Venuti consider whether invisibility might be something that all parties involved in the translation process, and particularly translators themselves, actually desire and benefit from. But is invisibility really *that* bad? Or, to phrase the question slightly differently, precisely what kind of visibility should translators desire? Throughout all future research into this area, it seems important that scholars bear in mind that invisibility can be considered a positive thing by various players in the translation chain.

With reviewing practices in particular in mind, we have already seen that Daniel Hahn, translator and reviewer of translations himself, does not always mention the translation or engage with the translation at all. He asserts that he does 'not often mention the translator of a book I'm reviewing. I don't feel any obligation to do so. In a five-hundred-word review there will be any number of things I'm not going to write about' (Hahn 2011: online). Hahn claims that a reviewer should engage with the work of the translator if the reviewer is assessing how the text reads in the target language, but takes no issue with translators being invisible if the review simply does not involve the work of the translator. But what about the rest of the translation chain, the way that translators translate and the way in which translations are commercialised by publishers? Another translation scholar, Penny Johnson, believes that translations may not be marketed as such as it 'might be a way to enter the target culture; a way for readers to acquire a taste for foreign literature; and a way for the author to reach a wide audience' (Johnson 2005: 139–40). If a translation is clearly marketed as such, in other words, it may well result in fewer readers picking up the work to read in the first place. In this scenario, although the translation and subsequently the translator is more visible in terms of how the work is commercialised, the fact that readers may not read the work at all would ultimately reduce the visibility of the work as a whole in the target culture.

If, however, such a work is not marketed as a translation, and more readers pick up the work and enjoy it, there is a greater chance that readers will want to find out more about the book, which may lead them to discover that it has been translated; ultimately, this would result in greater visibility overall for the translation and a stronger chance of readers recommending the work to their friends. According to Johnson, then, by attempting to make translation more visible on what we have termed a superficial level, we could actually be achieving precisely the opposite and making it more invisible as a whole.

A similar idea applies to the *activity* of translators as well, namely the way in which they translate works. If a translator were, for example, to follow Venuti's 'call to action' and experiment with discursive variations, then the translated work may not have as much success as if the translator adopted a more fluent approach, or indeed it may not get published at all. The translator would be textually more visible, and the reader would perhaps realise that they are reading a translation, but as above, if the work is not widely successful and is negatively received by general readers and reviewers, then this makes the work generally more invisible or contribute to the notion that translation is always going to be problematic or poor. Venuti's own translations of Tarchetti's works in which he adopts foreignising practices were appreciated by some niche reviewers, but criticised by more general mainstream reviewers. Whilst Venuti made himself visible within the text, the fact that the works were not terribly well received would in all likelihood have prevented others from reading them. If, however, Venuti had translated them in a more homogenous, fluent manner, then perhaps they would have had a greater success in the Anglo-American world. By making the translator more visible within the text itself, this leads to the work itself being less consumed and thus less visible on the market.

This is a view which is echoed by the *grande dame* of translation, Anthea Bell, who actively came out in support of translators and translation being invisible, at least in their translation activity. Bell (2004) laid out her stance at a translation conference at Brunel University London, the subject of which was precisely the visibility of translation. She considers herself to be an invisible translator but is not unhappy about this. She began her keynote speech as follows:

> I might as well tell you at once that in any debate between visible and invisible translation I am an unrepentant, unreconstructed adherent of the school of invisible translation, and I cannot change an honestly held opinion because it is out of fashion. I have called these remarks 'Translation as Illusion', because, all my professional life, I have felt that translators are in the business of spinning an illusion: the illusion is that the reader is reading not a translation, but the real thing. (ibid.: 14)

Bell elaborates upon this notion of translation as *illusion* and comments both upon the activity of translators, in other words how the translators themselves translate, and upon the manner in which translations are then commercialised and reviewed. She argues that if a translator is invisible through the whole process, enabling the reader to enjoy the reading experience, since the translation can be 'read as easily as if it had been originally written in English' (ibid.: 16), whilst still opening themselves to a foreign text, then the translator has ultimately done their job. She sees her goal as making readers enjoy the translated work 'as much as if they could read it in the original, without placing too many obstacles in the way of that enjoyment' (ibid.). Despite the fact that Bell has done her best to make herself invisible within her own translations initially, this has paradoxically led to her becoming one of the most *visible* translators in the English-speaking world; she has variously been described as the 'doyenne of translators' (*The Telegraph*), a 'magnificent translator' (*The Guardian*), and of course the 'grande dame of literary translation' (*The Times*). Whether Bell would have enjoyed the notoriety and cultural visibility that she does today had she made herself more visible textually is questionable. Ultimately, just because a translator makes themselves invisible in their own *activity* does not mean that they will be invisible in terms of their *situation*. This further highlights the need to break down the currently accepted notion of invisibility into various areas.

Bell continues to make the argument for invisibility and illusion as she progresses through her speech, but her attitude towards translated works becomes explicitly clear in her final remarks in which she argues:

> Translation is not, by its very nature, a high-profile craft. If you have spun your illusion successfully, then you are quite rightly invisible. If reviewers don't comment on a translation, it has worked. For to my mind the translator is constantly walking a tightrope, owing an equal duty to the original author and to the readers of the

> translation, trying not to fall off that tightrope between languages, but to preserve the illusion that what was thought and written in one can be read and understood in its essentials in another. (ibid.: 26–27)

Bell accepts what Venuti asserted back in 1995 about translation not being a highly acknowledged craft and translators often being invisible; however, she does not criticise this status quo. Bell also continues in the same vein as Hahn, by outlining her belief that reviewers do not need to comment on the translation, and even should not be expected to comment on the work of the translator if it has been done well.

## Final remarks

This conclusion has two main aims, both of which seek to enhance, or even reshape, our understanding of crucial notions within this area of translation studies. It has firstly reiterated the findings and discoveries of this study with regard to reviewing practices. Reviewing practices have evolved since the publication of *The Translator's Invisibility* and subsequent studies of the field: reviewers are now generally more likely to acknowledge the translator and frequently engage with the work of the translator to at least some extent. This development can be considered to be positive in terms of visibility, with translators now more visible within reviews. However, equally importantly, it has demonstrated that just because translators are more visible within reviews does not necessarily mean that they are more visible in general. The aim in the latter part of the conclusion has been to debunk commonly accepted notions around invisibility, to demonstrate why it is problematic to use the term invisibility as an umbrella term for all that it currently encompasses. I have outlined potential avenues for future research into the field, broken down into various aspects of the translator's *activity* and *situation*, which should allow a greater understanding of what translators do in their work and how translators and translation are perceived. The conflation of the notions that I have discussed into the one umbrella term of invisibility over the past thirty years has allowed an initial reflection on the status and standing of translation and translators in Anglo-American cultures and brought a key issue to the fore in translation studies; however, the problematic nature of grouping these notions under such an umbrella has been outlined. Ultimately, we should treat individual aspects of visibility separately, rather than grouping them, in any future research. And this may lead us to question precisely what the fight for 'visibility' is hoping to achieve: do we want visibility in terms of the translator's *activity* or the translator's *situation*? Or even certain elements within each of those categories? After all, if visibility is desired in either of the sub-categories, it may detract from visibility in the other.

# Bibliography

All websites were last accessed on 19 January 2024.

Actualitté Editorial. (2023). 'Qui sommes-nous ?', *Actualitté*, <http://tinyurl.com/bdd7a2zz>.

Adams, L. (2011). 'On reviewing translations: Lorraine Adams', *Words without Borders*, <http://tinyurl.com/ykhwnwmp>.

Albath, M. (2022). 'Untadelige Bilanzen', *Süddeutsche Zeitung*, <http://tinyurl.com/j5597 98t>.

Amazon. (2022). 'Customer review creation guidelines', <http://tinyurl.com/2p8btt77>.

Amazon France 1. (2022). *Vivement la suite!*, <http://tinyurl.com/4je9p8v9>.

Amazon France 2. (2022). *Le livre était vraiment dans son emballage d'origine*. <http://tinyurl.com/mr2esykm>.

Amazon France 3. (2022). *Je découvre Meyer!*. <http://tinyurl.com/4xvx85x2>.

Amazon France 4. (2022). *Les hommes ont peur de la lumière de Douglas Kennedy*. <http://tinyurl.com/566jzyzh>.

Amazon France 5. (2022). *Un polar historique intéressant et plein de suspense*. <http://tinyurl.com/4jx4hhuc>.

Amazon France 6. (2022). *Roman introductif*. <http://tinyurl.com/4je9p8v9>.

Amazon France 7. (2022). *Recueil de thrillers psycho très bien construit*. <http://tinyurl.com/8xndmw9x>.

Amazon France 8. (2022). *Un texte magnifique*. <http://tinyurl.com/24v9ktkt>.

Amazon France 9. (2022). *Nouvelle captivante*. <http://tinyurl.com/wvn8mae6>.

Amazon France 10. (2022). *Envoûtant*. <http://tinyurl.com/33w76sbc>.

Amazon France 11. (2022). *Un roman social parfois un peu fouillis*. <http://tinyurl.com/ydrm3brh>.

Amazon France 12. (2022). *Coup de coeur*. <http://tinyurl.com/waxayyfs>.

Amazon France 13. (2022). *Mauvaise traduction … dommage*. <http://tinyurl.com/4xzbncxs>.

Amazon France 14. (2022). *Remarquable*. <http://tinyurl.com/bdfh3vp8>.

Amazon France 15. (2022). *Pénible à lire*. <http://tinyurl.com/242s79ax>.

Amazon France 16. (2022). *Une très belle découverte*. <http://tinyurl.com/5dxhjn2h>.

Amazon France 17. (2022). *Une belle découverte*. <http://tinyurl.com/5ywycmfu>.

Amazon France 18. (2022). *Premier roman excellent*. <http://tinyurl.com/23j34u55>.

Amazon Germany 1. (2022). *Interessant.* <http://tinyurl.com/56m5b46m>.

Amazon Germany 2. (2022). *Tolles Cover, aber ….* <http://tinyurl.com/2mra5x6u>.

Amazon Germany 3. (2022). *Bucheinband war beschädigt.* <http://tinyurl.com/36kvebpx>.

Amazon Germany 4. (2022). *Wunderschön illustriertes Buch über China.* <http://tinyurl.com/mpu6hx55>.

Amazon Germany 5. (2022). *Feinsinnig.* <http://tinyurl.com/2jrfha23>.

Amazon Germany 6. (2022). *Ein langer Weg zu sich selbst.* <http://tinyurl.com/2sb6752h>.

Amazon Germany 7. (2022). *Düsterer und verstörender Debütroman.* <http://tinyurl.com/vwb4sp8b>.

Amazon Germany 8. (2022). *Sehr schwierig zu lesen aber inhaltlich interessant.* <http://tinyurl.com/2r39zw8s>.

Amazon Germany 9. (2022). *Berührendes Hörbuch.* <http://tinyurl.com/35pwenjd>.

Amazon Germany 10. (2022). *Ein etwas anderes Jugendbuch!* <http://tinyurl.com/3pkmwfv4>.

Amazon Germany 11. (2022). *Gut? So richtig gut!* <http://tinyurl.com/3pkmwfv4>.

Amazon Germany 12. (2022). *Das weibliche Mittelalter.* <http://tinyurl.com/35ctwjtd>.

Amazon Germany 13. (2022). *Atmosphärische Darstellung ohne Effekthascherei!* <http://tinyurl.com/4btthdj3>.

Amazon Germany 14. (2022). *Spannendes Setting und untergründiger Humor.* <http://tinyurl.com/4kt3f5fm>.

Amazon Germany 15. (2022). *Zur Erlösung vielleicht noch ein Heißgetränk?* <http://tinyurl.com/n6y9dfw2>.

Amazon Germany 16. (2022). *Schönes Buch mit Mängeln.* <http://tinyurl.com/3j769aec>.

Amazon Germany 17. (2022). *Schöne Illustrationen aber sehr viele Übersetzungsfehler.* <http://tinyurl.com/3j769aec>.

Amazon Germany 18. (2022). *Hübsch aufgemachte Märchen.* <http://tinyurl.com/3j769aec>.

Amazon Germany 19. (2022). *Schöne Bilder und Quellennachweis ABER nicht aus der ursprünglichen Sprache übersetzt.* <http://tinyurl.com/3j769aec>.

Amazon Germany 20. (2022). *Wunderschöne Illustrationen, schlechtes Lektorat und lieblose Übersetzung.* <http://tinyurl.com/3j769aec>.

Amazon Germany 21. (2022). *Richtig miese Übersetzung.* <http://tinyurl.com/yamv4f46>.

Amazon Germany 22. (2022). *Mit heißer Nadel gestrickt.* <http://tinyurl.com/yamv4f46>.

Amazon Germany 23. (2022). *Harter Tobak, nichts für mich*. <http://tinyurl.com/vwb4sp8b>.
Amazon Germany 24. (2022). *Good people*. <http://tinyurl.com/2u8e5ynw>.
Amazon Germany 25. (2022). *Höchst interessant*. <http://tinyurl.com/2b5tm72b>.
Amazon Germany 26. (2022). *Thematisch spannend, strukturell unausgegoren*. <http://tinyurl.com/vwb4sp8b>.
Amazon UK 1. (2022). *Dark look at content moderation*. <http://tinyurl.com/3m2prsze>.
Amazon UK 2. (2022). *Book*. <http://tinyurl.com/bdhy38tk>.
Amazon UK 3. (2022). *Arrived on time in good condition*. <http://tinyurl.com/mudm9ra9>.
Amazon UK 4. (2022). *The sands of Tomb were unbalanced*. <http://tinyurl.com/2vz8dd7y>.
Amazon UK 5. (2022). *Hard going*. <http://tinyurl.com/3ub7mpw4>.
Amazon UK 6. (2022). *An evil axis's Twilight Zone*. <http://tinyurl.com/kkj976h3>.
Amazon UK 7. (2022). *Visceral!* <http://tinyurl.com/2p8k4f8a>.
Amazon UK 8. (2022). *Did not finish*. <http://tinyurl.com/bdhy38tk>.
Amazon UK 9. (2022). *The writing flows really well and I ended up reading most of it in one day*. <http://tinyurl.com/e42jtfub>.
Amazon UK 10. (2022). *Something lost in translation*. <http://tinyurl.com/bdhy38tk>.
Amazon UK 11. (2022). *An exploration of grief from another culture*. <http://tinyurl.com/3xurnw8k>.
Amazon UK 12. (2022). *So well translated that you'd think the author's native tongue was English*. <http://tinyurl.com/3j5vfh73>.
Amazon UK 13. (2022). *Stunningly beautiful prose*. <http://tinyurl.com/5n7pjnec>.
Amazon UK 14. (2022). *Not your usual murder mystery*. <http://tinyurl.com/3xurnw8k>.
Amazon UK 15. (2022). *Japanese classic mystery novel very culture centred*. <http://tinyurl.com/bejbrxmr>.
Amazon UK 16. (2022). *A thorough job*. <http://tinyurl.com/49edac79>.
Amazon UK 17. (2022). *A very enjoyable and informative read*. <http://tinyurl.com/y63nxdvy>.
Amazon UK 18. (2022). *An interesting project*. <http://tinyurl.com/3c9acmr9>.
Amazon UK 19. (2022). *Political and religious history of France around 1800 to 1830*. <http://tinyurl.com/2afuzt9k>.
Amazon UK 20. (2022). *Two women, one story*. <http://tinyurl.com/2vz8dd7y>.
Amazon UK 21. (2022). *An exciting discovery for Rilke fans and followers of the Bloomsbury group*. <http://tinyurl.com/3c9acmr9>.
Amazon UK 22. (2022). *Problematic translation*. <http://tinyurl.com/5hczw7jk>.

Amend-Söchting, A. (2022a). 'Ehe-Exit und Brexit, Affekte und ihre Abstraktionen', *Literaturkritik*, <http://tinyurl.com/49yxcwd6>.

Amend-Söchting, A. (2022b). 'Rache als unzuverlässige Projektierung', *Literaturkritik*, <http://tinyurl.com/3wyz6dp2>.

Ancion, L. (2022a). 'Dandadan: renversant, fulgurant, sublime', *Actualitté*, <http://tinyurl.com/mr3vwuns>.

Ancion, L. (2022b). 'The Chilling Dead: les morts-vivants ont la vie douce', *Actualitté*, <http://tinyurl.com/5n6nzyxj>.

Ancion, L. (2022c). '17–21: l'éclat des œuvres de jeunesse de Tatsuki Fujimoto', *Actualitté*, <http://tinyurl.com/yc83f69t>.

Ancion, N. (2022a). 'De la tyrannie: comment éviter que le pire n'advienne', *Actualitté*, <http://tinyurl.com/ue52m7rk>.

Ancion, N. (2022b). 'Nettoyage à sec, de Joris Mertens: Bruxelles comme on ne l'a jamais lue', *Actualitté*, <http://tinyurl.com/mupwu5ej>.

Angelier, F. (2022). 'Le Livre noir des Mille et Une Nuits: les « Nuits » érotiques de Sir Richard Burton', *Le Monde*, <http://tinyurl.com/y936ddfv>.

Anthony, A. (2022). 'Zelensky: A biography by Serhii Rudenko review – from voice of Paddington to global giant', *The Guardian*, <http://tinyurl.com/4jz57m6m>.

Augart, J. (2022). 'Vom Einwandern und Ankommen', *Literaturkritik*, <http://tinyurl.com/2p8rns63>.

Banville, J. (2022). 'Yell, Sam, If You Still Can by Maylis Besserie review – Beckett's last days', *The Guardian*, <http://tinyurl.com/yy4v824w>.

Bell, A. (2004). 'Translation as illusion', *Brunel University*, <http://tinyurl.com/43usbadk>.

Bernofsky, S. et al. (2011). 'On reviewing translations: Susan Bernofsky, Jonathan Cohen and Edith Grossman', *Words Without Borders*, <http://tinyurl.com/mwnyvsu2>.

Bie Brahic, B. (2015). 'Saying', *The Times Literary Supplement*, <http://tinyurl.com/9j6fca3y>.

Bleutge, N. (2022a). 'Schicksal an Resopaltischen', *Süddeutsche Zeitung*, <http://tinyurl.com/2a768vr7>.

Bleutge, N. (2022b). 'Landschaft der Unfreiheit', *Süddeutsche Zeitung*, <http://tinyurl.com/2p8cdesm>.

Blitzer, J. (2011). 'On reviewing translations: Confessions of a book reviewer (of works in translation)', *Words Without Borders*, <http://tinyurl.com/4j49ew65>.

Bogdan, I. (2012). 'Von der Unsichtbarkeit', *Börsenblatt*, <http://tinyurl.com/2pna8n3f>.

Boisseau, M. (2016). 'De la traductologie aux sciences de la traduction?', *Revue française de linguistique appliquée*, 21 (1), <http://tinyurl.com/286358v6>.

Börsenverein des Deutschen Buchhandels. (2020). *Der Buchmarkt 2018*. <http://tinyurl.com/mrx3mvtu>.

Bouhadjera, H. (2022a). 'Les chevaux de feu: l'Ukraine des pasteurs et des esprits', *Actualitté*, <http://tinyurl.com/9kk7fdce>.

Bouhadjera, H. (2022b). 'Jack Kerouac: à chacun, ses ailes invisibles', *Actualitté*, <http://tinyurl.com/4u4th4a4>.

Boutang, A. (2022). 'Une nouvelle traduction de Des souris et des hommes: sous la dureté de John Steinbeck, la tendresse des sentiments', *Le Monde*, <http://tinyurl.com/bp5e8737>.

Boyd, M. (2014). 'Reviewing translations', *Diálog Intercultural Services*, <dialogos.ca/2014/03/reviewing-translations>.

Brown, L. (2014). 'The dos and don'ts of book reviewing', *Huffington Post*, <http://tinyurl.com/56cpncsa>.

Burgess, A. (1990). 'On Wednesday he does his ears', *New York Times Book Review*, <www.nytimes.com/1990/10/14/books/on-wednesday-he-does-his-ears.html>.

Bush, P. (2004). *Reviewing translation: Barcelona, London and Paris*, <http://tinyurl.com/58u7hyr4>.

Byers, S. (2022). 'Our share of night by Mariana Enríquez review – political horror', *The Guardian*, <http://tinyurl.com/3xfcum25>.

Calvani, M., and Emmons, M. L. (2008). *The slippery art of book reviewing*. Kingsport, TN: Twilight Times Books.

Chakraborty, A. (2022). 'Tomb of Sand by Geetanjali Shree review – the timeless search to be seen', *The Guardian*, <http://tinyurl.com/583zjvmj>.

Chong, P. (2020). *Inside the critics' circle: Book reviewing in uncertain times*. Princeton: Princeton University Press.

Christ, R. (1984). 'Translation watch', *PEN American Center Newsletter*, 53 (8).

Clermont, T. (2022). 'Paradaïze, de Fernanda Melchor: frères de sang', *Le Figaro*, <http://tinyurl.com/b4sytd7z>.

Conquer, R. (2022). 'Lost in translation', *Times Literary Supplement*, <http://tinyurl.com/4ycne5rx>.

Costantini, V. (2022a). 'Mordew: dans les bas-fonds, la magie', *Actualitté*, <http://tinyurl.com/mrxkjkn7>.

Costantini, V. (2022b). 'Le musée des promesses brisées: donner, pardonner, et vivre enfin', *Actualitté*, <http://tinyurl.com/4y7ee3y3>.

Costantini, V. (2022c). 'Nos vies en flammes: conte désenchanté dans les Appalaches', *Actualitté*, <http://tinyurl.com/8s9er6bn>.

Costantini, V. (2022d). 'Boo: journal intime de l'au-delà', *Actualitté*, <http://tinyurl.com/86wxvk7a>.

Dale, J. (2014). 'Here they are: The rules for book reviewing', *The Conversation*, <http://tinyurl.com/yc8au4w8>.

De Haan, M. (2011). 'The translator's (in)visibility', *Hof/Haan*, <http://tinyurl.com/4bak6ndn>.

De Larminat, A. (2022). 'Contes de Noël, de Dino Buzzati: éloge de Noël', *Le Figaro*, <http://tinyurl.com/bdh9jmhh>.

Dennis, A. (2022). 'Mother is my skivvy', *Times Literary Supplement*, <http://tinyurl.com/bdd6czv3>.

Deshusses, P. (2022a). 'Anton Beraber, John McGahern, Sarah Moss, Helga Novak … Les brèves critiques du « Monde des livres »', *Le Monde*, <http://tinyurl.com/mwcv8b93>.

Deshusses, P. (2022b). 'Garçon au coq noir, de Stefanie vor Schulte: il était une fois un jeune redresseur de torts', *Le Monde*, <http://tinyurl.com/3dxtnxkr>.

Develey, A. (2019). 'Pourquoi nous avons encore besoin de traducteurs', *Le Figaro*, <http://tinyurl.com/33tmx9nz>.

Develey, A. (2022). 'Euphorie d'Elin Cullhed: l'incandescente Sylvia Plath', *Le Figaro*, <http://tinyurl.com/5n7ebxyv>.

Donahaye, J. (2012). *Three percent? Publishing data and statistics on translated literature in the United Kingdom and Ireland.* <http://tinyurl.com/2d973azj>.

DS Autorinnen und Autoren. (2022). 'Ukrainische Krimis, Familiengeschichten, stille Heldenporträts', *Der Spiegel*, <http://tinyurl.com/4kt9sxpk>.

Dziadosz, A. (2022). 'I wouldn't say I *love* Finland', *London Review of Books*, <http://tinyurl.com/337rvp3x>.

Ebel, M. (2022). 'Karussell der Gräuel', *Süddeutsche Zeitung*, <http://tinyurl.com/3yr3nhak>.

El Ouassil, S. (2022). 'Warum handeln wir nicht im Angesicht der Klimakatastrophe?', *Süddeutsche Zeitung*, <http://tinyurl.com/4rb9w8df>.

Elven, L. (2022). 'The dining-room table', *London Review of Books*, <http://tinyurl.com/4s9ycms3>.

English PEN. (2011). 'Literary translation centre', <http://tinyurl.com/24dkbfb7>.

English PEN. (2020). 'International translation day', <http://tinyurl.com/3u86na2u>.

English PEN. (2022). 'ITD 2022 –nationwide programme', <http://tinyurl.com/3298f3bk>.

Esposito, S. (2011). 'On reviewing translations: Scott Esposito', *Words without Borders*, <http://tinyurl.com/34uvzn99>.

European Commission. (2012). 'Studies on translation and multilingualism: The status of the translation profession in the European Union', <http://tinyurl.com/msvc2h2f>.

Evans, J. (2022). 'Shards of language', *Times Literary Supplement*, <http://tinyurl.com/wsz7f4hj>.

Fasseur, B. (2022). 'Rendez-vous du renard #2 : il va y avoir du sport … et de la lecture', *Actualitté*, <http://tinyurl.com/2mz5s3e6>.

Fawcett, P. (2000). 'Translation in the broadsheets', *The Translator*, 6 (2), 295–307.

Fay, S. (2012a). 'Book reviews: A tortured history', *The Atlantic*, <http://tinyurl.com/mvnrc3nn>.

Fay, S. (2012b). 'Could the Internet save book reviews?', *The Atlantic*, <http://tinyurl.com/bdesbemr>.

Federmair, L. (2016). 'Warum ich keine Literaturkritik mehr schreibe', *Begleitschreiben*, <http://tinyurl.com/44cfh9f2>.

Feeny, M. (2022). 'The Pachinko Parlour by Elisa Shua Dusapin review – sleepless in Tokyo', *The Guardian*, <http://tinyurl.com/yvy7b7ra>.

Ferney, J. (2015). 'Des traducteurs à bout de souffle: Enquête', *La Croix*, <http://tinyurl.com/43k8m24f>.

Fillon, A. (2022). 'Dans les rêves de Delmore Schwartz: un injuste oubli', *Le Figaro*, <http://tinyurl.com/muun9bbr>.

Flad, B. (1996). 'Kritik und Markt französischer Literatur aus Sicht eines Publikumsverlages'. In F. Nies (ed.), *Literaturimport und Literaturkritik: das Beispiel Frankreich* (pp. 38–47). Tübingen: Gunter Narr Verlag.

Forbes. (2018). *Amazon continues to impress with rapid growth*, <http://tinyurl.com/2s3vkmcn>.

Foster, H. (2022). 'Anyone can do collage', *London Review of Books*, <http://tinyurl.com/28sdtmu5>.

Fox-Martens, E. (2022). 'The land speaks', *Times Literary Supplement*, <http://tinyurl.com/2rkk2c72>.

France, M. (2022). 'Tightening the vice belt', *Times Literary Supplement*, <http://tinyurl.com/yj43fr3y>.

François, V. (2012). 'La critique littéraire est-elle si "Net"?', *Marianne*, <http://tinyurl.com/mrxfkp3p>.

Freund, N. (2022). 'Eine Niere: 100 000 Dollar', *Süddeutsche Zeitung*, <http://tinyurl.com/4fmbar9r>.

Frieling, R. (2015). 'Wie schreibt man eine Rezension?', *Literaturzeitschrift*, <http://tinyurl.com/y75v2bfb>.

Gabbert, E. (2018). 'Is there such a thing as a good book review?', *Electric Literature*, <http://tinyurl.com/ynmfmvj3>.

Gebhardt, L. (2022a). 'Eine postmoderne Lamentatio', *Literaturkritik*, <http://tinyurl.com/yc459ct6>.

Gebhardt, L. (2022b). 'Endlich sich selbst akzeptieren', *Literaturkritik*, <http://tinyurl.com/6k57rhbv>.

Gebhardt, L. (2022c). 'Irrgarten mit Mädchen', *Literaturkritik*, <http://tinyurl.com/4jmwwmwf>.

Gibson, S. (2014). 'Book reviewing is an art, in its own way', *The Conversation*, <http://tinyurl.com/2vh535fw>.

Gooding, F. (2022). 'Wolf, turtle, bear', *London Review of Books*, <http://tinyurl.com/mmwye4uf>.

Gras, C. (2022). 'Dersou Ouzala, de Vladimir Arseniev: le dernier des Mohicans sibérien', *Le Figaro*, <http://tinyurl.com/2pr2wmee>.

Gray, M. (2018). 'Examining the "Invisible": How are published translations reviewed in the United Kingdom and France?', *Mémoires du livre/Studies in Book Culture*, 9 (I), <http://tinyurl.com/rh23wcp6>.

Greenlaw, L. (2022). 'Out all day with his axe', *London Review of Books*, <http://tinyurl.com/ymwbxx3u>.

Ground, I. (2022). 'I fell apart!', *Times Literary Supplement*, <http://tinyurl.com/2jh4acxd>.

The Guardian Editorial. (2017). 'The Guardian view on translation: An interpretative and creative act', *The Guardian*, <http://tinyurl.com/y2d77fzv>.

Hahn, D. (2011). 'On reviewing translations: Daniel Hahn', *Words without Borders*, <http://tinyurl.com/ynvdturc>.

Hahn, D. (2018). 'Translators are the vanguard of literary change: We need better recognition', *The Guardian*, <http://tinyurl.com/24ymb2sp>.

Hall, C. (2022). 'Understanding our origens', *Times Literary Supplement*, <http://tinyurl.com/33w8t7xj>.

Häntzschel, J. (2022). 'Galerie der Seelen', *Süddeutsche Zeitung*, <http://tinyurl.com/3w6k8ve6>.

Harding, J. (2022). 'You're with your king', *London Review of Books*, <http://tinyurl.com/3ar5zzvx>.

Harrison, B. (1994). 'Once in Love with Giorgio', New York Times Book Review. In: Venuti, L. (1998). *The scandals of translation: Towards an ethics of difference*. London: Routledge.

Harrison, M. (2022). 'Retrospective by Juan Gabriel Vásquez review – Mao, movies and me', *The Guardian*, <http://tinyurl.com/yc6yj2dx>.

Helmes, G. (2022). 'Ein Abgrund mit Namen Familie, ein Aufbruch im Namen der Freiheit', *Literaturkritik*, <http://tinyurl.com/jw8yd5wx>.

Heydt, V. (2016). 'Mehr Licht auf Übersetzer', *Börsenblatt*, <http://tinyurl.com/4z5a7jz7>.

Hinsliff, G. (2022). 'Zelensky: A biography; Putin: His life and times reviews', *The Guardian*, <http://tinyurl.com/4cyn7but>.

Holdstock, N. (2022). 'Guinea pigs for dystopia', *Times Literary Supplement*, <http://tinyurl.com/2vyj3na2>.

Holmes, A., and Parker, J. (2015). 'Is book reviewing a public service or an art?', *New York Times*, <http://tinyurl.com/3rv4f6wa>.

Horváth, F. (2022). 'Die Würde der Rosen', *Literaturkritik*, <http://tinyurl.com/57e43und>.

Hughes, S. (2022). 'Novelist as a vocation by Haruki Murakami review – lessons in simplicity', *The Guardian*, <http://tinyurl.com/yc6netjy>.

Informationsgemeinschaft zur Feststellung der Verbreitung von Werbeträgern. (2018). *Werbeträgerdaten*, <http://tinyurl.com/4fmjee4h>.

Janker, K. (2022). 'Wenn die Steine weinen', *Süddeutsche Zeitung*, <http://tinyurl.com/yeywy8y2>.

Janssen, S. (1997). 'Reviewing as social practice: Institutional constraints on critics' attention for contemporary fiction', *Poetics*, 24, 275–97.

Johnson, P. (2005). '"Capturing the Spirit": Reviewing literary translation'. In I. Klitgärd (ed.), *Angles on the English-speaking world volume 6: Literary translation, world literature or 'Worlding' literature?* (pp. 129–44). Copenhagen: Museum Tusculanum Press.

Kaddour, H. (2022). 'Un bouquet d'anecdotes ou opus incertum, d'Hans Magnus Enzensberger: grandir au temps des nazis', *Le Figaro*, <http://tinyurl.com/bdcnpnkb>.

Kim, J. (2022). 'Don't tell the flowers', *Times Literary Supplement*, <http://tinyurl.com/y2aa8ead>.

Kittel, H., and Poltermann, A. (2009). 'German tradition'. In M. Baker (ed.), *Routledge encyclopedia of translation studies* (pp. 411–18). New York: Routledge.

Klappstein, W. (2022). 'Dante lesen', *Literaturkritik*, <http://tinyurl.com/38kbh4b9>.

Klein, L. (2014). 'Name the translator', *Words without Borders*, <http://tinyurl.com/3tv3t7y6>.

Koelb, T. (2022). 'Wives to widows', *Times Literary Supplement*, <http://tinyurl.com/4txcy2f9>.

Lanschützer, C. (2010). 'Zwischen „kongenial" und „holprig": Übersetzungskritik im Feuilleton'. In N. Bachleitner and M. Wolf (eds), *Streifzüge im translatorischen Feld: zur Soziologie der literarischen Übersetzung im deutschsprachigen Raum* (pp. 159–75). Berlin: Lit Verlag.

Lapaque, S. (2022a). 'Supermarché, de José Falero: maîtres et esclaves', *Le Figaro*, <http://tinyurl.com/5brw6un5>.

Lapaque, S. (2022b). 'Vivre les animaux au Moyen Âge de Chiara Frugoni: des bêtes douées de parole', *Le Figaro*, <http://tinyurl.com/33wx99sh>.

Laurens, C. (2022). 'Un amour, de Sara Mesa: le feuilleton littéraire de Camille Laurens', *Le Monde*, <http://tinyurl.com/47emc3ee>.

Lavault-Olléon, E. (2018). 'Regard diachronique et prospectif sur un demi-siècle de traductologie pragmatique', *ASp*, 74 (1), <http://tinyurl.com/bdzfpbjv>.

Le Figaro Editorial. (2022). 'La nouvelle traduction de Franz Kafka dans la Pléiade montre qu'il se méfiait de l'allemand', *Le Figaro*, <http://tinyurl.com/yc4dn3wh>.

Le Roy, A. (2022). 'L'indépendance des États-Unis ou le jeu de dupes des nations', *Actualitté*, <http://tinyurl.com/ysxs9abn>.

Lennon, J. (2022). 'Doppelflugzeug', *London Review of Books*, <http://tinyurl.com/3a2ktdee>.

Lensing, L. (2022). 'The deer hunter', *Times Literary Supplement*, <http://tinyurl.com/mvxysj6f>.

Lentz, C. (2022). 'Zwischen Lebensrealität und Mystik', *Literaturkritik*, <http://tinyurl.com/4ppc3xxv>.

Lewis, T. (2011). 'On reviewing translations: Tess Lewis', *Words without Borders*, <http://tinyurl.com/mr86dme6>.

Leyris, R. (2022). 'Les Idéalistes, de Kristopher Jansma: tutoyer la grandeur avec Waldo', *Le Monde*, <http://tinyurl.com/5n8f5d7x>.

Löchel, R. (2022a). 'Lovecraft in Manhattan', *Literaturkritik* , <http://tinyurl.com/4ftkafym>.

Löchel, R. (2022b). 'Weder Bild noch Ornament', *Literaturkritik*, <http://tinyurl.com/5n6p4n63>.

Lockwood, P. (2022). 'Strap on an ox-head', *London Review of Books*, <http://tinyurl.com/mva266nj>.

The London Book Fair. (2023). 'About the London Book Fair', <http://tinyurl.com/49zzze6v>.

The London Book Fair Hub. (2019). 'Katy Derbyshire, esteemed German-English translator, to be LBF 2020s literary translator of the fair', <http://tinyurl.com/mh8tms6a>.

Lucas, A. (2022). 'Italy's greatest novel?', *Times Literary Supplement*, <http://tinyurl.com/23kpwzt4>.

Mach, M. (2022). 'Das „Grüffelo" – Erfolgsduo ist zurück', *Süddeutsche Zeitung*, <http://tinyurl.com/bddn4z34>.

Magenau, J. (2022). 'Kopfabreiße mit Stil', *Süddeutsche Zeitung*, <http://tinyurl.com/twzzzzyn>.

Maidt-Zinke, K. (2022). 'Späte Leichtigkeit des Seins', *Süddeutsche Zeitung*, <http://tinyurl.com/4dwy2sxk>.

Maier, C. (1990). 'Reviewing Latin American literature', *Translation Review*, 34 (5), 18–24.

Mars-Jones, A. (2022). 'Quantum influencers', *London Review of Books*, <http://tinyurl.com/2czzy3nr>.

Mazenauer, B. (2022). 'Biere zischen, Rumba tanzen', *Literaturkritik*, <http://tinyurl.com/4b5w2wbp>.

McDonald, R. (2022). 'So what is the good of book reviewing? A review of a review of the reviewers', *The Conversation*, <http://tinyurl.com/4z7hbvs8>.

McGuinness, P. (2022). 'Time Shelter by Georgi Gospodinov review – the dangers of dwelling in the past', *The Guardian*, <http://tinyurl.com/kkf48cha>.

Menasse, E. (2022). 'Neuer Roman von Stardramatikerin Yasmina Reza: Was ein existenzieller Donnerschlag!', *Der Spiegel*, <http://tinyurl.com/295efvem>.

Menden, A. (2022). 'Kleine Wellen nagen am Pfirsich', *Süddeutsche Zeitung*, <http://tinyurl.com/muwuevvf>.

Mengeringhaus, M. (2022a). 'Hommage à Sophia', *Literaturkritik*, <http://tinyurl.com/55nj7tj6>.

Mengeringhaus, M. (2022b). 'Ein wilder Detektiv', *Literaturkritik*, <http://tinyurl.com/zm7xhzn8>.

Miller, L. (2022). 'Wife, mother, worker', *Times Literary Supplement*, <http://tinyurl.com/442jw8zd>.

Mimiche. (2022a). 'L'étrange bibliothèque, une nouvelle endiablée', *Actualitté*, <http://tinyurl.com/5fn84ua2>.

Mimiche. (2022b). 'Le dernier loup de Laszlo Krasznahorkai', *Actualitté*, <http://tinyurl.com/5v5dtw8x>.

Ministère de la Culture. (2014). 'Les Assises de la traduction et de l'interprétation', <http://tinyurl.com/427u5bj4>.

Mitchell, J. (2022). 'Exclusivement Française', *London Review of Books*, <http://tinyurl.com/2m8nuf5n>.

Mohr, P. (2022a). 'Kubakrise und Klavierlehrerin', *Literaturkritik*, <http://tinyurl.com/mtbebfd3>.

Mohr, P. (2022b). 'Blick im mexikanische Seele', *Literaturkritik*, <http://tinyurl.com/2xcy4mte>.

Moorhead, C. (2022). 'Command in her blood', *Times Literary Supplement*, <http://tinyurl.com/3nz5wdxw>.

Moos, H. (2022). 'Glückskekse in der Bronx', *Süddeutsche Zeitung*, <http://tinyurl.com/5n6mxr3s>.

Morrison, B. (2022). 'Oops, I'm trapped', *London Review of Books*, <http://tinyurl.com/3mnajfd5>.

Moss, S. (2022). 'Prams in the hall', *Times Literary Supplement*, <http://tinyurl.com/2mc5wpsu>.

Müller, L. (2022a). 'Im Bauch des Murmeltiers', *Süddeutsche Zeitung*, <http://tinyurl.com/3rdadrpu>.

Müller, L. (2022b). 'Rosen für den Weltfrieden', *Süddeutsche Zeitung*, <http://tinyurl.com/2cernb85>.

Munday, J. (1998). 'The Caribbean conquers the world? An analysis of the reception of García Márquez in translation', *Bulletin of Hispanic Studies*, 75 (1), 137–44.

Munday, J. (2012). *Introducing translation studies: Theories and applications* (3rd edn). Routledge: Oxon.

Müntefering, M. (2022). 'Bestsellerautor Zhou Haohui: Chinas Thriller-Star', *Der Spiegel*, <http://tinyurl.com/2hfhe8s9>.

Naiman, E. (2022). 'Proust, minus Dickens', *Times Literary Supplement*, <http://tinyurl.com/v5rv94bz>.

Neuhoff, E., de Larminat, A. et al. (2022). 'Les meilleurs livres de genre de poche à lire cet été', *Le Figaro*, <http://tinyurl.com/mxdfwh2f>.

Nicholls, A. (2022). 'One demigod to another', *Times Literary Supplement*, <http://tinyurl.com/yc8jursk>.

Nielsen. (2012). *Consumer trust in online, social and mobile advertising grows*. <http://tinyurl.com/bdjeszny>.

Noiville, F. (2022a). 'Gabriel Byrne, Félicité Herzog, Hersh Smolar … Les brèves critiques de la rentrée littéraire', *Le Monde*, <http://tinyurl.com/ysnfj7xr>.

Noiville, F. (2022b). 'Revolusi: la geste indonésienne de David Van Reybrouck', *Le Monde*, <http://tinyurl.com/28u94cru>.

Observatoire de l'économie du livre. (2020). *Le secteur du livre: chiffres-clés 2018–2019*. <http://tinyurl.com/46u5ahjp>.

Orwell, G. (1946). 'Confessions of a book reviewer', *The New Republic*, 115 (5), 144.

Paloff, B. (2022). 'Great sonatas' ghosts', *Times Literary Supplement*, <http://tinyurl.com/bdzfdhb5>.

Palou, A. (2022). 'John Sherman, de William Butler Yeats: les harmoniques du coeur', *Le Figaro*, <http://tinyurl.com/kfj3jnt9>.

Parks, T. (2022). 'The beast he was', *London Review of Books*, <http://tinyurl.com/r7ey3xex>.

Parole de Libraires. (2022). 'Plongée en eaux troubles avec la saga *Blackwater*', *Actualitté*, <http://tinyurl.com/3tc5acka>.

Parr, B. (2011). 'On reviewing translations: Rigoberto González', *Words without Borders*, <http://tinyurl.com/ympmr8ps>.

Pym, A. (1996). 'Venuti's visibility', *Target*, 8 (2), 165–77.

Racz, G. (2022). 'Reflections of a *Translation Review* editor', *Translation Review*, 112 (1), 138–40.

Randol, S. (2013). 'Interview with Susan Bernofsky', *Words without Borders*, <http://tinyurl.com/bn44brvx>.

Reiss, K. (1971). *Möglichkeiten und Grenzen der Übersetzungskritik; Kategorien und Kriterien für eine sachgerechte Beurteilung von Übersetzungen* (1st edn). Munich: Hueber.

Reza, A. (2022). 'I write in Condé', *London Review of Books*, <http://tinyurl.com/2h3z462v>.

Ries, A. (2018). 'La déontologie du traducteur: quelques règles de bonne conduite', *Master TSM*, <http://tinyurl.com/bdhbynu3>.

Roberts, M. (2022). 'Chic lit', *Times Literary Supplement*, <http://tinyurl.com/36232wdc>.

Rönsch, R. (2022a). 'Keine Hoffnung, kein Fest', *Literaturkritik*, <http://tinyurl.com/4rrdtakn>.

Rönsch, R. (2022b). 'Kein Eheglück für Yingzhi', *Literaturkritik*, <http://tinyurl.com/yc6dthzj>.

Rönsch, R. (2022c). 'Ichsüchtige Mutter, herzschwacher Vater, übermäßig geliebter Sohn', *Literaturkritik*, <http://tinyurl.com/yvw3epca>.

Rönsch, R. (2022d). 'Doppelte Identität und flegelhafter Psychiater', *Literaturkritik*, <http://tinyurl.com/cp4b9hjv>.

Rönsch, R. (2022e). 'Schwefelwasser und Stolperfalle', *Literaturkritik*, <http://tinyurl.com/4jxdr37f>.

Saint-Victor, J de. (2022). 'Comment devenir dictateur, de Frank Dikötter: la légende de l'adhésion des peuples à la dictature', *Le Figaro*, <http://tinyurl.com/sc2th7sj>.

Sammet, K. (2022). 'Vom Reichtum zur Verzweiflung?', *Literaturkritik*, <http://tinyurl.com/bddcbxht>.

Samoyault, T. (2022). 'L'herbe brille au soleil, de Beppe Fenoglio: le feuilleton littéraire de Tiphaine Samoyault', *Le Monde*, <http://tinyurl.com/78fzcd3t>.

Schell, L. (2014). 'Tips for reviewers: The politics of reviewing translations', *Reading in Translation*, <http://tinyurl.com/e477k9f2>.

Schimmang, J. (1996). 'Eine Übersetzungskritik findet nicht statt'. In F. Nies (ed.), *Literaturimport und Literaturkritik: das Beispiel Frankreich* (pp. 26–9). Tübingen: Gunter Narr Verlag.

Schmidt, M. (2022). 'Die Zeit vergeht nicht', *Süddeutsche Zeitung*, <http://tinyurl.com/yk8vca5j>.

Schulte, R. (2000). 'Editorial: Reflections on the art and craft of reviewing translations', *Translation Review*, 60 (1), 1–4.

Schulte, R. (2004). 'Editorial: Reviewing translations: A history to be written', *Translation Review*, 67 (1), 1.

Schulte, R. (2022). 'Present and future horizons of *Translation Review*', *Translation Review*, 112 (1), 1–5.

Scott, M. (2022). 'The book of modern love', *Times Literary Supplement*, <http://tinyurl.com/2s3njeyv>.

SDZ Autorinnen und Autoren. (2022a). 'Bücher des Monats August. Vergangenheit, die uns verfolgt', *Süddeutsche Zeitung*, <http://tinyurl.com/4wryfbp8>.

SDZ Autorinnen und Autoren. (2022b). 'Bücher des Monats Oktober. Neues vom Herdenleben', *Süddeutsche Zeitung*, <http://tinyurl.com/bp5ubr35>.

Sedgman, S. (2013). *Reviewing translation*. <http://tinyurl.com/bdhwadwm>.

Seiler, S. (2022). 'Die fünf Zacken des Pentagramms', *Literaturkritik*, <http://tinyurl.com/4ecbamfh>.

Self, J. (2022). 'The best recent translated fiction – review roundup', *The Guardian*, <http://tinyurl.com/2pvc74nn>.

Shaller, C. (2022). 'Logik der Paranoia', *Süddeutsche Zeitung*, <http://tinyurl.com/2khukjtd>.

Shaw, L. (2022). 'Life soup', *London Review of Books*, <http://tinyurl.com/35p4dv93>.

Shulman, P. (1992). 'Faux Poe', *Village Voice*. In: Venuti, L. (1998). *The scandals of translation: Towards an ethics of difference*. London: Routledge.

Singer, A. (2022). 'Le Fleuve des souvenirs, de José Maria Merino: genèse d'une séparation', *Le Monde*, <http://tinyurl.com/v9ehk7yd>.

Sirviö, K. (2006). *'Le roman est agréablement traduit': Etude comparative sur la visibilité des traductions et des traducteurs en Finlande et en France à travers des critiques de livre*. Helsinki: University of Helsinki.

Society of Authors. (2018). 'Name the translator', <http://tinyurl.com/2pysd2y6>.

Society of Authors. (2020). 'Translators association AGM', <http://tinyurl.com/2euya4fy>.

Spengler, T. (2022). 'Vor unsichtbaren Zeugen', *Süddeutsche Zeitung*, <http://tinyurl.com/2zycx38u>.

Stegelmann, K. (2022). 'Schwierige Geschwisterliebe: Happy End trozt Loch im Kopf', *Der Spiegel*, <http://tinyurl.com/yfswav88>.

Steinfeld, T. (2022a). 'Er will nichts werden', *Süddeutsche Zeitung*, <http://tinyurl.com/583rnusz>.

Steinfeld, T. (2022b). 'Im Bett suchen wir unser Ich jeden Morgen wieder neu zusammen', *Süddeutsche Zeitung*, <http://tinyurl.com/4a8hkbsy>.

Stephan, F. (2022a). 'Nicht im Ernst', *Süddeutsche Zeitung*, <http://tinyurl.com/7e2wpcax>.

Stephan, F. (2022b). 'Wall Street, Wahn und große Geister', *Süddeutsche Zeitung*, <http://tinyurl.com/4kpt7ufc>.

Strebel, V. (2022). 'Von der Schuld der Unumerziehbaren', *Literaturkritik*, <http://tinyurl.com/34npx3ud>.

Tahourdin, A. (2015). 'Abroad in English', *The Times Literary Supplement*, <http://tinyurl.com/yc7n2x5c>.

Támas, R. (2022). 'The best recent poetry – review roundup', *The Guardian*, <http://tinyurl.com/3hck9s82>.

Thomas-Corr, J. (2022). 'Portrait of an Unknown Lady by Maria Gainza review – Bolaño-esque art mystery', *The Guardian*, <http://tinyurl.com/5haft49f>.

Toury, G. (1995/2012). 'The nature and role of norms in literary translation'. In L. Venuti (ed.), *The translation studies reader* (pp. 168–81). Oxon: Routledge.

United Nations. (2017). 'International translation day: 30 September', <http://tinyurl.com/mr2939nw>.

Updike, J. (1975). *Picked-up pieces*. New York: Random House.

Vanderschelden, I. (2000). 'Quality assessment and literary translation in France', *The Translator*, 6 (2), 271–93.

Varno, D. (2011). 'New series: On reviewing translations', *Words Without Borders*, <http://tinyurl.com/mtsewzse>.

Venuti, L. (1995). *The translator's invisibility: A history of translation*. Oxon: Routledge.

Venuti, L. (1998). *The scandals of translation: Towards an ethics of difference*. London: Routledge.

Venuti, L. (2012). *The translation studies reader*. Oxon: Routledge.

Verband deutschsprachiger Übersetzer literarischer und wissenschaftlicher Werke. (2018). 'Zum Umgang mit der Nennung von Übersetzernamen', <http://tinyurl.com/7x6e9fx9>.

Voigt, C. (2022). 'Jugend im San Francisco der Achtziger: Die ewige Sehnsucht nach Aufmerksamkeit', *Der Spiegel*, <http://tinyurl.com/mry6wnxn>.

Von Bitter, R. (2022). 'Mond über Liebende', *Süddeutsche Zeitung*, <http://tinyurl.com/ymuyv4za>.

Von Cranach, X. (2022). 'Nobelpreis für Annie Ernaux: Schock als Nebeneffekt', *Der Spiegel*, <http://tinyurl.com/4y3c9he5>.

Wasserman, S. (2007). 'Goodbye to all that', *Colombia Journalism Review*, <http://tinyurl.com/5n8eur63>.

Weber, O. (2022). 'Unsere Schuld', *Süddeutsche Zeitung*, <http://tinyurl.com/59a2hwbc>.

Weidermann, V. (2013). 'Literaturkritik im Netz. Wer steht hier am Abgrund?', *Frankfurter Allgemeine Zeitung*, <http://tinyurl.com/25ma7ep6>.

Weill, N. (2022). 'Les Bésicles, de Johannes Reuchlin : la Renaissance d'une controverse', *Le Monde*, <http://tinyurl.com/caykkrp6>.

Welle, F. (2022). 'Kleines Weibsbild', *Süddeutsche Zeitung*, <http://tinyurl.com/5a3c5p8p>.

Wheatley, D. (2022). 'The best recent poetry – reviews roundup', *The Guardian*, <http://tinyurl.com/2srkpk39>.

Wilke, I. (2022a). 'In den Häusern aber wird geschwiegen', *Süddeutsche Zeitung*, <http://tinyurl.com/5n8syym6>.

Wilke, I. (2022b). 'Staatenlos', *Süddeutsche Zeitung*, <http://tinyurl.com/33bbm32y>.

Wilke, I. (2022c). 'Wer eine Wahrheit verschläft', *Süddeutsche Zeitung*, <http://tinyurl.com/yx5e3urj>.

WIPO. (2020). *The global publishing industry in 2018*. Geneva: World Intellectual Property Organization.

Wood, M. (2022). 'Cage in search of a bird', *London Review of Books*, <http://tinyurl.com/ykv8hds8>.

Wood, T. (2022). 'Aristotle on the metro', *London Review of Books*, <http://tinyurl.com/59wzu7v5>.

Wright, C. (2016). *Literary translation: Routledge translation guides*. Oxon: Routledge.

Wright, C., and Freely, M. (2017). 'Translators are the jazz musicians of the literary world: Translating Pamuk, literary translation networks and the changing face of the profession', *The Translator*, 23 (1), 95–110.

# Index

# New Trends in Translation Studies

In today's globalised society, translation and interpreting are gaining visibility and relevance as a means to foster communication and dialogue in increasingly multicultural and multilingual environments. Practised since time immemorial, both activities have become more complex and multifaceted in recent decades, intersecting with many other disciplines. *New Trends in Translation Studies* is an international series with the main objectives of promoting the scholarly study of translation and interpreting and of functioning as a forum for the translation and interpreting research community.

This series publishes research on subjects related to multimedia translation and interpreting, in their various social roles. It is primarily intended to engage with contemporary issues surrounding the new multidimensional environments in which translation is flourishing, such as audiovisual media, the internet and emerging new media and technologies. It sets out to reflect new trends in research and in the profession, to encourage flexible methodologies and to promote interdisciplinary research ranging from the theoretical to the practical and from the applied to the pedagogical.

*New Trends in Translation Studies* publishes translation- and interpreting-oriented books that present high-quality scholarship in an accessible, reader-friendly manner. The series embraces a wide range of publications – monographs, edited volumes, conference proceedings and translations of works in translation studies which do not exist in English. The editor, Professor Jorge Díaz Cintas, welcomes proposals from all those interested in being involved with the series. The working language of the series is English, although in exceptional circumstances works in other languages can be considered for publication. Proposals dealing with specialised translation, translation tools and technology, audiovisual translation and the field of accessibility to the media are particularly welcomed.

Vol. 1 Meng Ji: Phraseology in Corpus-Based Translation Studies
251 pages. 2010. ISBN 978-3-03911-550-1

Vol. 2 Josu Barambones Zubiria: Mapping the Dubbing Scene: Audiovisual Translation in Basque Television
191 pages. 2012. ISBN 978-3-0343-0281-4

Vol. 3 Elisa Ghia: Subtitling Matters: New Perspectives on Subtitling and Foreign Language Learning
234 pages. 2012. ISBN 978-3-0343-0843-4

Vol. 4 Anabel Borja Albi and Fernando Prieto Ramos (eds): Legal Translation in Context: Professional Issues and Prospects
325 pages. 2013. ISBN 978-3-0343-0284-5

Vol. 5 Kieran O'Driscoll: Retranslation through the Centuries: Jules Verne in English
302 pages. 2011. ISBN 978-3-0343-0236-4

Vol. 6 Federico M. Federici (ed.): Translating Dialects and Languages of Minorities: Challenges and Solutions
245 pages. 2011. ISBN 978-3-0343-0178-7

Vol. 7 Silvia Bruti and Elena Di Giovanni (eds): Audiovisual Translation across Europe: An Ever-changing Landscape
289 pages. 2012. ISBN 978-3-0343-0953-0

Vol. 8 Tong-King Lee: Translating the Multilingual City: Cross-lingual Practices and Language Ideology
176 pages. 2013. ISBN 978-3-0343-0850-2

Vol. 9 Laura Incalcaterra McLoughlin, Marie Biscio and Máire Áine Ní Mhainnín (eds): Audiovisual Translation. Subtitles and Subtitling: Theory and Practice
301 pages. 2011. ISBN 978-3-0343-0299-9

Vol. 10 Xiaohui Yuan: Politeness and Audience Response in Chinese–English Subtitling
250 pages. 2012. ISBN 978-3-0343-0732-1

Vol. 11 Isabel García-Izquierdo and Esther Monzó (eds): Iberian Studies on Translation and Interpreting
401 pages. 2012. ISBN 978-3-0343-0815-1

Vol. 12 Claire Ellender: Preserving Polyphonies: Translating the Writings of Claude Sarraute
250 pages. 2013. ISBN 978-3-0343-0940-0

Vol. 13 Pilar Sánchez-Gijón, Olga Torres-Hostench and Bartolomé Mesa-Lao (eds): Conducting Research in Translation Technologies
329 pages. 2015. ISBN 978-3-0343-0994-3

Vol. 14 Claire Ellender: Dealing with Difference in Audiovisual Translation: Subtitling Linguistic Variation in Films
221 pages. 2015. ISBN 978-3-0343-1816-7

Vol. 15 Anna Jankowska and Agnieszka Szarkowska (eds): New Points of View on Audiovisual Translation and Media Accessibility
316 pages. 2015. ISBN 978-3-0343-1842-6

Vol. 16 Charlotte Bosseaux: Dubbing, Film and Performance: Uncanny Encounters
251 pages. 2015. ISBN 978-3-0343-0235-7

Vol. 17 Guadalupe Soriano-Barabino: Comparative Law for Legal Translators
220 pages. 2016. ISBN 978-3-0343-1725-2

Vol. 18 Şebnem Susam-Saraeva: Translation and Popular Music: Transcultural Intimacy in Turkish–Greek Relations
184 pages. 2015. ISBN 978-3-03911-887-8

Vol. 19 Celia Martín de León and Víctor González-Ruiz (eds): From the Lab to the Classroom and Back Again: Perspectives on Translation and Interpreting Training
371 pages. 2016. ISBN 978-3-0343-1985-0

Vol. 20 Carla Mereu Keating: The Politics of Dubbing: Film Censorship and State Intervention in the Translation of Foreign Cinema in Fascist Italy
191 pages. 2016. ISBN 978-3-0343-1838-9

Vol. 21 Susanne M. Cadera and Andrew Samuel Walsh (eds): Literary Retranslation in Context
252 pages. 2017. ISBN 978-3-0343-1996-6

Vol. 22 Kayoko Nohara: Translating Popular Fiction: Embracing Otherness in Japanese Translations
248 pages. 2018. ISBN 978-3-0343-1963-8

Vol. 23 Pierre-Alexis Mével: Subtitling African American English into French: Can We *Do the Right Thing*?
256 pages. 2017. ISBN 978-3-0343-1897-6

Vol. 24 Micòl Beseghi: Multilingual Films in Translation: A Sociolinguistic and Intercultural Study of Diasporic Films
256 pages. 2017. ISBN 978-1-78707-159-9

Vol. 25 Michal Borodo: Translation, Globalization and Younger Audiences: The Situation in Poland
248 pages. 2017. ISBN 978-1-78707-473-6

Vol. 26 Eugenia Dal Fovo and Paola Gentile (eds): Translation and Interpreting: Convergence, Contact and Interaction
308 pages. 2019. ISBN 978-1-78707-750-8

Vol. 27 Nana Sato-Rossberg and Akiko Uchiyama (eds): Diverse Voices in Translation Studies in East Asia
224 pages. 2019. ISBN 978-178874-022-7

Vol. 28 Sarah M. A. Reed: Translating Cultural Identity: French Translations of Australian Crime Fiction
260 pages. 2019. ISBN 978-1-78874-007-4

Vol. 29 Blanca Arias-Badia: Subtitling Television Series: A Corpus-Driven Study of Police Procedurals
274 pages. 2020. ISBN 978-1-78707-796-6

Vol. 30 Károly Polcz: Speech Acts, Directness and Politeness in Dubbing: American Television Series in Hungary
270 pages. 2020. ISBN 978-1-78874-232-0

Vol. 31 María Dolores Rodríguez Melchor, Ildikó Horváth and Kate Ferguson (eds): The Role of Technology in Conference Interpreter Training
262 pages. 2020. ISBN 978-1-78874-407-2

Vol. 32 Ali Almanna and Juan Jose Martinez Sierra (eds): Reframing Realities through Translation
300 pages. 2020. ISBN 978-1-78997-228-3

Vol. 33 Alícia Moreno Giménez: The Translation of Irony: Examining its Translatability into Narratives
262 pages. 2022. ISBN 978-1-78997-984-8

Vol. 34 Esther de Boe: Remote Interpreting in Healthcare Settings 290 pages. 2023. ISBN 978-1-80079-373-6

Vol. 35 Ali Almanna and Juliane House (eds): Translation Politicised and Politics Translated
268 pages. 2023. ISBN 978-1-80079-446-7

Vol. 36 Carmen Pena-Díaz (ed.): The Making of Accessible Audiovisual Translation
202 pages. 2023. ISBN 978-1-80079-677-5

Vol. 37 Michela Canepari: Specialized Languages and Graphic Art: Translating Specialized Discourse Intralingually and Intersemiotically
288 pages. 2023. ISBN 978-1-80079-858-8

Vol. 38 Almudena Nevado Llopis and Ana Isabel Foulquié Rubio (eds): Medical Interpreting: Training the Professionals
266 pages. 2024. ISBN 978-1-80079-321-7

Vol. 39 Martyn Gray: Making the 'Invisible' Visible?: Reviewing Translated Works
228 pages. 2024. ISBN 978-1-80374-030-0

www.ingramcontent.com/pod-product-compliance
Lightning Source LLC
Chambersburg PA
CBHW071105100726
47908CB00008B/2267

* 9 7 8 1 8 0 3 7 4 0 3 0 0 *